For Dawn
Watch ∽

PRO BONO

a Hit Lady for Hire novel

LAURYN CHRISTOPHER

Camden Park Press

Pro Bono

I don't usually do pro-bono work.

I've got bills to pay, just like everyone else. And it takes a great deal of time and effort to dig up dirt on someone, peeling back the thin, civilized veneer to reveal the ugliness lurking beneath the surface for all the world to see.

It takes time to make someone wish you'd gotten it over with, and just killed them, quickly and painlessly.

Of course, there are also people who don't deserve the easy way out.

So while it's not my policy to work for free, once in a while, I'll make an exception, and donate my time to a worthy cause, pro bono.

I think of it as a public service.

— Meg Harrison
Hit Lady for Hire

Chapter 1
Present day: Thursday, 3:00 a.m.

It was three a.m. and *Here Comes the Sun* was playing on my cell phone. There's only one person I associate with that song: Deborah Markham. A former member of one of Philadelphia's power-families, now a pediatric nurse and single mom, Deb's sunny nature made the ringtone a logical choice.

Three a.m. calls are rarely sunny.

I was instantly alert, shifting around into a fully upright, sitting position on the edge of the bed as I reached for the phone on the nightstand. It's a conditioned response, developed through years of practice and numerous middle-of-the night calls requiring immediate attention. I answered the call less than thirty seconds after the phone started ringing, raising it to my ear before George Harrison got to his first *"it's all right"* of the tune.

"Deb? What's wrong?"

"He's dead, Meg," Deb's voice was half whisper, half gasp.

"Who?" I asked. Deb's father had passed away the previous summer, and she wasn't seeing anyone that I was aware of. Her son was in his late teens, though – had the boy been out with friends and gotten killed in a car accident? My mind raced, searching for answers.

"Stephen," she said, her voice still barely above a whisper.

Stephen Markham. Deb's ex-husband and deadbeat-dad to their two teenaged children. Holy hell. I ran my fingers through my short hair, scraping the nails along my scalp, biting back the "good riddance" that sprang to my tongue.

"How?" I asked.

"I don't know. Mother Markham just called… all she said was that they found him in his office."

In the middle of the night? That seemed strange to me. Honestly, though, I was surprised Deb's former mother-in-law had bothered to call her at all, instead of letting her get the news from the obituary column sometime next week.

"What can I do?"

"I don't want to wake the kids," Deb said. "Not yet. I need to sort myself out first… before I tell them. Oh, Meg, I don't want to be alone right now. Can you come over?"

"Of course," I said. "I'm on my way."

"Thanks. I know it's a lot to ask—"

"Not a bit," I said, cutting her off. "Put the teapot on. I'll see you soon."

I stared at the phone in my hand for a long moment after the call ended. My initial surprise at learning that Stephen Markham was dead was already fading, a new reaction replacing it: curiosity.

I'd been watching him for a long, long time. Biding my time. Waiting.

Clearly, I'd waited too long.

I wondered who had gotten to him first.

Chapter 2
12 years ago

No one openly turned to stare when the newcomer walked into the small street gym that chilly October evening, but everyone noticed. The slim brunette had arrived about ten minutes ahead of the Tuesday evening women's self-defense class.

Meg spotted her right away. Watched to see if she'd lose her nerve and leave, or if she had the guts to stick around.

The brunette hesitated near the bulletin board, pretending to read the notices pinned there – the usual collection of used car ads, pleas from those looking for jobs of any sort to keep them off the street, an advertisement for the tacky little apartment upstairs.

Meg had looked at the apartment once herself and wouldn't recommend it to anyone who wasn't desperate – the landlord insisted that the faint odor of moldy bread, sour milk, and rotten produce were courtesy of the previous tenant, and would air out soon enough, and he might have been correct.

But Meg's nose told her otherwise, and she suspected they were actually the time-worn residue of the gym's former days as a mom-and-pop grocery before the big-box store appeared a few blocks over, pushing a dozen or more small businesses on this side of Philadelphia out of operation. It had been ten or eleven years since the store had died, but the faded signs indicating the bakery, produce, and dairy sections still clung to the walls, though the shelves below had long-since been replaced with punching bags, weight benches, and thick, protective floor mats.

Meg nodded in approval as the newcomer left the bulletin board without tearing off the phone number for the apartment, and drifted over to the coat rack. She spent an inordinate amount of time choosing a hanger, but when she finally hung up her thin jacket, it seemed that the entire gym let out a collective sigh and went back to getting ready for the upcoming class.

Hanging up the jacket was a good sign. It signified a level of commitment some newcomers didn't reach too early on. A lot of them kept their coats or sweaters on all the way through their initial workout, ready to bolt the moment the session got to be more than they could handle.

Since it was a come-as-you are gym, no one said anything.

But everyone noticed. And everyone understood.

So the newcomer had decided to stick around, give the gym a chance.

Meg finished her pre-class stretch, bowed, and backed off the mat, pushing back the damp wisps of hair that had slipped out of her long blonde ponytail. Grabbing a towel from her gym bag, she walked over to the newcomer, dabbing at the perspiration beading her forehead and trickling down her neck, the front of her tank-top already marked with a dark "V" of perspiration even though she'd only been there twenty minutes herself.

"Heater's busted," she said, by way of greeting. "Doesn't seem to know when to shut down. Ian keeps promising to send someone over to fix it. In the meantime, he just tells everyone he installed a group sauna. Thinks that makes the sweat smell sweeter or something." She stuck out her hand, "Meg Harrison. Corporate slave by day, volunteer self-defense class instructor most Tuesday nights."

The newcomer took the offered greeting.

"Deborah Markham," she said softly. Her hand was tiny, bird-light in Meg's, but with a hint of strength that she would need if she was going to work out here.

Deborah was of medium height – a couple of inches shorter than Meg at about five four or five – and too-slim, like a dancer, or someone who had been ill. She was wearing a cheerfully-patterned pair of hospital scrubs, but the optimism the little butterflies and flowers attempted to convey didn't reach her eyes, which were wary, guarded. Eyes that watched Meg for any reaction to her name, which connected her to one of Philly's top-tier families.

Watched for any reaction to the dark shadows under her eyes and along one cheekbone. Her face had very little color to it, and what was there had not only come out of a bottle, but had been expertly applied to cover the bruising.

But even make-up can only hide so much.

Meg didn't react to the name, didn't stare at the bruises. She'd seen that face before. Worn it herself on more than one occasion. Knew that the pain and fear that brought people to the gym, inspired them to learn to protect themselves, was irrespective of their relative social status.

That was why most of them were here. Why Meg made it a point to be at the gym every Tuesday night, no matter how long her regular workday had been.

"Class is about to begin," she said. Other women were arriving around them, some hanging their coats and claiming spots along the benches to change shoes or drop off gym bags, others moving directly to the mat to begin warming up. "Have you had any martial arts training? Or is this your first visit to a class? We teach all levels, but it helps to have an idea what your experience is."

"I did some gymnastics in college," Deborah replied. "But that's about it. These days, I mostly run around after little children."

"Your job?"

"That, too. But I was mostly thinking about my kids." She smiled weakly, but her eyes clouded when she said that. There was clearly more to that story – there always was – but Meg didn't press. Deborah would tell it when she was ready.

Or not. Her choice.

Some people never chose to share. Meg knew all about that, too.

"Well, like I said, we teach all levels," she said, gesturing for Deborah to follow her to the mat. "Trouble doesn't wait until you're trained."

♦

Deborah fit in well with the self-defense class. In her first few months, she rarely missed a week, except when one of her jobs interfered.

She had two jobs – a waitressing gig that sometimes had her running in only seconds before class began, her curly brown hair still pulled back in a tight knot. A couple of times she was even still wearing her apron, which prompted a bit of good-natured ribbing from other members of the class.

Her other job was as a nurse's aide at the local Children's Hospital, where she worked a night shift caring for kids with leukemia. On those nights, she'd show up in colorful scrubs, with her hair pulled back in a loose ponytail.

Meg found herself watching Deborah. Studying her. She found something about her intriguing, more so than most of the other women at the gym.

Each of the women in the self-defense class had her own story. Some were painfully open about the situations they'd been in, their reasons for coming to the class. Others were more reticent.

The talkative ones found in each other their own support group. Meg didn't worry about them. Teaching the self-defense class was just something she did on the side, after-hours. She had a day job, a consulting business with high-powered, sometimes temperamental corporate clients that were her responsibility to look after. She wasn't at the gym to be a counselor, mentor, or even friend to the women who trained here.

But she watched the quiet ones.

Deborah was quieter than most.

Instead of that haunted sort of quiet Meg had seen so many times, the kind that turned a woman in on herself, making her fearful and jumpy, Deborah had a quiet kind of grace, a way of carrying herself that said sure, she'd been through some tough times, but she wasn't giving up. After a while, Meg decided it was that grace that caught her attention from early on.

Deborah never talked about herself or her own troubles, but always had a kind word or a gentle touch for women who came into the gym in pain, bleeding from emotional wounds that others couldn't see.

Deborah had a gift. She genuinely cared about people in ways Meg had long since forgotten how to do.

Ways Meg had found to be too painful.

So on one mid-January night, about four months after Deborah had joined the class, Meg noticed right off that Deborah wasn't herself. It was the way she stopped at the bulletin board – like she'd done that first time she walked in – pretending to read the notices pinned there, but really taking a deep breath as though steeling herself for something difficult to come.

When she turned from the board, a quiet smile on her face, and made her way to the coat rack, Meg froze in mid-stretch, one foot on the sit-up bench, resting her chin on her knee, the other leg planted firmly on the floor behind her.

The smile pasted on Deborah's face was as false as any Meg had ever seen in the gym. As false as any she'd ever worn herself.

Something was very wrong.

And Meg was certain that Deborah would never say a word about it to anyone.

At least, not anyone in the gym. She'd never arrived with anyone or left with anyone. So far as Meg knew, she'd never struck up a friendship with any of the other women in the self-defense class. Not that that was a problem, but when you were wearing a face like that – an emotionless mask with a smile painted on it – you needed someone to talk to.

Meg was hyper-aware of Deborah all evening, but she only faltered once, and landed on her butt because of it. The rest of the time, she was focused and alert, practicing the moves, and even helping another newcomer who was struggling.

That was Deborah. Always looking out for someone else.

Meg wondered who looked out for her.

As the self-defense class members were trickling out at the end of the session, Meg tugged on her coat and walked up to Deborah, slipping her arm in hers, girlfriend-like, as she turned toward the door.

"You look like you could use a cup of coffee," Meg said conversationally, matching her stride to Deborah's shorter one.

Deborah pulled her arm away and looked up at Meg as though the usually stable self-defense instructor had gone mad. She was wearing that carefully-constructed expression again. The one that all but screamed 'trouble' to Meg.

"I can't," she said. "I have to get home."

"Is there someone with the children?"

"Yes... Yes. They're at my parents'.... we live with my parents...."

"Good. Then you have time for coffee." Meg snagged Deborah's arm again, tucking it firmly into her own as they went through the doors.

After the warmth of the gym, the blast of icy cold air that greeted them as they hit the street was truly painful. Meg let go of Deborah's arm, and tugged her coat tighter around herself, glancing over at an all-night diner on the corner across the street.

Deborah followed her gaze, nodding silently as she wrapped her scarf around her face.

They made their way gingerly across the icy street, grateful for the lack of traffic that allowed them to save a few steps by jaywalking – but not so appreciative of the mounds of snow piled up along either side of the road by Philadelphia's ever-vigilant snowplows.

By the time they reached the diner, they were both half-frozen. A passing waitress took one look at them as they walked in, and nodded sympathetically.

"Sit anywhere you like," she said. "I'll bring coffee."

"Tea?" asked Deborah, her voice barely audible through her scarf.

"You got it."

They found an empty booth away from the window and as far removed from the door as they could get. The waitress appeared an instant later with mugs, a steaming carafe of coffee, and a small ceramic teapot with a couple of tea bags tucked under the edge, which she set in front of them like offerings, then placed a couple of laminated menus at the end of the table.

"I'll give you two a few minutes to thaw out," she said. "Just shout if you need anything before I get back."

They sat there in silence for several minutes, Deborah stirring her tea until Meg thought the teabag would break, spilling the leaves all through the mug. Meg watched her, basking in the warmth of her coffee, and only occasionally taking a sip while she waited for the silence to draw Deborah out of her shell.

It was nearly five minutes before the silence finally reached the breaking point and Deborah began to talk, first about her failed marriage and her divorce, then her struggles over the past five years as a single mom. She started slowly, her momentum growing as she talked. It was like a dam had burst, Meg thought, all the pent-up emotions carrying her helplessly along in a flood of words. When Deborah finally paused to take a breath, she got flustered at the idea of having opened up so deeply to someone she barely knew, and spent several minutes studying the menu.

But Meg didn't like that haunted look in her eyes. Deborah was holding something back and needed to talk, not bottle up whatever it was. Break through the reserve of her upbringing.

"So about your divorce," Meg began, once Deborah was settled with a fresh cup of tea to ignore. "Who decided to call an end to things once and for all?"

She sighed. "I did. One day Stephen's mother asked him what was going on between us; he's always been close to her, and I guess she'd sensed our tension, or something. He told her we were effectively separated and probably splitting up. I panicked, and filed for divorce the next day."

Meg put down her coffee. "Why the rush? You'd already waited for months, right?"

"Over a year, actually. But I was terrified of his family – they're well-connected, not just here in Philly, but across the whole region. Know a lot of people in high places. Lawyers. Judges. I don't have any connections – there was no one with any clout who would stand up for me, if it came to it."

Meg leaned forward, putting her elbows on the table, resting her chin on her hands. "What did you think they'd do?"

"I don't know," Deborah said. "I just didn't want to give his family a chance to circle the wagons. A friend recommended a lawyer, and we pushed the paperwork through in record time. Stephen signed everything and hardly said a word. Had to be one of the fastest divorces in history."

"Except for the year or more leading up to it."

"Yeah, except for that part." She drew her finger through a drop of water that had splashed on the Formica, playing connect-the-dots with the speckled pattern.

"So what has you so freaked-out tonight?"

The tears finally spilled over, streaming down Deborah's face. She ignored them, reaching into her purse and pulling out a heavy, white envelope and holding it out to Meg. "He's threatened it before, but now he's really doing it. He's suing me for custody."

Her voice was thick, full of undisguised anguish as Meg took the envelope.

"Stephen wants to take my children away from me."

◆

By the time Meg got home, her head full with Deborah's worries, it was already quite late. As she pulled her car past the oversized trash bin occupying the other half of the driveway and into the garage, she wondered how much longer it would be before the renovations to her mother's old house would be complete. It had been nearly three months since she'd moved in, taking over the house – and the renovations from the former tenants when their financing fell through – and she was getting tired of never really knowing what she was going to find when she got home. At least the construction workers had finally stopped leaving their equipment in her parking spot.

She pushed her way through the door into the kitchen, and flipped the light switch several times, to no avail.

"Oh, goody," she muttered, switching on her phone's flashlight app so she could look around.

Most of the cabinetry and appliances, including the new stove, were clustered together, just beyond the kitchen in the small space that would eventually become the breakfast room. Their blocky outlines loomed ahead like an oddly-proportioned skyline.

Behind the boxes and cabinetry, a wall of windows stretched across the back of the house like a dark, cold void. The flashlight reflected back at her off the glass. Meg winced, half-blinded by the sudden brightness, and angled the flashlight down at the floor. As her eyes adjusted, dim lights from neighboring houses barely visible through overhanging tree branches shone through the windows, providing the slightest possible illumination.

Dim shadow was better than pitch dark.

"There's nothing to worry about," she murmured, her voice sounding loud in the stillness. She shook her head, trying to shake the fear away. It was irrational. She was in her own home. The workers had switched off the power to the kitchen while they worked, that was all.

It wasn't like before. The memory sent icy fingers down her spine.

"No, it's *not* like before," Meg said, annoyed at the tremor in her voice.

She'd known, when Deborah started talking about her deadbeat husband and her fears about losing her children, that it would stir up memories of her own deadbeat father, her own mother's fears. Those topics always left her stomach in knots. And these walls had borne witness to too much pain and far too many secrets to let her slip in quietly. Meg didn't believe in ghosts, but she was all too familiar with personal demons – and most of hers had been born in this house.

She straightened her shoulders, shining the phone's tiny light into the darkness, trying to discern the shapes and shadows. As a child, she'd known every square inch of this house. Could traverse it front to back, from attic to cellar, with her eyes closed. Had on more than one occasion.

But the new layout was unfamiliar, most of the main floor still a work in progress. Meg edged forward, fingers of her left hand trailing along the wall. When she got to the end of the wall, she stepped across the small space to the cluster of appliances, her hand coming to rest on the smooth, metallic curve along the edge of the stove.

That was when the memory hit her.

She was thirteen years old, making herself a fried egg sandwich. It was a Saturday afternoon, and her stepfather, Eddie, had gone to play golf with his business friends while her mother took her little brothers to a Little League game. Her big sister, Shelia, was spending the weekend with a girlfriend. She did that a lot lately, but it was probably more interesting to go to the mall or listen to music with other teenagers than to sit around with her younger siblings all the time.

That left Maggie at home, alone, which was perfectly fine with her. The house was peaceful, without the twins zooming up and down the stairs, and she only got to put her own music on the stereo when everyone else was gone.

She'd taken a break from the book she'd been reading to make herself a sandwich, leaving the music playing at full volume in the living room. It was while she was standing at the stove, singing along to the music, when Eddie grabbed her from behind, one hand cupping her small breast while the other groped between her legs.

It wasn't the first time he'd done that kind of thing, and though she hated him for it, she usually tried not to react. But this time, because she'd thought she was alone in the house, Maggie was so startled that she shrieked at his touch, twisting around, accidentally jerking the frying pan off the burner. The eggs flew up and hit Eddie in the face, grease sizzling as the still-gooey yolks dribbled down onto his shirt.

Eddie smacked the frying pan out of her hand and shoved Maggie backwards against the stove, swearing at her as he fumbled with the button on her jeans. She squirmed, trying to pull away from him, at the same time arching her back in a desperate effort to stay as far as possible from the searing heat of the burner, inches behind her. But her struggles only succeeded in pressing her body more tightly against his, arousing him further.

Maggie was never sure whether it was the heat singeing her back through her thin t-shirt as Eddie tugged her pants down and shoved his way into her, or the acrid smell as the ends of her hair started to burn that caused her to flail about. Desperate, she struggled to free herself while he laughed, ignoring her pitiful efforts to fight him off.

The fork she shoved into his shoulder, though – the one her groping fingers found and grabbed onto as she searched for something on the counter she could use to defend herself – that he noticed.

Swaying, almost dizzy from the sudden onslaught of the memory, Meg jerked her hand away from the stove. It wasn't hot – of course not, it wasn't even connected – but she could almost feel the heat, smell her hair burning.

Panting, she turned her back on the stove and on the memory. Following her small flashlight, Meg slowly, deliberately found her way to the foot of the stairs and flipped the light switch there.

Light flooded the stairway and upper hall, banishing the darkness.

Breathing a sigh of relief, Meg climbed the stairs on shaky legs. She was soon cocooned in the safety of her bed, burrowed under the blankets while throughout the house the lights blazed brightly, keeping her demons at bay.

Chapter 3
Present day: Thursday morning

We sat at Deb's kitchen table, steaming mugs of tea cooling between us. Her eyes were puffy and red, her nose swollen.

She saw me looking at her, and gestured at her face. "This isn't all for Stephen," she said, her voice ragged and hoarse. "You'd think the sinus meds I'm on would at least slow down the drippy nose."

"Over the counter?"

She shook her head. "Prescription. I can't go back to work until I'm not contagious."

"I think going on a crying jag overrides the meds – even the strong ones," I said.

"Probably right. Someone should do a study."

She reached for a napkin and dabbed at her nose. "I should go find a box of tissues," she said. "But I think we're out. Sinus infection." She rose, tossed the crumpled napkin into the trash, and washed her hands before coming back to the table.

The conversation drifted. Deb talked about her conflicting feelings of grief and relief at Stephen's death, wondering how to tell her children about their father. As she spoke, my thoughts went back to that first conversation, long ago, when we'd sat across from each other at another table, drinks untouched and forgotten.

While Stephen had managed to make Deb's life difficult one way or another for over a decade, at least taking her children away was no longer an issue. In my opinion, she was better off without him.

Emotions aren't logical things. I try to avoid them whenever possible, but at the moment, that wasn't an option. Logical or not, Deb was grieving.

"It's not like I was still in love with him or anything," she said. "It's been years since I cared for him at all." She pushed her tea away. "Okay, that's not exactly true – but 'cared' is the opposite of how I felt, and 'hated' is too trite. Loathed him, sure. Despised him and the way he'd treated both me and the kids. Wanted him to just make the support payments and otherwise stay out of my life. Call his kids once in a while. That wasn't too much to ask, right? But that didn't mean I wanted him dead."

"If everyone I wanted out of my life was dead," I said, "there would be a lot of dead people around." I took our teacups to the sink and dumped them out. A lot of the people I wanted out of my life actually *were* dead. But not all of them. Not yet. But that was a different conversation, and not one I could have with Deb.

I really suck at the whole consoling thing. I tried again.

"About the support – are you going to be okay without it?"

She waved it off with a laugh that turned into a coughing fit. I poured her a glass of water, but it still took a couple of minutes before she could even take a sip.

"Okay, it was funny, but not *that* funny," Deb croaked, when she could finally speak. "I haven't seen a penny of the child support in three, maybe four years."

I looked up in confusion. "He'd stopped paying again?" My random spot-checks of his accounts showed the regular support garnishment from his paycheck. Had he managed to re-route the payments somehow…? Thankfully, Deb answered before I got too far in my speculations.

"Oh, he paid every month, regular as clockwork. The university saw to that. And the money was no sooner in my account than it was out again, on an automatic payment to my lawyer. I swear I bought that man his last car, just in legal fees. Probably a couple new suits, too. But he was worth it – made sure the support kept coming, and let me spread out the payments instead of try to pay in big lumps. So there was that much at least." She took another swallow of water.

"But the kids never benefitted from the money like they were supposed to, and that always made me mad. I get that Stephen wanted to punish me for leaving him, but did he have to hurt the kids, too? They never did anything to him."

She teared up, and all I could do was pull my chair over and put my arm around her while she leaned her head against my shoulder and cried.

Stephen had given her a raw deal, there was no denying that. I thought I'd been helping her by letting him live as long as I had. Now I wished I'd gotten rid of him sooner.

There's a lot to be said for hindsight.

At least, once the tears dried, he'd finally be out of her life for good. That couldn't be a bad thing.

◆

I sat with Deb until morning, slipping quietly out of the house when her daughter, Cassie, came downstairs a little after seven o'clock. Almost twenty, Cassie was a sophomore at the University of Pennsylvania, while her younger brother, Josh, was a high-school senior. With the news their mother had for them, I suspected neither would be going to school that day.

On the other hand, I had meetings today that it would have been bad business to cancel for anything short of a dire emergency. So for me it was a quick trip home to shower, dress for the day, and grab some coffee before heading to the office.

I work in mergers and acquisitions for a privately-held boutique agency, and as I'll happily tell anyone who asks, my 9-

to-5 isn't as glamorous as the movies make it out to be. It's seldom just 9-to-5, either. When I first started out, a typical workday might be dawn-to-dawn for several days in a row, wrapped around grad-school classes and the occasional quick nap, and followed by mere fourteen-hour days during the lulls between one deal closing and the next one ramping up. And while I've moved up through the ranks, can come and go pretty much as I please, and now delegate out a large share of the grunt work I used to do to the junior associates on my team, I still take the time to study every deal in-depth.

Blending two companies is a little like rock-climbing. Only instead of looking for flaws in the rock that will flake off in your hand if you grab onto them, and hoping to find the tiniest handholds that will support your weight as you move to the next impossibly narrow ledge, you're trying to find a way to match the strengths and weaknesses of often disparate financial patterns to create a stronger whole.

I have a knack for it. Hence my rapid rise in the ranks. I'd started out as an intern while working on my MBA, hired on full-time right after graduation. Within three years, I was a junior partner.

A few years back, the firm offered me a senior partnership. And while it was tempting, I opted to break away from the firm altogether and open up my own consulting firm. Maybe someday I'll sell out and spend my winters on a sunny beach instead of slogging through the Philadelphia slush.

But for now, it's a living.

A *legitimate* living.

As they say about "all work and no play," it's not the only thing I do. I've also turned a college side job as an under-the-table information broker into an extremely lucrative moonlighting career. Now, when not negotiating deals in stuffy corporate boardrooms, I'm facilitating agreements that blur legitimate boundaries. I take on illicit research jobs that require absolute confidentiality, troubleshoot messy problems, and eliminate obstacles. I handle these jobs personally. No secretary, no support staff. No one's ethics to compromise but my own.

I don't mind. That particular set of clients pays well for the privilege of keeping their hands clean.

Very well.

I also own a few things I'd rather not have anyone else knowing about. Mostly documents of a sensitive nature – this is the Information Age, after all, and I'm still every bit an information broker. I collect documents I'm not supposed to have, but which I'm happy to sell if the price is right, and store electronic copies on flash drives in multiple locations, one of which is a small, fireproof safe hidden in a secret compartment in an antique-styled cabinet in my bedroom.

I have trust issues.

In service to this secondary career, I typically work from home once or twice a week, whether I need to or not. I'll occasionally cancel or reschedule meetings at the day job seemingly on a whim, or take off and go out of town for several days with little or no notice.

It's all part of a carefully constructed façade I have built over the years. An image that allows me the freedom I need, and keeps anyone at work from noticing my unscheduled comings and goings as being anything out of the norm. A persona equipped with alternate identities, a clandestine skillset, and the ability to disappear into the shadows at a moment's notice.

Like I said. Trust issues.

•

When you think about how long you've known someone, it always seems like you've either just met them or known them forever – at least that's how it seems to me.

The twelve years I've known Deb feel like a lifetime.

In almost every way that matters, I can trace the direction my life has taken back to the beginnings of my friendship with

Deb and her challenges with Stephen. Not that I blame her in any way – I made my choices, first on her behalf, and then for myself, and I stand by them.

Still, as I left the office at the end of the day, a voice from the past echoed in my head:

Women are getting stiffed by deadbeats all the time. What's so special about this one?

At the time when the question was asked, I hadn't been in a position to help Deb in any meaningful way. I barely knew her, but had wanted to help, truly I had. But more than that, I wanted to punish Stephen, *hurt* him.

For Deb and the children he abandoned.

I eased my navy blue Altima into the press of suburban Philadelphia's rush-hour traffic, clenching my teeth and clutching the steering wheel tighter, as though that might somehow help me get a grip on my emotions. It had been a long day, with too little sleep the night before and too many ghosts from the past coming back to haunt me. "Frayed" didn't begin to describe the state of my nerves.

Who are you really doing this for?

The mental picture I had of Deb, exhausted and afraid as we sat over cold tea in the diner twelve years ago, dissolved into my own mother's image. A woman who'd proudly held her head up in society after my father disappeared, stubbornly portraying a façade of solvency while struggling behind the scenes to make sure my siblings and I were properly provided for.

This isn't about me.

I couldn't punish my father – he'd dropped off the grid years ago and my efforts to locate him had all come up empty. But Stephen Markham had been right there, practically begging to be burned in effigy for my father's sins.

It had changed my life.

I had secretly taken the torch to Stephen time after time in the past several years, like a shadow tormentor poking pins into a voodoo doll. Had watched from the wings while Stephen suffered for both my father's misdeeds and his own – but it had never really made me feel any better.

His death had finally brought closure for Deb, but there was none for me.

The tears welled up, unexpected and unbidden, from the deep well I'd buried them in so many years before. I tried to blink them away, but it was pointless. They spilled over, streaming down my face as the pain of a child who didn't understand – had never understood – why her father left one day and never came home again, nearly overwhelmed me.

I didn't try to stop the tears or wipe them from my face. And when my vision blurred beyond my ability to blink it clear, I pulled to the side of the road and rested my head against the steering wheel, letting the sobs take over.

My Aunt Ruthie, who took in my siblings and me after our mother's death, regularly touted the virtues of a good cry. *"It'll wash away your troubles, let you see things clearly,"* she always said.

Maybe she wasn't all wrong.

While the sudden deluge of tears hadn't washed away either my troubles any more than Deb's tears this morning had eased her sense of guilt at feeling relieved by Stephen's death, it went a long way toward releasing the tension that had been building up inside me all day. Tension that had been clouding my judgment, interfering with my objectivity for longer than I wanted to admit.

I took a deep breath to collect myself and pulled back into traffic. I needed a drink, a workout, and a long, hot shower, and I didn't much care in which order.

Chapter 4
Present day: Thursday, afternoon

The evening commute had gotten heavier during my little meltdown, and I found myself growling as I slipped from one pocket of stalled traffic to the next.

During one of these forced lulls in forward motion, I dug my wireless headset out of my purse and clipped it to my ear, then tapped a speed-dial number on my cell. Traffic started to move again as the call connected, so I dropped the phone in my empty cup-holder and moved forward a few inches.

"Hello?" a silky voice purred in my ear, a smooth contralto edged with just a hint of Jersey.

"Hi, Bonnie."

"Meg!" she said, her greeting immediately followed by a burst of colorful expletives.

"Well, if that's how you feel about it, I'll call another realtor," I said, laughing.

Bonnie Kauffman and I go way back — two decades ago she was my sister Shelia's best friend, and barely noticed me. A couple years' difference in ages was a huge deal in high school. But when my mother died and Shelia OD'd and my brothers and I moved in with Aunt Ruthie, my life pretty much went to shit, as far as I was concerned and I'd all but forgotten Bonnie existed.

Then, a few years ago — only a couple years after I'd met Deb, actually — we bumped into each other again. Bonnie was representing a rowhouse I'd taken a liking to, which was conveniently located only minutes from my downtown office. We bonded over shared appreciation of classic architecture and interior design, and I bought the house. Since then, we've become good friends ourselves. She and her wife, Peggy, are like the adult sisters I wished Shelia had lived to be.

"You wouldn't dare replace... hold on...," she growled. "*Get the hell out of my way...!*"

I winced as the blast of a car horn drowned out her shout, the sound crystal-clear in my ear. Bonnie may be a petite five-foot-four, but she had a way of packing a punch when she got riled up. The echo of the car horn faded quickly away, though I still heard Bonnie muttering under her breath for several seconds before she came back to the call.

"Sorry about that," Bonnie said finally, her voice once again come-hither smooth, with only a touch of her earlier frustration.

"Rush hour?" I said sympathetically.

"*The crawl* is more like. You?"

"Same. Roads are a mess. That's why I called — you doing anything tonight?"

"Oh, God, I hope so," she said with a husky laugh. "Peggy's away at a conference, and I've been going stir-crazy. What'd you have in mind?"

"McGillin's?" I suggested. "I'm heading to the gym now, but could meet you there around ten."

"You're on. Everything okay?"

"Yeah, why do you ask?"

"No reason. Just wondering..." She let the unasked question hang there, fill the silence on the line.

"It's been a long day," I said finally.

"I hear you. See you tonight. We'll kick back and knock the day on its ass."

"I like the sound of that," I said. "Don't kill anyone on your way home."

"No promises," Bonnie said with a laugh. "Idiots better just stay outta my way."

We said our goodbyes and I pulled the headset from my ear and tossed it back in my bag. I was feeling better already.

◆

I found a parking spot about halfway down the block from the gym – the tiny lot at the back of the building was full – and put an hours' worth of coins in the meter.

It was only as I was hanging my coat on the rack that I realized I'd come without a change of clothes. I stood there for a minute, feeling slightly out of place in a silk blouse, business slacks, and dress shoes while everyone around me was in sweaty workout clothes.

With a shrug, I kicked off my shoes. Flexibility and adaptability were part of the gym's core philosophy – and I'd just have to adapt. I tucked my socks and jewelry into an inside coat pocket, then slipped out of my blouse and draped it over my coat like a scarf. No sense ruining a good silk blouse when I was wearing a perfectly serviceable camisole underneath.

Beyond the large, group space at the front where the self-defense class spent most of their time, the gym provided a range of other facilities. Four smaller practice mats, designed for no more than a half-dozen people each, ran down the center of the room, and there was a boxing ring in the back corner, to one side of the double-doors leading to the parking lots. Free-weights and benches sat near a small forest of punching bags in the opposite corner near the ramp leading to a running track above. As I got ready for my own workout, a pair of runners pounded overhead along the grated track that clung improbably to the wall, anchored by steel cables that rose to the high ceiling.

I moved to an unoccupied practice mat, bowed, and then spent the next several minutes moving through some a combination of yoga stretches and modern dance moves designed to stretch muscles stiff from a day mostly spent sitting behind a desk. Following the warm-up, I moved on to a more energetic kickboxing routine I hoped would help me work off the tension that had settled right between my shoulder blades.

"You look about as relaxed as a pile of barbed wire," Ian said, coming to the edge of the mat. He was an active owner of the gym, on the floor with the members as much as — if not more than — he was in the office, minding the books.

I ignored him and continued pummeling the air in a series of sharp punches.

"And as prickly, I see," he said with a grin. "Want a sparring partner? Or is shadowboxing doing the job?"

Ian Mitchell is more like Vin Diesel than Master Yoda, a veteran of multiple tours of duty in the Middle East, who had walked away from Special Ops when a slow-healing injury made him more of a liability to his team than an asset. But by then he'd seen too much, done too much to ever really walk away.

When he returned home, he bought the broken-down old store and turned it into a gym, teaching martial arts and self-defense as a way to combat — and control — his inner demons. We'd clicked early on. Even dated briefly when we first met, before deciding — okay, I decided, he disagreed at the time, but knew better than to fight me on it — that we were better as friends.

Ian probably knows me better than anyone else.

I responded by stepping back a couple of paces and gesturing for him to join me on the mat.

He bowed and stepped onto the mat, his long legs covering the distance between us in an instant and engaging me immediately. We sparred silently for several minutes — kick and dodge, jab and feint, moving quickly from proscriptive training routines to the unstructured, anything-goes fighting style that characterized the gym.

"What's got you so wound up?" Ian asked, slipping out of a shoulder hold and rolling me across his back. "I haven't seen you like this since…" he spared a glance around the room, dark eyes noting the location of everyone within possible earshot, before continuing, "…since *before*."

The 'before' he was referring to was twelve years ago – just after I first found out about Deb and Stephen. And here I was again. Full circle. Clearly their situation was a trigger subject for me.

I have serious issues when it comes to deadbeats – even Ian only knows about some of it. The small nest egg my own mother had squirreled away before my father abandoned us hadn't lasted long, leaving her with no marketable skills and four young children to care for. Whether she was ashamed or simply too proud to admit that she needed help, I'll never know. I do know that she'd put on a false front with her family, convincing them that she was doing just fine. Ultimately, she'd been forced to remarry – with disastrous results – just to make ends meet.

The Deb-and-Stephen situation had pushed my buttons when I first learned about it, and was doing a number on me all over again, making me relive memories I'd thought long-buried. Even knowing Stephen was dead, I still wanted to protect Deb, punish the guy who had left her to fend for herself.

Now, though? I had no clear reaction, only anger. There's just not that much you can do to punish a dead guy.

"Same shit, different day," I growled.

"I'm not following."

I landed on the floor in a crouch, swiping at his leg. "My father," I said, practically spitting out the words.

"You found him?" He dodged my swipe and caught my arm in a scooping motion, linking our elbows and pulling me to my feet. "Where?"

"No." I twisted away, putting some distance between us. "He ditched my mom. Abandoned us."

I bounced from foot to foot, looking for an opening. Ian was several inches taller than me, and nearly twice my weight, all broad-shouldered muscle and quick reflexes. And though he'd taught me pretty much everything I know about fighting, I was faster. It was my only advantage against him, and we both knew it.

Ian frowned, staring at me intently. "Your mom died, Meg. A long time ago."

"Yup," I said. I took advantage of his slight distraction and dove at his midsection. He didn't dodge or block the attack, and we tumbled to the mat, Ian landing on his back, me sitting on his stomach. He raised his hands, palms toward me, and I began to punch them – my left to his right, my right to his left, one-two, one-two, round after round until Ian finally caught my fists and held them.

I squirmed, but his grip was tight, and by then I'd used up most of my anger, so I didn't really try to fight him. We sat there like that for a couple of minutes, breathing hard, sweat beading on our skin. A droplet slid from my hair and landed on his face, where it was quickly absorbed by the perpetual five o'clock shadow that ran from his short goatee to his closely-cropped hair. He ignored it, his eyes locked to mine.

He was using the same tactic on me that I'd used on Deb and so many others, waiting patiently for me to fill the silence.

The difference was, unlike someone who really needed to talk, I didn't. Talking wasn't going to help. Beating the crap out of Ian, metaphorically speaking, had come as close to making me feel better as I was going to get.

"Old wounds," I said finally, knowing Ian would understand. Of all of my friends, he knew better than most about hidden triggers that could rip the tender flesh off long-ignored emotional injuries – I won't say long-*healed*, because they never really heal, just sit on the shelves of our minds and hearts like souvenirs; dusty, dried-up scabs we don't know how to dispose of, some of which still bleed when jostled.

My father's leaving was the first and deepest in my personal collection, a gash that had left my child-self vulnerable to other hurts until I'd discovered that if you don't care, you don't feel pain. Not caring had become a shield, a protective cocoon I'd wrapped around myself.

But it was a fragile defense at best.

I took a long, slow breath, forcing myself to relax on the exhale. Understanding what was going on in my own head didn't make it hurt any less, but it had helped to clear away the haze clouding my thinking.

Ian must have felt the tension easing, because he released his grip on my fists. "You good?" he asked.

"Good? No," I said, standing. I held a hand out to help him up. "But better. Thanks."

He nodded. "I hear you. I've split a few punching bags finding my way back to 'better.' It's preferable to smashing in faces."

"Hardly as satisfying," I said.

"Perhaps in the sheer primal sense of it," he said, slipping into his variation of streetwise Zen master. "But if you go too far, you reach a point where it passes satisfaction and you simply lose yourself. That's when you get sloppy."

He was looking down at me, a frown knitting his eyebrows together. "You never want to go there, Meg. Find your focus, your center, and it will help you maintain control of your emotions, of your actions."

He leaned closer, his mouth near to my ear, speaking softly so no one else could hear. "You can't afford to get sloppy. It could get you killed. Or worse."

Like I said, Ian knows me pretty well.

◆

I'd checked in with Deb a couple of times during the day, and texted her again as I left the gym.

You okay? I asked.

Weird, she replied. *I still really don't know how to feel.*

Big surprise.

LOL.

Need anything?

Lunch tomorrow maybe? My house? Still on the sinus meds. Not sure if today's sniffles & burning eyes are one last hurrah from the infection or from crying. Will give it another day to be sure. Won't risk taking it to the floor with all those little kids.

Sure thing. Will bring chicken soup. Call if you need me before then. I *mean* it.

I will. :/

Chapter 5
Present day: Thursday evening

I headed back downtown, parked in the underground garage beneath my office, and took an Uber the few blocks to McGillin's — a more practical option than trying to find on-street parking in the narrow streets and alleys near the bar. With as much back-and-forth as I was doing today, I should have just left my car home.

McGillin's is a classic old Irish pub that fills up early and just gets louder and more crowded as the evening wears on. It's one of those places where you can have a perfectly private conversation even though you're practically shouting to the person sitting next to you. As watering holes go, it's one of my favorite in the city.

The Uber driver let me off across the street from the pub, and I was waiting to cross the street when someone opened the door and a burst of raucous laughter filled the air. The sound cut off just as abruptly as the door swung shut behind them. It was barely ten p.m., and the crowd was clearly in full-force, no doubt cheering on their favorite karaoke singers.

Of the fifty or so people that packed the main floor open area, seated at the long rows of tables, squeezing between the chairs pushed back into the narrow aisles, talking, drinking, and generally having a good time, only about a dozen glanced my way when I entered the pub. Half of them looked away again almost immediately, having decided that I wasn't whoever it was they were waiting for. The rest took their time sizing me up. It's nothing sexist – male or female, we all decide whether or not a newcomer is a companion or a threat, worth trying to hit on, or likely to be more attractive to our current partner than we are. Half of my appraisers looked away within about ten seconds; as I had made a similar quick assessment of them, I didn't take their dismissal personally.

While the initial quick scan-and-evaluation of a stranger is a normal part of social interaction, the longer look moves the exchange to the next level. Part of my success in the corporate world was based on my ability to read body language and correctly interpret the signals my clients were inadvertently sending during a meeting. They told me whether I should press my advantage or ease back and try another approach, and when to swoop in and close the deal, like a bird of prey snatching an unsuspecting rodent.

On the clandestine side, this ability had saved my life more than once. Of all the lessons Ian had taught me over the years, reading a room was one of the most critical.

Two steps into the pub, only three people – two men, and a woman – were still looking my way.

The first man, an executive type, was seated with two others of the same general category at one of the tall, round tables between the large windows to my left, but appeared to have little interest in their animated conversation. I noted the basic details – dark hair touched with gray at the temples, an obviously tailored navy suit jacket, the slightly lighter blue point of his discarded tie poking out of the breast pocket, top button of the dress shirt unbuttoned, and collar loosened. He raised a half-full tumbler as though in salute, but the smile that touched his lips didn't reach his eyes.

I turned away without acknowledging the gesture.

My second observer was younger, more casually dressed, in jeans and a button-up with the sleeves rolled up and a warm-looking coat slung over the back of his chair. He caught my eye more because he appeared to be trying not to let on that he was looking at me, sneaking sidelong glances so the woman seated across from him wouldn't notice. I made a mental note of his face as well.

I would recognize either if I ever saw them again.

And then there was the woman – Bonnie Kauffman – now waving vigorously to me from a table across the room. I couldn't help but smile.

She was the center of attention – as usual – fit and trim, and casual in a pink and green plaid shirt that she somehow managed to make look stylish, the ends of her short blonde hair swishing softly around her face as she beckoned me over. A small cluster of men and women surrounded her, mesmerized by her infectious laugh and sparkling blue-green eyes. I returned her wave, feeling my own spirits lift as I did so. Bonnie just had that sort of an effect on people.

I pointed to the bar.

Bonnie nodded and returned to her conversation-in-progress while I moved over to the counter and ordered one of McGillin's locally-brewed house ales. Once fortified, I joined Bonnie, slipping into the seat she had saved for me at the end of the table.

I nodded politely as she introduced me to our tablemates. There was a Jim and a Nancy, someone named Kevin, and two women and another man whose names I missed in the general chaos. The woman seated opposite Bonnie, and to my left, was black, and the man next to her was noticeably older than the rest of us; but in the hubbub, and without nametags or a seating chart, I couldn't match the names to the faces two minutes later, much less safely say who was connected to whom.

Clearly, Stephen's death and the ghosts that had awakened for me, had shaken me more than a good cry and a workout had been able to repair. I took a long drink of my beer, hoping the alcohol would relax me, keenly aware of the nails I was digging into the palm of my free hand.

I don't like being rattled.

I like being well-organized, but flexible; feeling prepared for whatever came my way. Detached enough from the emotions of the situation to be able to respond quickly and logically. Aware enough to create mental nametags.

"Hey, Meg? You in there?" Bonnie was waving her hand in front of my face, the swishing blue and white of her shirt sleeve breaking me dizzily out of my introspection. "Long day?"

"Yeah," I replied. "Sorry. Got a lot on my mind."

"Share?"

My first thought was to wonder who had replaced Bonnie with a body double. 'Sharing' isn't my thing – especially in public – and she knows that.

Then again... I looked around the table at the impromptu focus group: six total strangers, in addition to Bonnie, eager faces all staring expectantly at me. *Why not?* My own baggage had colored my reactions to Deb's situation for the past twelve years. Maybe I was overreacting.

Their reactions could be instructive.

"A friend of mine is a single mom with two kids," I said, presenting Deb's original situation as it had been when I first met her, and watching the facial expressions around the table as I spoke. "Her ex stiffed her on child support for about four years – then threatened to take the kids away from her if she kept trying to make him pay up."

The shift in body language was unanimous. If we'd been sitting around a boardroom table discussing a possible merger, instead of in a noisy bar, chatting about the day's events, I'd have read the collective expressions of shock and outrage that colored the faces of my companions as an indicator that they'd just been handed an extremely bitter pill.

Interesting. Maybe it wasn't just me.

"Does he see the children?" asked one of the other women, a blonde with short hair like Bonnie's, only curly instead of straight. I think she was the one named Nancy.

I started to reply, but the black woman answered first.

"Doesn't matter," she said. "Support and visitation are completely separate issues. Withholding one as leverage for the other isn't allowed."

"For the sake of argument," I said, "let's assume that the father has access to the kids, but chooses not to exercise it, and that he has the means to pay child support, but refuses to do so. What should my friend do? What would *you* do?"

"Go after him with a baseball bat," said the brown-haired woman opposite Nancy. She had an athlete's build, and looked like she might know how to use a bat. "Nothing debilitating, mind you – he needs to keep earning a living – but a well-aimed blow, where it hurts most…" She gestured vaguely toward her lap.

All three men groaned sympathetically in protest.

"I'm thinking along slightly less physical lines," said Bonnie. "If he owns property, she could put a lien on his house."

"That would hurt him if he ever tries to sell it," I countered. Bonnie was a realtor and thinking like one, looking at the property for its resale potential, rather than as a place where the owner might choose to stay. "But it wouldn't do her any good in the short term."

"She doesn't have a lot of options," said one of the men – Kevin, I think. He was sitting to Bonnie's right. "She can fight him in court, and hope her attorney's good enough to play up the deadbeat angle. With luck, the judge will view that against him and rule in her favor—"

"With luck?" the blonde burst out, leaning forward, slamming her glass onto the table with a sloshing thud. For a moment, I thought she was going to lunge over the table toward

Kevin. "*He's* the deadbeat, and she needs to *get lucky* to keep her children? That's just wrong."

"On multiple levels," Kevin agreed. "But it's not a simple question of black or white, who's good and who's bad. There are all sorts of other factors that go into the decision…"

I watched silently as the four other women at the table turned to face him, expressions ranging from shock and outrage to pure fury.

Outnumbered, Kevin shrank in his seat a little, raising his hands in defeat. "Hey, hey, you wanted the truth, right? Don't kill the messenger."

"It isn't pretty," I agreed, turning the attention away from Kevin.

Bonnie reached out a small hand to squeeze mine. "There's more isn't there?"

At her words, I had to force myself to not shudder.

"Oh, yeah. His opening shot, the way he let her know of the threat? He sent her a copy of the court paperwork. He wanted to freak her out with it."

"Okay," said the brown-haired bat wielder. "Gimme his address. I'm going after him."

"I'll hold him down while you swing," said the blonde. They clinked glasses. "Maybe take a few practice swings of my own."

"That's what had you so bugged," said Bonnie. "I didn't think it was just him being a deadbeat."

"'Deadbeat' is too good a name for him," said the third man. He was sitting at the far end of the table, opposite me, and had been quiet for most of the conversation. "There are all sorts of more appropriate names: slimeball, jerkwad, sleazebucket…"

The conversation took a turn for the weird as everyone contributed their own beer-enhanced epithets to the list of nicknames.

I said nothing, just sat back and drank my ale, listening to them to rant about the unknown deadbeat and their overall disdain for deadbeats in general.

Whether it was the collective vindication of my own reaction the group had provided, or simply the ale, I actually felt myself relax a little.

◆

"So you want to tell me what the hell that was all about?" Bonnie asked. We'd left the bar and gone in search of coffee, finding it in an all-night diner a couple of blocks from the pub.

"What *what* was about?" I asked.

"You were talking about Deb Markham – don't deny it, we both know I'm right – but all that stuff you told everybody happened *years* ago."

"You asked me to *share*," I said, putting emphasis on the word. "It was on my mind."

"Why?"

"Stephen Markham is dead."

Bonnie nearly dropped her coffee. "No way!" she said. "I always figured he'd live forever. He was too mean to die."

"Guess he was nicer than we thought," I said. My coffee was bitter, even with cream and sugar. I pushed it away.

"How'd he die?"

I shook my head. "Not sure. All Deb knows is that some student on the night janitorial crew found him in his office and called 911."

"He probably gave some student a bad grade, and the kid took it personally."

"Who knows? Deb's been trying to get more information, but the family won't talk to her, the university is giving her the runaround, and all the police will say is that they're not at liberty to discuss it."

"What a mess. How's Deb taking it?"

"She's conflicted. Glad he won't be tormenting her anymore, guilty for feeling that way. He was her children's father and all."

"No need to feel guilty for losing the sperm donor," Bonnie said. She took a sip of her own coffee and made a face. "Why did we stop here instead of just going to your place? At least you have halfway decent coffee."

"I don't know. We should have, I suppose," I said, ignoring her attempt at humor. I leaned back in the corner of the booth and wrapped my arms around myself, as though trying to hold on the faint rays of sunshine I'd felt in the pub before the gloomy clouds I'd been battling all day closed in on me again.

"You that worried about Deb?" Bonnie asked. "Or is something else wrong?"

I shrugged. "Stephen… Deb… it's too much like what my father did to my mother," I said finally. "The whole thing ties me up inside."

Bonnie nodded and waited.

I had nothing more to say.

Bonnie and Shelia had been pretty close during high school, so she knew enough of our past not to pry. And I'd never seen the need to burden her with the details.

"Meg?" Bonnie said.

I jumped, startled, hitting my knee on the underside of the table, jostling the still nearly-full cups of coffee and rattling the silverware. A butter knife clinked back into place alongside the small pile of empty sugar packets, the light from the bright fluorescent tubes overhead glinting off its blade.

I shivered and looked up at Bonnie, wondering if I looked as pale and cold as I felt.

"I need a new house," I said.

♦

I slept poorly, and woke late, squinting as the morning sun streamed in between the slatted window blinds. While I'm usually up and about while it's still dark out, one thing I do love about the rowhouse is the way the morning sun lights up my room.

I must have been out of my mind to tell Bonnie that I wanted to move.

There was a rustle and a tugging at the blanket where it hung off the side of the bed, and then a scaly, brownish-green head appeared, golden eyes blinking balefully at me.

"Hi, Glau," I murmured.

The iguana – whose name was actually "Glaurung" after the wingless dragon-king in a Tolkien story – just blinked at me, then scrambled the rest of the way up onto the bed, took two steps forward, and head-butted me in the chest.

"Oof! Yeah, yeah, it's morning. I know!" I reached out and caressed the rough patch of scales at the top of his head. Glau stretched upward, pressing his head into my hand, his eyes closing and his mouth opening in a lizard-ish approximation of a smile.

I've never really been one for pets, but Glau suits me.

I'd rescued him from my former sister-in-law, Janine, after their young daughter died and my brother committed suicide. Janine always said the lizard creeped her out, and was constantly threatening to leave the door open so he could *accidentally* wander off. With Gary gone, I thought she might actually do it, so I went over that same day and collected Glau and all of his gear. I did it for Gary. Janine didn't protest.

Glau was well-socialized to being around people – Gary had handled him a lot and put a lot of time into his training. As a result, he adapted quite well to living with me.

Or maybe he just likes that I only restrict him to the second-floor bedroom I'd had converted into a combination greenhouse-terrarium when I'm out of town, and otherwise give him the run of the house. My three-story rowhouse offers plenty of places for him to climb, stair railings and decorative ledges where he can perch and imagine he's up in the tree-branches watching the comings and goings of the humans below, and a few prime spots for basking in the sun on warm afternoons.

He really is a dragon-king. All six and a half feet of him.

And at the moment, the diminutive dragon king was sitting on my bed and letting me know that it was long past time for me to get up and give him his breakfast.

I sighed, shifted past the lizard, and got out of bed.

Deliberate introspection really isn't my thing, but as I padded downstairs, Glau rushing ahead of me toward the kitchen, I wondered what had possessed me to tell Bonnie I wanted a new house.

Old habits die hard, I decided.

Back when Bonnie and I connected over real estate, it was when I was desperate to get out of the house I'd been living in.

Now I looked around my sunny kitchen, smiling at its vintage charm. I'd liked this house when I first saw it, and I still did. I had no reason to leave it.

Other than a handful of changes necessary for modern living – like insulation, double-paned windows, updated plumbing and wiring, and a state-of-the art heating and air-conditioning system – both the former owners and I had chosen to retain as much as possible of the rowhouse's late 19th century style both indoors and out. The tall ceilings sported elaborate medallions and crown moldings, and the interior doors were all topped with stained-glass transoms, letting light from the front and rear windows flow through the house.

Like most of its neighbors, the rowhouse opened directly onto the sidewalk, with only a few steps up to the front porch. But at the back, French doors opened onto a small garden and short, tree-filled alley, providing a private oasis from the busy, day-to-day world. And while some parts of the neighborhood had become ridiculously young and over-gentrified in the past few years – I'm only in my early forties, yet I sometimes feel like a middle-class old lady when I take Glau for a walk down the tree-lined sidewalk or in one of the nearby parks – I have no bad memories associated with this house any more significant than the bathroom pipes bursting one winter.

It has its quirks, but it's convenient to just about everything – work, trains, shopping, restaurants. Besides, if I sold it, then I'd have to pack, and there's nothing quite like the prospect of hauling everything you own down three narrow flights of stairs to keep you in one place forever.

I'd have to call Bonnie later and tell her I'd been drunk or something. If I didn't, she'd have twenty properties lined up for me to look at in the next week, and I'd end up having to buy one of them just for the sake of friendship.

I had just dropped a handful of kale leaves into Glau's shallow food dish and refilled his water when my cell phone rang. It was Deb's daughter, Cassie.

"Aunt Meg?" she said, sounding very much like she was trying not to burst into tears. "I hope I'm not interrupting you or anything."

"What is it, Cassie?" I asked.

"Can you come over?"

"Of course. What's wrong?"

"The police were here... they arrested Mom... They're saying..." she choked on her words and had to try again. "They're saying she murdered Dad."

And here I'd thought there was nothing else Stephen Markham could do to hurt Deb.

Chapter 6
12 years ago

Over her second cup of coffee, Meg studied the results of the database queries she'd set running the night before. Deborah's account of her divorce had been heart-wrenching, but Meg knew better than to accept a sob-story at face value. She wanted to know Stephen's side of the story – or as much of it as she could get without asking him directly.

She had just enough time to review the reports and form a mental image of Deborah, Stephen, and his second wife, Malia, before she went to work. She didn't know what she was looking for, but hoped she'd recognize it when she saw it.

If she'd never met Deborah, Meg would have been able to guess at much of her history just from her financial reports. A fairly stable picture for several years that dropped sharply at the time of her divorce, and then took another plunge a couple years later, when the child support stopped. Bank accounts for the past three years always hovering just above empty. No credit to speak of. No personal property of record that could be leveraged for its equity.

Stephen's financial profile was consistent with the pampered son of a prominent family. High-end cars, replaced after a year or two, multiple credit cards, all close to their limits, an investment portfolio loaded with speculative ventures that tanked more often than they paid out. A home in the city – in an older, established neighborhood popular with university professors – and the requisite vacation home in the Hamptons. Both mortgages were up-to-date, but each had a scattering of late payments.

The properties were both in Stephen's name alone, and not held jointly with his new wife, a former model with a very messy financial history up until their marriage, three years before. Of course, in a family like the Markham's, pre-nuptial agreements were probably de rigueur as a protection against gold-diggers. Understandable, if a bit cold.

But it also explained how Deborah had left the marriage with no assets of her own.

Everything they had owned as a couple had stayed with him. She left with what she brought – which was very little, in terms of real property.

And the children, of course.

Meg pondered the data while she washed up her breakfast dishes in her makeshift kitchen – with the renovation in full-swing downstairs, she'd set up the guest bathroom with a mini-fridge, coffee maker, and toaster oven and repurposed the linen cupboard into a temporary pantry.

She was just drying her hands when her cell phone rang.

She smiled when she saw the name displayed on the Caller ID. James Paoletti was a top-flight attorney who had just been elected as Pennsylvania's Attorney General. He and his wife, Maureen, were long-time friends of Meg's family.

"Hi, Uncle Jim," she said. "What's up?"

"Maureen says you've moved back into your mother's house," he said.

Meg looked at the stacks of boxes piled around her. "You could call it that. Moved in over New Year's," she acknowledged. "Still sorting things out. Aunt Ruthie tell her?"

"Who else?" he asked. "Gave her an earful."

Meg heard the smile in his voice. Aunt Ruthie was an acknowledged gossip – and liberally seasoned the family news with her own opinions. And Aunt Ruthie's opinions with regard to Meg's moving back into her childhood home were strong, to say the least.

"I can just imagine."

The humor in Jim's voice faded as he continued. "You okay?"

Meg shrugged off his concern, unwilling to admit just how unsettling it was to be living in her dead mother's house. The house she grew up in. A house filled with memories she'd just as soon forget.

"I didn't want to renew the lease on my apartment, and the house was sitting empty," she said. "This is just temporary, until I find a place of my own. In the meantime, I'll be around to oversee the rest of the renovations."

"'Temporary' has a way of lasting a while," Jim said. "And renovations always take longer than you expect. You can always stay with us until you find your next place."

Aunt Ruthie had made the same offer, but Meg had spent enough years under her aunt's roof, and had no desire to relive the experience.

"Thanks, Jim. I'll keep it in mind," Meg said. Downstairs, the doorbell rang. Meg went over to the window and looked through a gap in the curtains. "But I'm okay here. Really."

"Was that the door? Do you need to get that?"

Meg watched the uniformed delivery driver walk back down the sidewalk to the unmarked gray van. "No," she said, letting the curtain fall closed as the van pulled away from the curb. "Just a delivery. The driver must have left it on the porch."

"Oh, okay. How about if Maureen and I come over on Sunday afternoon?" Uncle Jim suggested, changing the subject. "We can help you finish settling in, open a bottle of wine, bring over your birthday gift, and have a quiet little housewarming. I'm curious about the renovations anyway."

"I'll rearrange some boxes so we all have a place to sit down," Meg said, heading down the stairs. "And I'll take care of dinner – if you're okay with Chinese takeout. I don't actually have a kitchen yet."

"Love it," Jim said, his voice warm. "And so does Maureen."

"Sounds great. And no black balloons or teasing about my age," Meg added, knowing he'd notice if she'd ignored his comment about her upcoming birthday.

"Black balloons are for fifty, not twenty-somethings," Jim said, "or so Maureen claimed a few years ago, though I question the reliability of her sources. Kids your age get something gentle – like fuzzy slippers – to ease them across the threshold into adulthood."

Meg opened the door, stooping to retrieve the unlabeled manilla envelope that leaned against the doorframe. "I think a couple bottles of wine should do the trick," she said, closing and locking the door behind her before tearing open the envelope. A slim black flash drive fell out in her hand.

"Are you even twenty-one yet?"

Meg rolled her eyes. "Twenty-*six* on Sunday, silly."

She chatted with her uncle for a few minutes more, toying with the thumb drive while they talked. By the time the call ended, Meg was practically grinning at the irony of receiving illegally-sourced information while carrying on a conversation with the state's new Attorney General.

She loved her uncle, but as she plugged the flash drive into her laptop, Meg was feeling more like herself than she had in days.

The drive contained a single file – Stephen Markham's personnel file from the University. She had no idea who the courier had been, but the data had come from a less-than-legitimate information broker she knew only as the Researcher.

Despite the comic-book anonymity of his preferred name, the material he provided was always well worth the fees she willingly paid.

Meg scrolled through the file, shaking her head as she read. Deborah had been lucky to get away from Stephen. He'd been accused of plagiarism of multiple research papers. Complaints from female students about inappropriate behavior had been hushed up and swept under the rug, but never purged from his employment record. Reprimands for excessive paid time off littered the record – the most recent only a few weeks before. Only tenure and his family name were keeping him from losing his position.

Steven Markham was enough less-than-squeaky-clean to provide plenty of leverage that might help Deborah's case. Leverage that, if properly applied, would force him into shaping up his act, while leaving him capable of providing for his children.

But Meg had to be careful.

If she pushed Steven Markham too hard, she could end up doing more harm than good. Too much pressure, and he might just quit his job entirely, sell one of his houses, convince his wife to go back to modeling, or even come up with a way to work under the table to keep from bringing in an income that could be garnished for support. No, it was better to nudge him toward semi-decent behavior than push him over the edge.

Semi-decent was the best she thought she could expect of him.

Deborah didn't need the additional burden of having the entire truth about her ex-husband dumped on her all at once, if at all. Slime bag or no, he was the father of her children, and his betrayal already hurt her enough for one day.

Enough for a lifetime.

However, according to her sources, Steven Markham cared very much about his mother's good opinion of him. Meg thought that might be something she could use against him, even though she knew it was something Deborah's sensibilities would never allow her to do or condone.

Deb still had qualms about breaking long-standing family taboos.

Meg had gotten past that a long time ago.

♦

Eleanor Markham was the real power behind the Markham family, and everyone even remotely connected to Philadelphia society knew it. While the money had originated a few generations back along the paternal line, it was the Markham women who had developed the network of connections that propelled the family into its current position of prominence.

Armed with that knowledge and more, Meg pulled up to the wrought-iron gate that protected the Markhams from the curiosity of idle passers-by shortly before six o'clock. She put down her window, and reached out to press the intercom button attached to one of the great brick pillars framing the entry.

"Margaret Harrison to see Eleanor Markham," she said in response to the bland security greeting. "I'm expected."

"The drive splits just inside the gate," came the tinny reply. "Follow the left fork. Park in front of the house."

She'd expected the grounds to be pretentious, considering the elaborate nature of the gate and reputation of the family. Instead, she was pleasantly surprised to find herself winding through a natural wood, reminiscent of a nature preserve. The barren branches of a variety of deciduous trees arched over the plowed and salted road, casting deep shadows in the early evening; a squirrel darted across the road across her path.

The house was a large, three-story affair, built in a modified Tudor-style. Thick swaths of ivy climbed one wall, individual leaves barely visible under a dusting of snow, and all but obscured an upper window. Copper chimney pipes long-since covered with a green patina, hinted at the building's age. Enormous oak trees that were probably little more than saplings when the house was built extended their branches over the eaves.

Meg parked the car, then made her way up a brick-lined path, a fresh scattering of blue ice-melt crystals providing traction even as they crunched under her shoes.

Eleanor Markham answered the door herself, elegant, with her silver hair piled loosely on her head and wearing a sweater heavily embellished with a cascade of flowers tumbling over one shoulder.

After inviting Meg in, Eleanor seemed to be studying her as she removed her coat and hung it on the antique mirrored coat rack that dominated the vaulted entry.

"I knew your mother," she said, matter-of-factly. "I was very sad when she died. You don't look a thing like her; well, except maybe for the hair."

"Mine's lighter than hers was. I favor my father's side of the family," Meg replied.

Eleanor nodded, gesturing her toward a sitting room adjacent to the entry.

The furniture in this room was pleasant to look at, but functional rather than comfortable – hard, thin cushions intended to minimize the duration of the visit. Meg took a seat on a small loveseat, laying a slim portfolio on the cushion next to her.

"I presume you have a specific purpose to your visit," Eleanor said, seating herself opposite in a tapestry-covered Queen Anne chair and folding her hands across her lap. "And that this is not purely a social call."

Meg liked her direct manner, and responded in kind.

"Yes. I confess, I traded on your acquaintance with my mother to gain the appointment. I wasn't sure if you would see me otherwise."

"That depends. Why are you here?"

"I'm here on behalf of your daughter-in-law, Deborah."

Eleanor's demeanor darkened. "That bitch!" She practically spat out the words, then composed herself instantly. "Forgive my outburst. We welcomed Deborah into our family with open arms, and her response was to turn her back on us. She hurt my son terribly, and continues to do so – did you know that she refuses to allow him to see his own children? She has cut off all contact with our family – forcing those children to grow up without their grandparents, aunts, uncles, cousins in their lives."

There are always two sides to every story. Clearly Stephen had chosen to share his own version of the situation with his family, to Deborah's detriment.

"When was the last time you spoke to her?"

"It's been at least three or four years," Eleanor replied.

"Then how do you know these things about her?"

Eleanor drew herself up stiffly. "I speak with my son and his wife regularly," she replied. "I know everything I need to know about Deborah." She spoke her name as though she was discussing bodily waste. "The woman is intolerable. What could you possibly have to do with her?"

"Let me start by saying that Deborah doesn't know that I'm here; probably doesn't know most of what I'm here to tell you, and almost certainly wouldn't approve of my being here if she did know."

Eleanor raised an eyebrow. "Please continue."

"I met Deborah a few months ago," Meg said. "Among my other pursuits, I teach a women's self-defense class."

"What would Deborah be doing at a self-defense class?"

"Steven hit her."

The air in the room seemed to close around them. Meg was suddenly aware of orchestral music playing softly in the background.

Eleanor's eyes went hard. "That is impossible. My son would never do such a thing."

"But he did. And I suspect that not everything he's told you about his relationship with Deborah has been...," Meg paused, searching for the best word. "...entirely accurate. If you want to see your grandchildren, I recommend contacting Deborah directly, rather than going through your son. But don't expect to be welcomed with open arms. From what I have been given to understand, she has every right to mistrust anyone bearing the Markham family name."

Eleanor stood, rising out of her chair in a smooth, fluid motion. "We have nothing further to discuss," she said stiffly. "I regret that you lack your mother's sensibilities."

Meg stood as well, picking up the portfolio, and extending it to her.

"Don't take my word for it," she said. "See for yourself."

"Please leave," said Eleanor, ignoring the proffered portfolio and refusing to meet her gaze. "And do not call on me again."

"If this information isn't true, there's no reason to be afraid of it," Meg said.

"How dare you stand in judgment against my son," Eleanor hissed. "Whatever lies Deborah has told you, whatever you think you know, it's nothing."

"Perhaps. Or perhaps your son simply believes himself to be above the law."

Eleanor snatched the portfolio from Meg's hand and tossed it onto the table. "When one achieves a certain station, one *is* above the law," she snapped. "It is truly regrettable that your mother passed away before she was able to teach you that simple, yet vital lesson."

"Then I consider myself fortunate that you have taken it upon yourself to supplement my education," Meg said, keeping her voice calm, her manner businesslike, without a trace of the vulnerability she had attempted to generate.

Eleanor Markham was not the first person to try to intimidate her, nor was she the most powerful. And the barb she'd thrown by bringing up her mother's untimely death had been the only weapon in her undoubtedly vast arsenal that stood even the slightest chance of scoring.

Meg indicated the portfolio with a slight nod. "It should go without saying that these documents are not the originals."

Eleanor escorted her to the door in silence, not bothering with the pleasantries of departure. The door closed firmly behind her as soon as Meg crossed the threshold.

As she started down the driveway, Meg saw a motion in the rear-view mirror. Eleanor Markham stood at the sitting-room window, curtain pulled to one side, watching her drive away.

◆

The meeting with Eleanor Markham had left Meg unsettled, though not in the ways Eleanor had clearly intended. Meg encountered too many powerful people on a daily basis through her work for Eleanor's attempts to intimidate her to seem any more than routine. And Meg had long since dealt with any residual emotion surrounding her mother's death for her cutting remark to have left anything more than a scratch.

Rather, it was the inefficiency of the entire encounter that had Meg pacing the upstairs hall from bedroom to stairs and back in the middle of the night. She'd been able to delve into Stephen's financial records easily enough, but had had to rely on the Researcher to provide the deeper information she'd needed to use as leverage. And then she'd had to go to Eleanor Markham herself, rather than use that leverage against Stephen in a more direct – and more stealthy – manner.

None of it sat well with her.

Meg was comfortable operating in morally gray areas; that wasn't the problem. It was the need to involve so many other people – people who knew who she was and what she was doing – that bothered her. What was to keep the courier from mentioning occasional deliveries of unmarked envelopes? Or Eleanor Markham from turning her visit into an amusing anecdote at a garden party?

She caught the shadow of her reflection as she passed the darkened guest bathroom-turned-kitchen, and froze, staring at the vague silhouette.

The Researcher worked in anonymity. She should do the same.

Meg went back to her room, scooped up her cell phone, and dialed a number.

"Don't you ever sleep?" His voice was raspy, harsh from too many years of cheap cigarettes and shouting at underlings – or so she'd always imagined. Large machinery whined and clanked in the background. What he was doing at this hour Meg had no idea, and didn't want to know.

"I want you to teach me."

"It's easy. Lay down and count sheep until you wake up."

Meg ignored the joke. "I want you to teach me how to do what you do."

"It will be cheaper for you if we just continue—"

"It's not about the money."

"Then what *is* it about?" The rough voice was all business, and the machinery sound was more distant, as though he'd moved into another room. "Many consider corporate espionage to be a career-limiting choice, but you've done well – moving up quickly in your... *legitimate* profession. So I have to wonder, what's changed?"

"My reasons are my own," Meg said. "I don't need to explain them to you."

"You're asking me to take you on as an apprentice," he snapped. "Teach you my trade. Introduce you to my contacts. That exposes me in any number of ways. In exchange, I don't think wanting to know why I should take that kind of risk is too much to ask."

Meg sank down to the floor at the foot of her bed, running a hand through her hair. She barely knew what she was thinking, much less how to answer the Researcher's question. "It's just time," she said finally. "Time for me to up my game. Stop relying so much on other people to do my work for me."

There was a long silence before the Researcher finally spoke.

"Don't make me regret this."

Chapter 7
Present day: Friday morning

Deb? Arrested for murder? I couldn't wrap my head around it.

I'd thought about killing Stephen myself many times – he represented so many things I found personally offensive. But I'd refrained, out of respect for my friend. As long as Stephen was paying child support, he was more useful to her alive.

Then again, he was always dragging her back to court, repeatedly challenging her over the support amount. And after what she'd said about the support money going to pay the never-ending legal bills…

I almost dropped the phone when I realized that I actually *could* contemplate the idea of Deb having a possible motive for killing her ex-husband.

Cassie was still crying on the other end of the line.

"Calm down, Cassie," I told her. "Do you know where they took her?"

"Um… I think…," she began, then paused shouting away from the phone, "Gran? What did you do with that business card?"

There was some additional talking and noise in the background, then a new voice said, "Hello, Meg? It's Barbara."

Deb's mother sounded much more composed than Cassie had been.

"Hi, Barbara," I said. "Cassie was looking for the district station address where they took Deb—"

"I told Deb not to say a word until her lawyer got there, just like they show on *Law and Order,*" she said. "And then I got on the phone with her lawyer's office before they'd even pulled out of our driveway. But that prissy secretary I talked to said they don't handle criminal cases – can you imagine that? Her calling Deb a *criminal?*"

"It's nothing personal," I told her. "Different situations require specialized legal training – this comes under the category of criminal law. Did she recommend another attorney?"

Barbara huffed in displeasure. "No, she didn't. She just said that the court would appoint someone if Deb didn't have her own attorney. Really! After all the money Deb has paid them over the years, you'd think they could have been more helpful. When Deb comes home, I'm going to tell her to find a new lawyer right away... oh, but she won't need them anymore now that Stephen is dead. So that's a good thing, anyway."

This line of conversation wasn't going to help Deb any. I tried to turn the topic back to my original question.

"Do you know where they took Deb?" I asked.

"Oh, yes, I have that right here. One of the officers left a card." Barbara read off the officer's name and the station address. "Are you going over? You can take her cold medicine. They wouldn't let her take it with her. I don't see why not. It's prescription. She's supposed to take it four times a day. The hospital won't let her go back to work if she might infect any of those poor children..."

"I'm not sure," I said, ignoring Barbara's rambling about Deb's medication. "They're not likely to tell me anything or let me see her anyway. I'm going to make a couple of calls first, see if I can find an attorney who can advise Deb. That's the first thing she needs."

"He was such a horrible man," Barbara said.

"I'm sorry?"

"I told her she never should have married him," she continued, and then proceeded to catalogue Stephen's many faults.

I needed to get off the phone before Barbara wandered any further off-topic. She had a habit of snatching up random bits of information, suspicion, and outright speculation and tying them together in much the same the way a fisherman tied knots. Before you knew it, a simple greeting had turned into a lengthy conversation, and you were both tangled hopelessly in her net, without either of you having any idea what you'd been talking about in the first place.

"Barbara," I said, trying to get her attention. "Barbara, I've got to go."

"Hmm? Oh. Sorry. I was rambling again, wasn't I?"

"Yes," I said, "But not without good cause. Try not to worry too much, and tell Cassie that I'll let her know if I find out anything, okay?"

"I will," Barbara said. "And thank you, Meg. I don't know what we'd do without someone like you who can keep her wits about her. Deb's good at it, but Lord knows, I'm not."

It took almost five minutes to finally get off the call. I didn't want to be harsh – some people cry when stressed, others clam up. I knew the rambling was just how Barbara was trying to cope – but her entire understanding of the criminal justice system was based on years of watching television crime dramas, and barely bordered on reality. It was all I could do not to simply hang up on her.

The things we do for our friends.

♦

I dug my Bluetooth headset out of my purse and popped it in my ear as I headed back upstairs to get dressed. Naturally, because I was in a hurry, it seemed to take forever for the headset to link to my phone, but when it finally did, I dialed a number from memory.

I'd told Barbara that I was going to look for someone to represent Deb. In reality, there was only one person I had in mind.

My Uncle Jim – who other people know as former Pennsylvania Attorney General, James Paoletti – had grown weary of politics and "retired" back into private practice a few years back, at the end of his second term. Not many people know the Paoletti's home phone number. I've had it memorized for years. I just hoped Jim was still at home.

The phone only rang three times before the call was picked up.

"Uncle Jim? It's Meg," I said, pausing in front of the mirror to quickly run damp fingers through my short blonde hair and push the wayward strands into place. "I hate to call so early, but I need to ask a favor."

"What's wrong, Meg?" Jim asked, his voice full of concern.

"A friend of mine was just picked up for murder – her name's Deborah Markham..."

"Markham? As in 'Markham Enterprises?"

"Related by divorce, yes," I said, moving to the closet where I pulled out a charcoal gray, featherweight, wool suit. "Thought you'd recognize the name. Anyway, Deb's ex turned up dead yesterday, and Deb was arrested for the murder about an hour ago."

"I take it she doesn't have an attorney?"

From the background noises on Jim's end of the line, it sounded like he was cooking breakfast. Something sizzled; my stomach rumbled in response, and I could have sworn I smelled bacon.

"Only for family law – ongoing child support issues and such," I answered. I held up a white linen blouse next to the dark gray blazer but didn't like the look, and discarded it in favor of a black silk with thin pleats down the front. "Apparently they're totally arms-length for this."

"And...?" He left the question hanging.

"Yeah, well, that's why I'm calling you."

"You'd like me to look into it." Jim said. His voice had taken on a professional edge that I seldom heard. "You know I can't make any sort of promises, Meg."

"I know. And I don't have anything else in the way of details, but she's my friend, and she needs help. Someone to advise her, at the very least."

"Did she do it?"

I wanted to say 'No, absolutely not!' but that hint of uncertainty I'd felt earlier made me hesitate a heartbeat too long before I answered. "I don't think so. I've known her for a long time…"

"…But even people we think we know can be pushed into dark places, and do things we don't expect," Jim finished for me. "Not knowing is the right answer, Meg."

I nodded, fumbling with the buttons on my blouse, not that he could see either.

Jim was silent for a long moment – even the cooking sounds in the background had faded, as though he'd moved away from the stove. Most likely, he'd had Aunt Maureen take over for him and gone into his study.

"Okay," he said finally. "What else can you tell me?" He was in full attorney-mode now. I could almost see him at his big mahogany desk with a notepad and pen, poised to take down whatever I said.

As I finished dressing, I told him everything I knew, which wasn't much.

"Do you know where they took her?"

"Yeah." I gave him the arresting officer's information and the station number.

"I'll call now, and stop by on my way to the office. Talk to her, see what else I can learn."

"Thanks, Jim," I said. "Knew I could count on you. Advise her, do whatever it is you do to help make this right, and send the bill to me, okay?"

"To you? But she's a Markham."

"She's a *former* Markham, and isn't in a position to cover your retainer, much less pay you for full representation. I don't want her worrying about the cost." I slipped on a pair of black suede ankle boots, better for walking than the low-heeled pumps I usually wore. "I've had a good month, I'll cover it."

"This could get very expensive."

"Doesn't matter. She's my friend, she's got a problem, and there's precious little I can do about it. This is one thing I *can* do. I mean it, Jim. I want you to send me the bill." I pulled on the gray jacket and gave myself an appraising look in the mirror. Armani. Joie. Prada. The look was suitably don't-mess-with-me.

"You drive a hard bargain," Jim said with a sigh.

"That's what all my clients say."

♦

Bonnie and I had shared a taxi the night before, and I'd left my car in my office's downtown parking garage. Fortunately, the early autumn weather was decent, and the walk to the transit station was uneventful.

Rather than head directly downtown, though, I went in the opposite direction, and after a couple of transfers and another short walk, I found myself at a family-style restaurant located across the street from one of the city's many police stations.

If you're going to hack into local law enforcement servers, I've found it's convenient to do it from a location that's close enough that your signal is bouncing off the same tower as theirs. Takes them an extra couple of minutes to locate you – and there's a lot you can do in a couple of minutes.

Like get away, for one.

Locate and download case files for another.

Deb was my friend, and I wanted to help her. But before I did anything further on her behalf, I needed to know exactly what had happened to Stephen – how he died, what evidence the police thought they had that pointed at Deb.

I needed to decide if I thought she'd committed murder.

I ordered coffee – a cup to stay, and one to go – a fruit cup, and an English muffin, then pulled out my iPad and set to work. Nothing about the tablet tied it to me personally – I'd bought and registered it under a falsified corporate ID, which also paid the connection fees. I seldom use it, and figure if anyone ever catches on, I'll just reset it to factory defaults or toss it and pick up another.

Cost of doing business and all.

I'm not the world's greatest hacker, but I am good at what I do. I was in the police network before my toast got cold. Speed was essential at this point – security systems are tuned to notice breaches, but the quicker you're out, the harder it is for them to flag and find you.

I grabbed the files for all new cases opened in the past ten days, obscuring the fact that I was only after Deb's, copied them to the tablet, and was out of the system by the time the waitress returned with my check.

I paid in cash, left a reasonable tip – nothing memorable – and left the restaurant as a pair of uniformed officers walked in, clearly on a coffee break, chatting casually amongst themselves. One of them even held the door for me.

Chapter 8
Present day: Friday afternoon

I had a full calendar that morning, and a lunch meeting with a potential client, so I copied the police files to a flash drive and tucked both into a locked compartment at the back of my bottom desk drawer for safekeeping.

My lunch meeting had just broken up, and I was hoping to take advantage of some free time later that afternoon to look at the case files, when my phone buzzed in my pocket. I groaned when I saw Bonnie's name on the caller ID, and was momentarily tempted to let it go to voicemail.

But I knew that if I did that, instead of only a dozen houses, she'd have twice that many to show me when she finally reached me. I bit the bullet and took the call.

"Hey, so I don't know what I was thinking last night, but I don't want to move after all."

"Of course you don't," Bonnie said, undaunted. "But you're going to come look at these houses with me anyway."

"I've got things to do—"

"You're not busy now, or you wouldn't have answered the phone. I'll pick you up in fifteen minutes. You're at home?"

"No, just leaving Butcher & Singer."

"Okay…" she trailed off, and I heard someone speaking softly in the background.

Bonnie came back on the line a moment later. "You're going to love these houses," she gushed. "Well, most of them, anyway."

I sighed. "I'll meet you out front in fifteen."

♦

I called Uncle Jim's while I waited for Bonnie to arrive.

The call went to voice mail. It figured.

"It's Meg," I said. "Just checking in. Give me a call back when you have news."

I turned the ringer up to full volume before I dropped the phone back in my purse. I was itching to know what he'd learned from Deb. I didn't want to miss another call.

A bullet-gray Mercedes convertible with the top down squealed to a stop in the drive, a valet hopping back out of its path. Music surrounded it like a cloud, a boot-scooting country tune turned up so loud you could almost taste fried chicken and cornbread.

"Hop in!" Bonnie shouted over the two-stepping twang of a steel guitar.

I shrugged at the valet, who seemed to have recovered his composure, and walked over to the car. "You 'bout scared that poor boy to death," I said as I got in. We were moving almost before the door closed.

"Nah," Bonnie replied, a wicked grin on her face. "He's young. A little adrenaline is good for him. Keep him on his toes."

We pulled out into traffic, then turned at the next light. "So where are we headed?" I said, shouting over the combination of music and traffic sounds. It was a nice day, but having the top down was nothing new for Bonnie — as long as neither rain nor snow were falling from the sky, she almost always drove with the wind in her hair. I once saw her wearing a parka while driving with the top down in the middle of January.

Bonnie turned the music down, then nudged a folio wedged between the seats. "I've got a dozen possibles in there."

"I don't want to look at houses."

"Have you heard anything more about Deb?"

"No." I didn't bother to mention the case files I'd pilfered and was impatient to analyze. Bonnie may be one of my closest friends, but that doesn't mean I spill my guts to her about my work. It's safer that way.

For her.

Bonnie shoved the folio at me. "Choose three."

"I'm don't want to look at houses."

"You said that," she said as we merged into heavier traffic on 34th street and crossed the Schuylkill River at the University Bridge, heading west. "I was listening. That's why you only have to choose three."

We were standing in the formal dining room of the second house when Uncle Jim called, the melancholy strains of the ringtone's violin echoing in the large, empty room.

"It's been a long, crazy day," he said in response to my greeting. "And I have you to thank for it."

"Moi?" I said innocently, nodding as Bonnie pointed out the elegant butler's pantry – cherry paneling, built-in coffee station – connecting the dining room to the chef's kitchen.

"Yes, you. I hate celebrity cases, and you dumped one right in my lap."

"Deb's no celebrity. Far from it," I said.

"Not her; I've got the entire Markham clan 'blowing up my phone' as my secretary says. The family is already making demands – no autopsy, no bail, stiffest possible charge, death sentence; you name it, they're asking for it. As if the judge, jury, and executioner were all family members."

"It sounds bad," I said.

"It's not good."

I'd followed Bonnie into the kitchen, and we were standing on either side of the massive, marble-topped island. "I'm with another of Deb's friends, do you mind if I put you on speaker so she can listen in?"

"Go ahead," Jim said. I pushed the button, and his gravelly voice filled the room, slightly tinny from the phone's speaker. "It's not like I can tell you much – client-attorney privilege, after all."

"I understand," I said. "You're on speaker now." I made quick introductions, slipping into conference call habits.

"I have another call in five minutes, so only time to give you a quick summary. Stephen Markham was murdered, no question of that. There's evidence that places Deb at the scene during the period identified as the probable time of death; the police also have other evidence they're working to verify. The preliminary arraignment will be in about an hour; she's lucky they picked her up early, or she might have been here all weekend."

"What's she being charged with, Jim?"

"Manslaughter."

"My God," Bonnie breathed.

"It's a lesser charge," Jim said, his voice softening slightly as though trying to reassure us. "The family wants her charged with first-degree murder, which is a capital offense. On a manslaughter charge, she could be looking at as much as twenty years. But not the death penalty."

"Well, that's something," I said.

"I can say this," Jim continued, "there's more going on here than you led me to believe, Meg – not your fault, you would have had no way of knowing. I'll take the best care of her I can from the legal side, but it's going to be messy."

Bonnie and I looked at each other. The large pendant lights shining down on us suddenly seemed too intense.

"Are they going to let her go home today?" I asked.

"Bail has been set at 100 grand."

Bonnie and I replied in unison. "I'll cover it."

Jim laughed, but there was little humor in the somber tone. "I'll message you the details. Maybe you can split the bill."

"Thanks, Jim," I said.

"I don't know how well you ladies know her, or what your relationship is, but Deborah Markham could use a friend."

We said our good-byes, and I pressed the button to close the call. The large, tastefully appointed kitchen seemed cold and uninviting in the sudden stillness.

♦

It took some time to get things arranged, but Bonnie and I arrived at the police station about five-fifteen p.m. to post bail for Deb. The paperwork didn't take long.

Waiting for Deb to come out seemed to take forever.

The waiting area was small – four uncomfortable metal chairs with vinyl seats in the corner near the door, two along one wall, two with their backs to the reinforced glass panel that separated the public area of the station from other offices. A tall, spindly ficus tree with drooping, yellow-edged leaves stood between the chairs and the door, as though trying to soften the space.

If it hadn't been for the notices on the walls, it might have passed for a small clinic's reception area.

I have no problem with the police – in fact, I have the highest respect for them, in spite of my routine breaking of the law. I take comfort in knowing that they're out there, looking out for us, often putting their lives on the line.

But as much respect as I have for the police, I hate police *stations* with that special kind of loathing that only comes from an unpleasant experience at an impressionable age. And as Bonnie and I walked from the parking lot and into the station, I felt the muscles in my neck and shoulders begin to tighten, and had to forcibly keep my fists from clenching.

I took a deep breath, holding it for a count of three as we

crossed the threshold, and releasing it slowly as we approached the desk.

I inhaled again, a long, slow breath, held and released like the first, while Bonnie talked with the woman at the counter. And then a third.

And a fourth.

I signed the necessary paperwork, then walked over to the waiting area and perched on the edge of one of the chairs with its back to the wall. Bonnie sat by the glass wall, in the chair by the pitiful excuse for a ficus tree, pulled out her phone, and began checking her messages.

I was too wound up.

Deep breathing. It wouldn't be long, and Deb would come out and we could go.

Finally, Deb came through the heavy door that separated the reception and waiting area from the inner offices and interrogation rooms and cells and whatever else is really down the hall in a police station. Movies and television shows try to make them look both pleasant and frightening at the same time, depending on the show. One look at Deb said frightening had won out.

Deb's face was pale as death, eyes and nose red-rimmed. Her hair hung limp and tangled instead of pulled back in a ponytail like she usually wore it. Her coat was draped loosely, as though only half-remembered over one arm. She held a crumpled tissue in one hand, while the other clutched a small plastic bag that held her wallet, keys, and cell phone.

The officer escorting Deb stepped past her and opened the small gate that was connected to the end of the reception counter, and indicated that she should go through it. She just stood there, staring blankly at him.

"Ma'am, you can go," he said again, holding the gate open.

I took a step forward. "Deb," I said, "we've come to take you home."

She looked at me, confusion written all over her face, then looked back at the officer. "I can go?" she asked.

"Yes."

Deb took a hesitant step toward the gate, then another, as though certain that it would close before she got to it, but unable to make her feet carry her any faster.

Bonnie and I came closer, waiting quietly just a few steps beyond the gate.

The officer held the gate until Deb passed through it, then closed and latched it behind her. She flinched as it clicked into place, but didn't look back.

As Bonnie came forward and wrapped her arms around her, I looked over Deb's shoulder and mouthed a silent 'thank you' to the officer. He nodded, then turned away and went back down the hall.

We took Deb home, and handed her over to her mother and daughter who fussed and cooed over her like a new baby. Barbara plied her with questions, most of which Deb answered in monosyllables, until Cassie finally rescued her mother from her grandmother and took her upstairs to her room.

"You must stay for supper," Barbara said.

"We couldn't," Bonnie said.

"We wouldn't want to put you out—" I began.

"It's no trouble at all," Barbara insisted. "I have a lasagna in the oven, and no room in the refrigerator for leftovers. So you see, you *must* stay."

Barbara is an excellent cook. We stayed.

Cassie came down while we were setting the table.

"Poor Mom," she said. "She's got an awful headache, and is all stuffed up from crying – or from what's left of her cold maybe. I gave her some of her cold medicine and told her to go to bed. She'll feel a lot better after she gets some sleep."

"God, I hate having a cold," said Bonnie. "My head gets all stuffy and I can't make sense of anything. Which side does the fork go on again? Peggy and I seldom set a table except for holidays and special dinner parties, and she's better at it than I am."

"Fork on the left, so you can cut with the right," I said absently. My mother had drilled it into our heads from an early age. To Cassie I said, "Did she say anything? She was pretty quiet on the way home."

Cassie sank down on one of the chairs, shaking her head. "She just kept whispering 'I didn't do it, I didn't do it,' over and over, like it was important that I believe her."

"*Do* you believe her?" Bonnie asked.

Cassie looked up, her eyes brimming with tears. "I want to, really I do. But he's been so awful to her for so long…" she trailed off, the tears spilling down her cheeks.

I went over to her and pulled her into my arms. "We'll get through this, honey," I told her. "Everything will be okay."

For once the lie didn't come easily.

Chapter 9
Present day: Friday evening

It was after ten when I finally got home, but there was no way I was going to sleep until I looked at Stephen's case file. I wondered how much had been added to it in the past twelve hours since I'd picked it up, but decided not to worry about that.

Whatever was in this morning's copy had been enough for them to arrest and charge Deb with the murder. Anything new that had come in today would just be an effort to confirm their initial findings.

The timer on my thermostat had already let the house begin cooling off for the night. I made myself a mug of tea, then grabbed a sweater on my way upstairs to my third-floor home office.

Glau was nowhere to be seen; he'd undoubtedly found someplace lizard-friendly to curl up for the night. I suppressed a shiver, envying his cold-blooded nature, and fired up my secondary computer.

Hacking my way into the police network and downloading the case files was no small task – and opening the files I'd retrieved in a form that allowed them to actually be readable was no less difficult.

Which is why it occasionally came in handy to have friends in low places who owe you favors. I'd called in on one of those favors a couple of years ago, resulting in a personal instance of the current criminal records system software which I'd installed on this computer. I kept this machine offline – it wouldn't do to have the software try to connect to the department network – and at some point, the regular updates would eventually render the software obsolete, but for now it was oh, so very convenient.

I connected the flash drive to the computer, transferred the files to the appropriate directory, then fired up the CRS application. A moment later, the blue Philadelphia Police Department badge flashed up on the screen. I entered my username and password, searched the available records for Stephen Markham's name, and sipped at my tea while the system pulled up the data.

So much more efficient than hacking my way in.

The detective who had been assigned to investigate Stephen's murder – a Lieutenant J. Thackery – was meticulous in his note-taking and keeping the case files up-to-date. I appreciated that, as it made reviewing the case file a much easier process than some I've had the misfortune to dig through.

First, the basics: Stephen had been bludgeoned several times in the face with a hard object – likely the baseball-sized geode found cracked and covered with blood on the floor near the body – resulting in loss of several teeth, a broken nose, a shattered left cheekbone, and damage to the left eye. Photos had been added to the record, taken from various angles.

His smashed and swollen face was barely recognizable.

The time of death had been tentatively established as Wednesday, between eleven a.m. and three p.m., pending the coroner's confirmation. However, from both the report and the photos, I was clearly not alone in assuming that the actual cause of death was not the beating he'd taken; rather, the letter opener that had been jabbed hilt-deep into his right eye.

I've seen plenty of dead bodies, and am not generally queasy about them. Whenever possible, I go out of my way to make death look natural, or the result of an accident – it raises fewer questions, which is better for business. But as analytical as I was in my study of the photos, the raw violence of Stephen's death was making my skin crawl. I scrolled past the images to Lieutenant Thackery's case notes.

He'd begun his investigation by establishing Stephen's usual routine – when he usually arrived on campus, the classes he taught, together with a list of all of his students, contact and background information for his teaching assistant. All very standard and by-the-book.

Next, he tried to track Stephen's movements on the day he died.

Malia had dropped Stephen off at the university at eight a.m. Wednesday morning, and saw him enter the building before she drove away. Apparently, this was a common occurrence. Campus parking being what it was, it didn't seem that unusual.

He'd taught his two morning classes, and been spotted in the department office shortly after noon, but failed to show up for either his afternoon or his evening class.

According to Malia, he was often quite late arriving home after the evening class, so she'd gone to bed about eleven p.m., not thinking his lateness was anything out of the ordinary until she received the middle of the night call from campus police.

Again, all very straightforward, with nothing pointing to Deb in any way.

I next turned to the surveillance footage.

According to the Campus Security guards Thackery interviewed, students were constantly tampering with the various cameras – covering them up, smearing peanut butter on the lenses, you name it, in an attempt to get away with the hijinks-of-the-moment. So no one thought twice about the fact that several of the cameras in and around the building where Stephen's office was located had been out of commission from about mid-afternoon Tuesday until late Wednesday morning.

Cameras for both of the neighboring buildings had also been tampered with, and maintenance crews had worked to restore them all as quickly as they could.

Footage from two cameras — one in a stairwell of Stephen's building, and one positioned just above a rear door — both showed a slim woman with medium length hair pulled back in a ponytail arriving at 12:27 p.m., going up the nearby stairwell, and then heading back down the same stairwell a few minutes later, departing the building at 12:52.

The exterior shot was blurred, but it was obviously the same person that had been seen in the stairwell.

I replayed the video of the woman running down the stairs, freezing the frame at the moment she looked back over her shoulder, and zoomed in on it.

Security cameras don't have the best resolution, and the images are distorted at the best of times. Still, I'd have bet money that the woman on the stairs, her movements nervous, her pale shirt covered with a dark smear not quite hidden by her partially zipped-up jacket, was Deb Markham.

Well, shit.

I quickly scanned through rest of Thackery's notes.

There had been minimal signs of a struggle in the office. There were a few papers on the floor between the body and the desk, but the blood spatter pattern suggested that most of them had been on the desk when the droplets flew and were probably knocked to the floor when Stephen fell.

Partial fingerprints had been found on the letter opener, doorknob, and one corner of the desk, though they hadn't had any success getting even a useful smudge from the geode.

They hadn't found the same prints on either the stairwell door, railing, or exterior door, but they didn't need them. The partials at the scene and on the murder weapon matched up on enough points with Deb's to be damning.

Stephen's office had a small window air conditioner, which was not uncommon in the older buildings on campus. What was unusual was that the machine had been turned to its coldest setting, and the window opened a couple of inches. Thackery speculated that the temperature had been turned down to slow the body's rate of decay, and the window opened to provide ventilation for what odors might otherwise have accumulated in the small room. That, combined with the fact that the student custodian had reported that the office door had been locked when he arrived, suggested a deliberate attempt to delay discovery of the body for as long as possible.

Finally, a search of Deb's locker at the hospital turned up a bloody scrub tunic, with a smear that matched the image on the security footage. The blood on the tunic was being DNA tested to compare with Stephen's blood.

It was going to come back as a match. I already knew that.

I pushed away from my desk and wandered around the room, running my hands through my hair as I tried to answer the questions that kept coming, thick and fast.

He'd been a thorn in her side for years, we all knew that. But why kill him now? Why not hold out for just a few more months until Josh turned eighteen and the never-ending child support battles were finally over?

Had he attacked her? Provoked her in some way? I had no trouble imagining that. And in a threatening situation, I could easily imagine her grabbing the nearest available weapon to defend herself. That was part of the self-defense training I'd helped teach Deb.

I looked again at Stephen's face, which was swollen and torn like a piece of rotten fruit, black and green and purple from the beating he'd taken. Bashing in someone's face – several times, according to Lieutenant Thackery's report – wasn't part of the self-defense training. Neither was jabbing them in the eye with a letter-opener.

If Deb actually had killed Stephen, why would she have stuffed the bloody tunic in her locker when she could have easily tossed it into a hospital laundry bin where it would have been just another bloody tunic among many?

And, the real question at the bottom of it all: why did she go to see him in the first place?

◆

I make a living buying and selling information. Occasionally, I kill people – sometimes because it's what I was hired to do, and sometimes because someone was in the wrong place at the wrong time. I used to feel bad about that; now I accept it as part of the cost of doing business. Collateral damage and all.

But despite what I do, I don't like it when bad things happen to my friends – especially when I'm one of those bad things. I go out of my way to protect them from anything I think might qualify as a 'bad thing' at the moment.

I go out of my way to protect them from *me*.

So, if I were to be completely honest with myself, I had to ask myself how much my years of harassing Stephen had played into Deb's current situation.

God, I hate soul-searching. It's high on the list of things I try to avoid doing whenever possible.

I took one last look at the image of Deb's terrified face, there on the stairwell, then shut down the system. I didn't want to think and was too wound up to sleep, so I changed into a track suit and headed out for a run, hoping the cool night air would do me some good.

Like most of Philadelphia's North Liberties district – or NoLibs – Orianna Street is a narrow street lined with rowhouses of various vintages and too many cars parked along the curb. I left my house and jogged to the corner then turned onto Poplar Street. I slowed briefly as I neared the small pub where I frequently unwound after a long day, but decided against stopping in and ran a few blocks more before turning again onto 5th, the bells at St. Peter's just beginning to ring midnight as I reached the corner where the large church stood. The streetlights on the Girard Street side of the church were reflecting off the stained glass windows, reminding me of a midnight mass I'd attended there one Christmas with some friends. I'm not a Catholic myself, but they certainly know how to build lovely churches.

Girard Street was too brightly lit for my current mood, so I quickly veered off, heading down Cambridge.

Now, Cambridge is okay a little further down – the whole district has been undergoing something the city likes to call "revitalization" for the last several years – but at this end it's pretty much a dark, narrow alley. The single streetlight at the end of the first block was on its last legs, faint yellow light flickering weakly, like a candle in the dark. The light at the 4th Street intersection, two blocks away, wasn't much brighter.

Coming this way was probably a stupid thing to do. Or maybe I was just looking for trouble.

It wasn't long before I found it.

As I approached the first intersection, a large shadow separated itself from the chain-link fence surrounding a small parking lot on the corner. As it moved toward me, it split into two shadows, one tall and slim, the other short and bulky.

I slowed, jogging in place when I reached the intersection, glancing up and down the cross street for any sign of other shadows waiting in the wings. To my left, another streetlight glowed a half-block away, illuminating another narrow street similar to the one I was on with a few cars parked along one side. There were no visible doors or windows in the brick walls on either side of the street.

To my right, the block was shorter, with the occasional car passing on the main road. But getting there would mean getting past Slim and Bulky, which wasn't going to happen easily.

"Heya," Slim called out. The pair had nearly reached the center of the street. "Didn't'cha know it's dangerous for a girl to be on the streets at night?"

Bulky took a last drag on a cigarette, the red glow a brief, bright spot before he tossed it to the ground. "Looks like we get to show her why," he said.

I stopped jogging in place and took a step back, positioning myself between the telephone pole and the brick wall of the building behind me. I hadn't been running long enough to be winded, which was good. My legs were limber. I shook my hands at my sides, flexing my fingers.

If they wanted a fight, they were going to get it.

As they came closer, the dim light overhead let me see them a little better. They both had black hair and I thought they were white, or possibly Hispanic, I couldn't tell in the dark.

Both wore jeans, tennis shoes. Slim was wearing a hoodie, the pullover kind with the hood pushed back. Bulky had on a leather, bomber-style jacket which sported an assortment of metal studs along the shoulders. I saw no clear indicators of gang affiliations.

Neither was openly carrying a weapon, though there was no way of knowing what either might have in his pockets.

They moved like they'd hunted together before. Separating slightly and moving slowly, approaching me from both sides.

I relaxed my breathing and waited, a slow smile touching my lips. I preferred to at least start out the fight on the defensive. See what they had.

Then, more quickly than his size would suggest, Bulky was coming at me, plowing into me like a freight train.

The momentum carrying us into the wall, forcing my breath out of me. Bulky held tight, and for a moment my face was pressed to the shoulder of his leather coat, metal studs digging into my cheek.

He had a solid grip on me, and had my arms pinned to my sides. But beyond just hold me, there was nothing he could do in that position.

I waited, not squirming.

And a moment later, when he realized his predicament and shifted, pulling one hand free so he could punch me in the ribs or something, I took advantage of our close proximity and slammed the top of my forehead into his nose.

He swore and jerked back, what remained of his hold on me relaxing. I slid out of his grip and dropped to the ground in a rolling escape, coming to my feet well out of his reach.

Bulky's attack had no finesse. He was shorter than me, and couldn't have been more than fifteen, but was probably half again my body weight, mostly muscle. His attack was all about brute force. I could work with that, use it against him if he came at me again.

Now for Slim.

He hadn't moved in during the few seconds I'd been engaged with Bulky.

He took a step toward me and I took one back, then he abruptly closed the distance between us, and we spent the next several seconds in a blur of jabs and blocks, *wax on, wax off*-style karate moves that would have made Mr. Miyagi proud.

He caught me with a fist to one cheekbone, then grabbed my arm on the downswing.

I twisted away – a dance move I'd discovered years ago could be modified for defensive purposes, rather than merely decorative. My arm slid out of the sleeve of my track suit, leaving him holding onto the empty jacket.

He threw it back at me.

I dodged, stepping off the curb and into the street, then scooped up a soda can and threw it at him. He batted it away easily. But instead of looking angry or combative, now he was grinning.

Slim had some skill. Good to know.

By this time, Bulky was leaning against the wall, still nursing his broken nose. "Get her," he growled.

Slim was taller than me, had a longer reach, and was probably half my age. On the other hand, I'd been training since he was in grade school. As far as I could tell, that made us fairly evenly matched.

He came toward me, feet scuffing lightly on the asphalt. I danced out of his way, moving away from the brick walls that surrounded us on my side of the street, while keeping from moving too far toward the chain link fences that flanked the opposite corners. I wanted plenty of room and a minimum of shadows, which the center of the intersection provided.

Slim didn't seem to like that idea, and I didn't blame him. He probably knew this area – and any hidden advantages it might provide – far better than I did.

Tough.

He came at me low and fast, reaching out with those long arms. I dodged, catching his right arm as he passed, and twisting it up behind him.

I reached out with my other hand to shove him down, but he spun into the twist, throwing me off-balance. I let go of his arm and rolled away, coming back to my feet just in time to use my own momentum to flip away a second time as he swiped at me.

We faced-off again, then, both panting as we circled each other.

"Where'dya learn to fight like that?" he asked, pushing a lock of hair out of his eyes.

"Around," I said. I spared a quick glance at Bulky who had slid down along the wall and was now sitting slumped against it, forehead resting against his pulled-up knees. For someone so big, I'd have expected more of a fight, but the bashed nose seemed to have done him in. If that was all it took to bring him down, the kid wasn't going to last long on the street.

I turned back to Slim. "You?"

"Same, I s'pose."

"Truce?"

"You're kiddin', right?"

"Thought I'd ask. Be a shame to wipe the street with you."

He grinned, the dim light reflecting off his teeth, and charged toward me.

I dodged, but Slim anticipated the direction and caught me full-on, plowing into me with both fists pumping.

I gasped for air under the onslaught, twisting and half-ducking under his nearest arm as he swung. He pinned me there, my head resting along his ribcage, so I rammed my fist up into the underside of his jaw. He grunted in pain, relaxing his grip on me just enough that I was able to wiggle free. But before I could make good on my escape, he grabbed me around the waist and threw me away from him.

I landed flat on my back, my breath knocked out of me and with no time to move. Slim was coming at me again, and as he dove at me, hands outstretched, I pulled my legs upward, catching him in the stomach with my feet and levering him over me and into the air. I'd practiced this move dozens of time with Ian – sending Slim flying was easy by comparison.

He hit the pavement with a solid *thwack*.

I was on my feet immediately, but Slim wasn't moving. In the dim light I could see that his chest was still rising and falling, so he was still alive, but he wasn't coming after me anymore, which was all I really cared about.

I walked over to the opposite curb and scooped up my jacket.

"Bee-yach," Bulky said. He was pulling himself to his feet as though he intended to come after me again.

But I'd gotten the need to fight out of my system, and had no interest in continuing the game. I spun around, landing a solid roundhouse kick to Bulky's jaw, driving him back against the wall.

He hit with an *oof* of outrushing air, then slid down the wall.

"Stay there," I said.

Jacket in hand, I jogged the rest of the way down Cambridge, crossing 4th Street and not pausing until I'd turned down 3rd and got close to Liberties Walk.

The crowds of shoppers and diners that filled the open-air mall during the day were long-since gone, but there was something comfortable about walking past the quiet shops. The adrenaline rush of the fight had faded, and my mind was finally beginning to clear.

As much as I hated to admit it, I knew I had to accept that Deb had killed Stephen. Probably not on purpose. More than likely, it had been completely accidental.

Still, while I knew from personal experience that it was entirely possible that Deb had, in fact, been pushed far enough over the edge to have committed murder, there was something in Thackery's case file that just didn't feel right.

It was something about the photo of her on the stairs. Something about the way her body was turned...

I came to a dead stop, right in the middle of the plaza.

"Oh my God," I breathed.

I sprinted home.

♦

I fired up the computer, logged into the police records system, then paced while the machine churned its painfully slow way through the records.

When Thackery's case file finally appeared on the screen, I scrolled back to Deb's blurred image, looking over her shoulder as she made her escape down the stairs.

I rewound the video clip and played it back several times, watching closely. Then I left my office and went to the landing at the top of the stairs. Using a pair of sticky notes, I put one on the wall, identifying where the door at the top of the stairs would have been, and a second one at the spot above me that best matched the position of the security camera.

Then I ran down six steps, trying to move just as quickly as Deb had in the footage.

I stopped, looking over my shoulder, as though I'd heard a

noise, or was worried about someone possibly following me, trying to mimic the reason why Deb might have looked back on her way out of the building.

In order to have both my face *and* my chest in full view of the camera, as Deb's had been in the recording, I had to turn nearly three-quarters of the way around. And holding my head at the same angle as hers had been had me looking not at the sticky representing the door at the top of the stairs, but directly at the one above.

At the camera.

I finished my re-enactment, making the turn, gripping the banister tightly to keep from falling, and looking at the camera. I counted to three – again matching the timing on the footage – then twisted back around to face forward, and ran the rest of the way down the stairs.

When I got to the bottom, I looked up at Glau who was watching me curiously from the upper banister, his tail dangling lazily between the balusters. "Well, what do you think?" I asked him.

He shifted slightly, resting his chin on his front feet, as though deep in thought, and blinked.

"Yeah," I agreed. "It was staged."

Chapter 10
10 years ago

Meg walked out of the Fortune 500 firm's Boston headquarters into the bright sunshine, the early spring chill doing little to erase the smug smile on her face. The client had been surprisingly reasonable to work with, the result of weeks of careful negotiating, and she'd anticipated most of the last-minute changes they'd asked for as the paperwork for the merger went around the table.

But the successful conclusion of another deal – and the resulting fee that would boost her bank account when the papers were signed the following morning – wasn't what had her smiling.

No, Meg was particularly proud of the fact that she'd managed to undercut the hedge fund that Stephen Markham had been siphoning money from for the past three years.

She had to give him credit. He'd managed to keep the fund's other investors unaware of his activities, and guided investments into assets where he would benefit from the improved portfolio, only to strategically liquidate his own holdings just as the asset's value peaked, leaving the fund to scramble to mitigate the risk as the asset collapsed. Meg had tested his system three times over the past year, using her own insider information to mirror his trades.

She'd made a tidy sum. But pulling the rug out from under her friend's deadbeat ex was far more satisfying.

Stephen might be paying the minimum ordered child support, but he always seemed to find a way to use his money and social status to make Deborah's life difficult – making unreasonable visitation demands, only to not show up to pick up the kids; providing clothing or other supplies in the wrong sizes; sending DCFS caseworkers to Deborah's house for surprise inspections – all things he did just because he *could.*

So Meg made his life difficult whenever *she* could. And divesting her client's firm of the less-than-stellar hedge fund had been too-easily accomplished not to give in to the temptation.

And whenever it seemed practical, Meg used Stephen Markham as the lab rat for the "homework" the Researcher gave her. The string of unpaid bills that sent his credit rate plummeting, the IRS audit on his finances, and even creating the report of an in-flight incident that resulted in his name appearing on a no-fly list for several months, all were capstone assignments from the Researcher. A sort of "final exam" intended to demonstrate her ability to access and tamper with the relevant systems without being discovered.

It had been a long two years – and there had been plenty of times when Meg thought her head was going to explode as she fought to wrap her thinking around computer queries and learning to read and alter code.

But she'd pressed on. The Researcher had grudgingly acknowledged her successes – and given her increasingly more difficult challenges as a reward. Today's deal had been of her own devising – extra credit, as it were – and would jab one more metaphorical pin into the voodoo doll named Stephen Markham.

One day she hoped to find her own deadbeat father. She'd jab the pins into him herself, make him pay for the hell he'd put her mother through, her entire family through.

Until then, punishing Stephen on his behalf would have to do.

◆

Meg caught an early afternoon flight, her thoughts still largely on the three days she'd just spent in Boston and the few clean-up tasks her firm would be responsible for now that the merger was complete. She made good use of the travel time, typing up instructions during the flight which she emailed to her assistant after she'd landed. By the time she pulled into her quiet, suburban neighborhood in the middle of the afternoon, she was contemplating nothing more complicated than relaxing with a little music, a little wine, and a good book.

She reached the intersection, signaling the right-hand turn that would take her to her house, two doors down, just as the school bus rolled by on the cross-street, yellow lights flashing.

Another car, heading in the opposite direction, gunned its engine, zipping past the bus as the yellow lights turned red.

Meg sat there, her blinker clicking, as the memory of another impatient driver racing past a waiting bus overlaid itself on her vision.

"Wait," the bus driver said.

Maggie looked past her at the silver Chevy sedan, tires squealing as it backed out of the driveway – her driveway – then sped off, passing the bus like it wasn't there, its red lights blinking.

"Some people just don't pay attention," the driver said. "We always have to watch for them. It's safe now, you can go." She opened the door, and the handful of junior high students, including Maggie, pounded down the steps to the sidewalk.

But it wasn't safe. The driver didn't know. That had been Eddie's car tearing out of the drive – and if he was in that big a hurry, he was upset about something. That was never good.

Maggie didn't stay to chat with her friends, but ran across the street to her house as soon as the bus pulled away. The front door wasn't locked, was open just a little, like he'd slammed through it, but it hadn't caught.

Meggie pushed the door open, then crept inside, closing it quietly behind her. Eddie might be gone, but she was still afraid.

She tip-toed through the downstairs rooms, but everything seemed normal, quiet, like any other day. Her little brothers wouldn't be home for an hour yet, Shelia was fifteen, and almost never came straight home from school anymore, and her mother was usually at Aunt Ruthie's or working on one of her charities most afternoons.

She'd just gotten to the bottom of the stairs when she heard something. She stopped and listened, then started up the stairs. Someone was crying.

There was a wide hallway at the top of the stairs, with two doors on one side going to the bathroom and her mother's bedroom, and three doors on the other, to her brothers' room, her room, and Shelia's room at the far end. At first Maggie thought all the doors were just standing open, like they usually did, but as she got to the top of the stairs, she realized that Shelia's door wasn't just open, it was broken, hanging sideways from the middle hinge. Pieces of splintered wood lay on the floor.

She ran down the hall, skidding to a stop at the threshold of Shelia's room.

Her sister could never be considered neat, but Maggie knew the difference between a messy room and one where there'd been a fight. Books and papers and makeup and clothing were strewn around the room like they'd been swept off the dresser, and a small desk lamp lay in a heap near the broken door. The bedding had been half-torn from the bed, and pillows and stuffed animals thrown to the floor.

There was blood on the sheets.

There was no sign of her sister.

"Shelia?" Maggie whispered, taking a step into the room.

Shelia didn't speak, but her answering whimper came from the half-closed closet.

Maggie dropped her pack in the doorway, then went to the closet and looked inside.

Shelia huddled there, half-naked and shivering, her hair a tangle around her bruised, tear-stained face.

Maggie grabbed one of the blankets and crawled into the closet with her sister, wrapping the blanket around her and cradling her in her arms as she sobbed.

"I had cramps," she said finally, through swollen lips. "I came home early. Didn't know he'd be here. When I didn't want to let him... he got mad. Real mad. Said I had no right..." She began to cry again.

Maggie did the only thing she knew how to do. She let Shelia cry.

Later, after she'd washed the blood from her sister's face and taken her to her own room and helped her find some pajamas and get settled in her bed, Maggie did her best to clean up the mess Eddie had made of Shelia's room.

A car horn behind her startled Meg back to the present. Her turn signal was still blinking, and the school bus had gone. From where she sat, she had a clear view of her house. Of the window that had once been her sister's room.

When the car behind her honked again, Meg eased around the corner. But instead of pulling into her driveway, she kept on going. It wasn't the first time she'd driven past her house, driven around the block, sometimes several times before settling her memories enough to go home.

She circled past the house a third time.

The renovations had changed the layout, but no amount of paint could erase the memories, and there was just no point in trying any more.

Why was she even still living there? What was she trying to prove? And to who?

◆

Meg woke with a start, her eyes snapping open, her brain racing to catch up. She'd heard something, like a thud or a clank, she wasn't quite sure. But she'd definitely heard something that had been wrong enough to have penetrated her sleep.

She got up, grabbed the robe from the chair near her bed, and swung it on as she went to the window and looked out. The street was quiet, the streetlights reflecting off the snow that had fallen that afternoon.

Meg moved quietly to the door, and opened it, wincing at the slight grinding noise of the knob. She smelled the hint of after shave meant to cover up the lingering trace of stale tobacco that drifted towards her as she opened the door.

Someone was in the house.

She paused at the top of the stairs, listening. The house was silent. Dark, except for a small pool of light from a nightlight at the foot of the stairs and the faint glow of streetlights coming in through the windows. In the past, the darkness had been peaceful; now, the shadows felt ominous.

Whatever woke her, she didn't hear it now. But the cigarette smell, that was definitely coming from downstairs. And unless she wanted to smack them with a hairbrush or jab at them with a hanger, she had nothing upstairs she could use as a weapon.

Poor planning on her part, but nothing she could do about it now.

She crept downstairs one step at a time, stopped frequently to smell the air, listen for breathing, hardly daring to breathe herself for fear of being heard.

And then, as she stepped off the bottom step and took her first steps into the living room, there was a flurry of movement, the sound of heavy boots thudding across the carpeted floor, and a large figure tackled her as solidly as a linebacker.

If there was one lesson she had learned at the gym, it was how to fall.

Meg let herself go limp, twisting as the momentum carried her down to keep from hitting the back of her head on who-knew-what might be behind her in the dark. The motion threw them both off balance, and sent them crashing into the small end table that sat just beyond the foot of the stairs.

By the time they finally hit the floor, they were laying on their sides, facing each other, Meg's chin pressed to his shoulder, the pungent odors of cigarettes and after shave filling her nose.

She shifted in his grasp, the slippery fabric of the robe the only thing that gave her any advantage. She squirmed, his grip around her waist loosening just loose enough for her to wriggle free before he was coming at her again. Meg scrabbled backward, trying to put some distance between them, kicking at him awkwardly as he grabbed one of her ankles, fingers squeezing tightly to keep their grip.

She kicked at him again and again with her other foot until he let go and backed off. They both got to their feet, watching each other's shadows to see what the other would do next.

Meg stepped back, wincing at a sharp pain from her bruised ankle, then he abruptly closed the distance between them. He was several inches taller than she was, and probably twice her body weight, mostly muscle. He caught her with a fist to one cheekbone, grabbing her arm on the downswing.

She moved around the room, dodging as she scanned the shadows for something she could use against him, trying to keep herself from getting trapped in a corner.

And then he lunged for her. As she darted out of his reach, she felt a tug as he managed to catch the edge of her silk robe. She didn't stop moving, pivoting on her bare foot as she pulled away. It was probably the only thing she still remembered from all those years of dance lessons her mother had made her take as a child, and the most useful thing she could think of to do now.

The robe tore.

"Aw, shit," she hissed, glaring at him as she backstepped to the opposite end of the room, keeping her eyes on his hulking form in the dim light coming in through the living room window. "I *liked* that robe."

Her anger boiled over.

He was in her house, and that was unacceptable. It was time for her to become the aggressor. But she had no idea how. He had too great a reach on her for Meg to feel confident going on the offensive with the few boxing routines she knew, and what little she remembered of her self-defense training wasn't doing her any good at all.

Then her back hit the edge of the wall dividing the living room from the entry. She glanced over her shoulder, knowing as soon as she did that she shouldn't have taken her eyes off him.

That was when he grabbed her hair. She'd braided it before going to bed, but as she turned her head, the long tail flipped over her shoulder, giving the intruder a perfect opportunity. He snatched at the braid and tugged, dragging Meg off-balance and toward him.

She stumbled forward, her head at an awkward angle, her body twisting so that her shoulder crashed against his chest.

He jerked her braid again, backward this time, encircling her exposed throat with his free hand.

Meg scratched ineffectually at his hand as he began to squeeze. She even stomped on his foot, but was fairly certain that the metal grommets of his heavy boots hurt her bare foot more than she hurt him.

She was running out of air.

Nothing she was doing was going to make him release her

throat. But in a sudden flash of clarity, she remembered Ian telling the class that an attacker's weakest point was their eyes. In a last, desperate effort, Meg reached back over her shoulder and clawed at his face

With a sound that was half-yelp, half-growl, he let her go, shoving her away from him. Meg hit the wall and careened off it, spinning to face him as she gasped for air.

Her nails had found their mark, and the intruder was standing there, in the center of the entryway, head bowed, one hand covering his right eye.

Meg didn't feel the least bit of remorse. Taking a deep breath, she landed a solid roundhouse kick to his upper thigh. It wasn't one of her better moves, but it was all she had the wind for, and it was just enough to knock him sideways.

He crashed against the front door with a grunt, but bounced right back, plowing into her with renewed vigor, both fists pumping as he drove her back into the living room.

Meg gasped under the onslaught, twisting and half-ducking under his nearest arm as he swung. He pinned her there, the back of her legs pressed against the low coffee table. The side of his head was right next to her face, so she bit down on his ear. She tasted blood and he grunted in pain, shoving her away from him. She dropped onto the table and slid backward on the smooth surface.

But before she could make good on her escape, he stepped around the table, reached down, grabbed her around the waist, and threw her across the room.

She hit the couch harder than she would have thought possible, her barely recovered breath knocked out of her.

He tossed the coffee table out of his way and dove at her, large hands outstretched.

Gasping for breath, Meg pulled her legs upward, the bottoms of her feet catching him in the stomach just like she used to do when she and her little brothers would wrestle. But that had been years ago, and he was much heavier than both of the twins combined.

The next moments were a blur.

His weight driving her knees forward, into the back of the couch.

Meg pushing back, screaming.

His momentum carrying him over the back of the couch.

The large, multi-paned window overlooking the yard, shattering as he hit the glass and fell through.

Meg rolled quickly to her knees and looked after him.

To her surprise, as he disentangled himself from the bushes and dusted the snow from his coat, she could have sworn she heard him laughing. Then he looked up, touched a finger to his forehead as though tipping an imaginary hat, and jogged off down the street, boots crunching through the frozen crust of snow as he passed beyond a neighbor's hedge and out of sight. A moment later, she heard a car door slam and a vehicle drive off.

Meg wrapped her torn robe around her and sank into the cushions, pulling her knees up to her chest and rocking back and forth as she shivered in the darkness

He could have killed her, if he'd wanted to.

She shuddered, letting the emotion wash over her for only a moment.

Was he gone for good? Or just coming back with reinforcements? It didn't matter. She couldn't stay here and find out. Not tonight. It was bitterly cold outside, and the house was cooling rapidly, her breath already coming out in little puffs.

Gingerly, she pulled herself up off the couch. A spike of pain shot from her ankle up her leg all the way to her thigh. Her throat ached. She already felt the bruises forming along her ribs, arm, and throat, was sure her face was swelling, and her forehead was throbbing. But in spite of all that, she didn't think she'd suffered anything life-threatening. Her self-defense training had kept her from panicking and probably helped her avoid serious injury – but mostly, the fight had shown her just how much more she had to learn.

Then she limped over and switched on the lights.

In addition to the shattered window, there was a large indentation in the dining room drywall where her attacker had crashed into the wall – she didn't even remember the fight even carrying them into that room, but the damage told a different story.

Most of the rest of the dining room had escaped unscathed, but two of the chairs and the small entry table were lost. Lamps, vases, and other decorative items lay in pieces on the living room floor, tracing the path of their fight.

A heavy canvas bag near the fireplace held a pair of antique silver candlesticks he'd taken from the dining room and a small packet of lock-picks. She'd clearly disturbed him before he'd found whatever he'd come for – not that she left had much worth stealing or that would be easy to fence out in the open.

All-in-all, she thought, it was nothing her homeowner's insurance wouldn't cover.

She grabbed the fireplace poker. It was purely decorative, thanks to the gas fireplace insert, and would probably break if she hit someone over the head with it, but for the moment it would do as a bedside weapon. Gripping the poker firmly in one hand, she limped to the kitchen and down the short hall to the garage door. It was locked, and the green LED lights on the security system touchpad were still blinking in 'active' mode.

"Useless piece of plastic," she muttered, turning away from the device without touching it. If the service hadn't registered either the intruder or the broken living room window, she didn't want to do anything now to set it off. She'd deal with it in the morning.

However, she did turn the thermostat to its lowest setting. No sense heating the great outdoors, but no reason to let the pipes freeze, either. She'd have to call her contractor first thing in the morning. Make repairs.

And put the house on the market, once and for all.

Meg headed upstairs, poker in one hand, a bag of frozen peas wrapped in a kitchen towel held in the other, pressed to her throat to ease the ache. She took the steps carefully, favoring her turned ankle, her thoughts bouncing between finding a hotel for what remained of the night and looking for a new place to live.

Halfway up the stairs she froze, a second realization dawning. She couldn't report the break-in.

For the same reason she hadn't dialed 911 as soon as she sensed someone in her house, she couldn't report it now. Not to her insurance company, not to the police. And when she talked to the contractor about the repairs, she would have to ignore his questions about what had happened.

More than that, she needed to clean up as much of the mess as she could herself – and she had to do that now. With a sigh, she turned and slowly limped back downstairs. She'd clean up, and then stage the damage so it looked like nothing more than the result of a party that had gotten a little out of hand. It was that or have inquisitive neighbors or a well-meaning contractor say something that could come back to cause problems for her later.

Reporting the incident would open files, raise questions, create a paper trail – and that was absolutely the last thing she wanted.

No, in all likelihood, she would never report anything to anyone ever again. As long as she was careful about what she did in her clandestine career, she could live a "normal" life. But she could do nothing to call attention to herself in any way that was outside the normal expectations for someone in her legitimate profession and socio-economic class.

The wrong sort of attention could get her – and anyone

associated with her – killed. Or worse.

    She'd always been careful in her less-than-legal dealings. Now she had to learn to be invisible.

Chapter 11
Present day: Saturday morning

I woke early, feeling surprisingly refreshed. Stephen was still dead, Deb still under suspicion for his murder; but knowing that she'd been set up put the entire situation in a new light.

Now there was a chance I could do something useful.

Armed with my largest coffee mug full of steaming brew, I went up to my office ready to take a deep dive into Lieutenant Thackery's notes. But instead of skimming it to see what he thought he had on Deb, this time I studied the file the way I would review information provided to me by one of my clandestine clients. I combed through the record, noting both the incriminating details as well as any anomalies.

Detail: partials of Deb's fingerprints had been found on the letter opener, doorknob, and one corner of the desk.

Anomaly: Deb was right-handed, but all of the partials were of her left index finger. In addition, when compared side-by-side in a graphics application, they were nearly identical in the portion of the print displayed.

Conclusion: Someone had attempted to lift a copy of Deb's fingerprints, but only got the partial, which they'd replicated at the murder scene.

Detail: Stephen's face had been severely beaten, presumably with the geode, just prior to his actual murder.

Anomaly: The swelling, amount of bruising, and varied coloring of the bruises suggested that he'd been beaten some time prior to his murder. Once the heart stops beating and blood is no longer circulating, it pools in the lowest place – and, of course, other effects of early lividity will be visible – but neither of those seemed to account for the level of bruising the body exhibited.

Conclusion: I wanted to know what the coroner had to say, but it was my opinion that the beating took place several minutes or more before Stephen's death.

Detail: The security footage showed Deb entering the building and coming up the stairs 12:27 p.m., then going back down the stairs and leaving the building at 12:52.

Anomaly: In addition to the artificially twisted posture of the woman in the stairwell – I no longer thought of her as Deb – I also replayed the footage showing her arrival at the building several times, at different speeds and resolutions. One frame at a time, I watched as she approached the door, slipped her left hand into her jacket pocket, then raised it slightly toward a small black rectangle on the wall just as she reached for the door with her right hand.

Conclusion: The woman in the video had used a security access card to enter the building.

I went on like that for a couple of hours, reviewing and annotating the file with case notes of my own, building the case for Deb's innocence one point at a time as the sky grew light. Thackery's notes were thorough, but he hadn't analyzed his findings – at least not so far as I could see. In his defense, he probably hadn't seen the need to. On the surface it was an open-and-shut case.

It was the first time I'd ever contemplated uploading an annotated file back into the police records system.

I saved the file and got up from the computer, stretching stiff limbs, and walked over to the French doors looking out onto my small, rooftop patio. The morning was gray, clouds in varying degrees of darkness rolling in with the promise of rain soon to follow. A breeze had chased a few stray reddish-gold leaves across the flagstone, swirling them into a corner formed by a built-in bench. I wrapped my sweater tighter around my body against the slight chill coming off the glass, and nodded in agreement with the wind – tapping into the police network to download the records had been risky enough, uploading modified files was nothing short of crazy. I'd likely end up as trapped as those leaves twisting in the wind.

Even if I could manage it without getting caught, knowing Thackery as I'd come to through the study of his notes, he was the type who would be compelled to launch an investigation into who had tampered with the records. It would undoubtedly do Deb more harm than good.

So no, I couldn't safely update the records… I would just have to figure out another way to make sure the incriminating evidence was properly analyzed.

In the meantime, I had some calls to make and errands to run.

♦

Before heading downstairs, I grabbed a disposable cell phone from the stash at the back of my linen closet. Then I fed Glau, fixed myself another mug of coffee – thinking fondly of the built-in coffee station in that much-too-fancy house Bonnie had shown me – and prepared a light breakfast.

All routine tasks which allowed me to concentrate on building a mental to-do list for the day.

The first thing on the list was to figure out who the woman in the security footage was, and the best way to start was to determine whose access card she'd used.

While I'm very good at digging up information, the Researcher makes me look like an amateur.

I shared a large portion of the fresh fruit I'd cut up with Glau, rinsed my hands, then pried an English muffin into halves and popped them into the toaster. While I waited for it to heat, I pulled the burner phone from my pocket and dialed the Researcher's number.

"Yeah?"

"I've got a project for you," I said, without preamble. "I need to know whose access card was used to get into a building at the University."

"*Pfft*," he chuffed. "Least you could do is make it challenging." he replied.

"I need it fast," I offered, putting the call on speakerphone before pulling the hot English muffin halves from the toaster and buttering them.

"You can have it fast, or cheap, or good," he said, quoting the old maxim, "but not all three."

"I'll take *fast* and *good*."

"Done. Details?"

I told him what I knew – the building name, which door, and the time of day, courtesy of the date stamp on the surveillance footage. "I'll pay extra for any information you have on the user for three days before and after."

He grunted in acknowledgement and told me how much getting the information was going to cost me. To clear Deb, I'd have paid twice what he asked, but I didn't tell him that.

"When?" I asked.

"Twelve-fifteen. Collins Park," he said. "Don't be late."

The irony of the meeting place wasn't lost on me – he wasn't kidding about this project being a walk in the park for him, and was rubbing it in. It would probably be more effort for him to contact one of his many runners, give them the data, and send them out to make the exchange, than to dig up the information I'd asked for.

"I'll be there," I said. "It's a pleasure doing business with you."

"As always," he growled. Then the line went silent.

I disassembled the phone and snipped the sim card into

small pieces with a pair of poultry shears before tossing the shards down the toilet in the guest bathroom. Then I collected my breakfast and carried it up to my room to nibble at while I got dressed for the day.

Sometimes it's that easy.

And sometimes it's not.

There are a number of ways to quickly and easily transfer funds from one person to another. Unfortunately, short of simply handing over a wad of cash, the vast majority of payment methods create a paper-trail connecting the payer, payee, and whatever institution was handling the transaction.

Payment for my under-the-table work comes in a variety of forms – stocks, property, jewelry, art, casino chips, cashier's checks, money orders, and occasionally bundled stacks of actual paper currency. As far as I'm concerned, it's about increasing my net worth, not the form of the payment, so I've learned to be flexible. And I've memorized the numbers for a few decent, discrete appraisers, just to be on the safe side.

No one wants to be taken advantage of.

Most of the cash payments never see the inside of a bank vault – except for reserve funds stored in a number of safety-deposit boxes around the country.

Another portion of the cash I convert into pre-loaded plastic. It's become almost a habit, actually, to pick up two or three VISA gift cards every week and stash them in a secure place until they're needed.

There are enough places to pick them up within a two-hour drive of my office –grocery stores, convenience stores, big-box stores – that I seldom have to go back to any location more often than once or twice a year. I pick them up whenever I go out of town as well.

Collecting gift cards from across the United States... I wonder if that counts as a hobby?

When I need to hire outside services from someone like the

Researcher and don't want the payment tracked back to me, I simply gather up enough gift cards to add up to the agreed-upon fee and deliver them as per his instructions.

And because they're paid for in cash up-front, there's no paper trail. Just the way I like it.

♦

I had several things to do, if I was going to help clear Deb's name, but before I went any further, I wanted to check in on her. She'd been such a mess when we brought her home Friday night; I wanted to make sure she knew we believed in her.

Or maybe I just needed to assuage my own guilt for having doubted her in the first place.

Either way, I showed up at her door, my arms loaded with a grocery-store bouquet of flowers, a box of pastries from my favorite bakery, and a few novels and old movies I'd pulled from my shelves that I thought she might enjoy.

"Nice!" Josh said, relieving me of the pastries as I came in the house. He was a tall, lanky boy, who had his father's sandy-brown hair and infectious smile and his mother's athletic build. He pulled out a Danish and took a huge bite of it. "If you're looking for Mom," he said around the sticky mouthful, "you're too late. She was out of here early. Pulling double-shifts this weekend to make up for so many days out this week."

"How many days did she miss?" I asked, following him into the kitchen.

"All week, I think. She was sick, and then Dad died, and there was the whole going to jail thing," he said with all the sensitivity of the average teenage boy. "I heard her telling Grandma that she ended up having to use her vacation time to cover it all. Sucks." He rummaged in the pasty box and came up with a cruller.

I took the box away from him and closed the lid. "Save some for the rest of the family," I said. "Where is everyone else, anyway?"

"Shopping. Should be home before too long. Cassie was gonna drop Mom off at the hospital, then she and Grandma were going to the grocery. She asked if I wanted to go, but, hey, it's the weekend and they were out *ear-r-r-ly*." He reached over and slid the pastry box across the table toward him. "All I wanted to do was go back to sleep."

"And yet, here you are, awake and eating all the pastries."

He grinned. "What they don't know about, they won't miss."

I shook my head, but didn't try to stop him. There were plenty to go around, even with a voracious teenager in the house. I put the stack of books and videos on the table and set the flowers in the sink while I rummaged through the cupboards for a vase. Josh found one for me – up on top of the cupboards – and I filled it with water and arranged the flowers in it before putting it in the middle of the kitchen table. I thought the pinks and purples of the flowers cheered a room that had seen too many tears that week.

"Anything I can get for you, Aunt Meg?" Josh asked. He'd put the pastry box next to the flowers and surrounded it with the books and videos, helping to make it all look festive.

"No," I said, then continued, indicating the table. "That's nice. Your mom teach you to do that sort of thing?"

"Grandma," he said. "She likes to set out surprises for us sometimes, 'specially if we've been down. Different kinds of stuff, but the same idea. Mom's been way down – really good of you to do this for her. She'll like it a lot."

He was a nice kid. And as I looked at him, standing there all knees and elbows, I saw a flicker of sadness cross his face.

"How are you doing, Josh? It's been a rough week for all of you."

He shrugged, grinding the toe of his sneaker against the floor. "Sucks," he said again. It seemed to be his word for the week. I couldn't disagree.

I waited, leaning back against the cool porcelain of the apron-front sink. He'd tried to play it cool, act casual, but there was a level of tension in his expression that suggested otherwise.

Finally, he looked up at me. "If I tell you something, will you promise not to tell Mom?"

I don't have kids, so I probably gave the wrong answer, but I did my best. "I won't say anything. But if I think she should know, I'll ask you to tell her yourself."

He considered that for a moment. "Fair enough," he said with a nod. "So, I've been friends with my dad on Facebook for a long time – it's no biggie, it just lets me say hi once in a while and sometimes he'll crack a joke or make some comment about the team—"

"The team?"

"Yeah, I run track. Thought you knew."

"Right. I'd forgotten. So your dad sometimes talks to you on Facebook?"

"Yeah. Not often, but sometimes."

"I don't think there's a problem with that. You might want to tell your mother at some point if…" I trailed off. I'd expected him to relax, but if anything, he'd grown even more tense. "That's not all, is it?"

He shook his head.

"Tell me."

"After everybody left this morning, I couldn't get back to sleep, so I got up and went onto Facebook," he pulled his phone out and started tapping at buttons while he talked. "Right there, on my wall, was a note from my dad. A new one. Posted early this morning."

He held the phone out to me.

He'd taken a screenshot of their conversation.

Stephen: *Don't think I'm going to make your meet next week. Sorry about that. I'm sure you'll do well.*

Josh: *Uh, Okay.*

Stephen: *I really wanted to do more for you and your sister, you know.*

Josh: *It's a little late for that now, don'tcha think?*

Stephen: *Probably. But if you ever need anything, just let me know.*

Josh: *WTF?? Who is this really?*

The conversation ended, with no reply.

I handed the phone back to him. "You're sure this was your father?"

His shoulders slumped. "Who knows? I mean, the guy's dead – so it can't be him. For all I know, it never was him all along. Probably his teaching assistant." His eyes welled with tears, but he somehow managed to keep his composure. "I wanted it to be him," he whispered, his voice quavering with misery.

I knew how he felt. I went over and put my arms around him, pulled his head down to my shoulder, and just held him as he sobbed.

After Josh regained his composure, we talked for several minutes more. We went back online to see if there were any more posts from Stephen – there weren't, and the conversation thread Josh had shown me had been deleted from the page.

I found that almost as interesting as the conversation itself.

Josh emailed me a copy of the screenshot he'd taken. I told him he might want to talk with his mom about things – all the 'feeling' stuff that Deb is so good at dealing with and I just fake my way through.

And then, when I couldn't think of anything else to say, I offered him another pastry.

Chapter 12
Present day: Saturday afternoon

I decided not to wait for Barbara and Cassie to come home, and headed into town for my rendezvous with the Researcher's courier. I left my car at a park-n-ride several blocks away and took a bus downtown, both to avoid having to deal with parking – which isn't great even on a Saturday – as well as to minimize the chance of being identified by anyone paying attention to little details like cars and license plates.

As a result, I ended up trudging three blocks toward Chestnut Street in the rain, my hat pulled down low and my collar turned up high in a vain attempt to keep the water from trickling down the back of my neck. By the time I reached Collins Park, I was cold and irritable.

Collins Park is a pocket park – one of the narrow slivers of hardscaping and potted trees that pepper the city. Its main entrance was tucked between a pizza shop on one side and a Japanese restaurant on the other, and the whole park was only about as wide as one of the restaurants. It gets used for weddings and private parties a lot during fair weather, but most of the park's daytime traffic is people who work in the nearby office buildings, taking an al fresco lunch break and listening to the splash of the block-style fountain near the Ranstead Street end of the park.

The fountain was quiet now, the water already turned off for the winter, and there wasn't enough foot traffic on this rainy October afternoon to support any of the food and coffee carts that populated the streets during better weather.

All the smart people were indoors.

I caught a whiff of baked dough and marinara and pepperoni as a small group of laughing people went into the nearby pizza shop and amended my thinking: all the smart people were indoors with good, hot food.

I pulled a thermal carafe of coffee from the outside pocket of my shoulder bag, and sipped at it. It wasn't hot any more, but it was still warm enough, and I was grateful for my own foresight as I paced back and forth along the edge of the fountain wishing for an overhang of some sort that I could duck under – or even a few sheltering leaves on the mostly-bare trees.

At precisely twelve-fifteen, a movement at the Ranstead Street entrance caught my eye. A man, medium height and weight, dressed in a beige trenchcoat, dark glasses, and a fedora, and carrying a battered leather briefcase, paused, glanced up and down the alley, then came into the park.

"A little theatrical," I muttered, shaking my head as I tucked my coffee away. "And that outfit – how obvious can you be?"

His hat was pulled down low, and he walked with his eyes down, as though trying to keep the rain from hitting his glasses. A wise precaution, but it had the result of him walking directly toward me. I took a step to one side as he approached.

Without missing a beat – or looking up – he altered his course so that he was once again heading directly toward me.

I moved in the opposite direction, edging toward the fountain.

Again he altered course.

He was only a couple of feet from me when I quickly moved down the shallow steps into the dry fountain.

He spun, as if the leather-sole of one dress shoe had slipped in a puddle at the fountain's edge. Like a dancer, he swung his briefcase in the opposite direction, using its weight to turn his body, pulling him away from the edge before the handle slipped from his fingers and the briefcase fell to the ground at my feet.

"Need to be careful, there," I said. I slipped the small envelope containing the money orders from my pocket and palmed it as I bent to pick up the case.

"Yes," he said.

I handed him the case, my envelope wrapped around the handle. He took it with his left hand, then shook my hand with his right. "Thank you," he said.

"Of course," I said. "That could have been a nasty fall."

As we shook hands, I felt him press something into my palm. I didn't remark on it, and it would be exaggerating to say we exchanged glances, one pair of dark glasses to another, but the hand-off was made with only the barest hint of a nod on either side.

He released my hand, touched a finger to the brim of his hat, and walked away, moving carefully along the less-sloppy parts of the paving stones. I slid my hand into my pocket, turning the small, flat flash drive he'd given me over in my fingers as I watched him go.

A few minutes later, I also left the park, and went directly into the adjacent pizza shop. I was cold and hungry, and the pizza shop seemed like the perfect solution to both.

◆

I'd barely made it back home and switched on my computer to study the information on the Researcher's flash drive when Patsy Cline started singing *Crazy* on my cell phone.

Bonnie's ringtone.

I groaned, looking at the phone and then up at Glau, but the lizard just blinked at me from his perch on the cat tree in the corner of the room. Silent as a stone, but I swear there was judgment in his golden-eyed gaze.

"You're supposed to be on my side," I muttered at him, accepting the call and pressing the speakerphone button. "Hey, there. What's up?"

"You know perfectly well 'what's up,'" Bonnie replied brightly. "I've picked out a dozen houses for us to look at this afternoon—"

"I thought I only had to look at three."

"That was yesterday. And we only saw two. So you're down one."

"I have things to do—"

"You always have things to do. And this weekend, house-hunting is one of them. Pick you up in an hour?"

"Are you like this with all your clients?" I asked. I'd logged into the computer while we'd been talking, and plugged in the flash drive. Its directory had opened automatically, displaying several files. An hour wasn't going to be long enough to go through this data.

"Only the ones I love," Bonnie replied brightly. "Your little rowhouse is charming, Meg, but it was an impulse buy and you know it. If my commission hadn't been so good, I wouldn't have let you do it. Frankly, I'm surprised you've stayed there this long. It's time you moved on."

"No fair using inside information," I complained.

"Don't get all S.E.C.-ish on me," she said. "In *my* industry, inside information is like gold. Of course I'm going to use it – but only to your advantage, to help you find a place that's perfect for you."

Considering the ethical tightropes I walked on a regular basis, my only response was to admit defeat.

"All right, already!" I said, looking at the list of files and weighing it against the responsibilities of friendship. I could start reviewing them now, spend some time with Bonnie looking at houses I didn't want to buy, and come back to the research later. It wasn't like Deb was going to be tried and sent to prison that afternoon.

"I'll go. But I'm not looking at a dozen houses. No more than six. Three would be better."

"Thought you'd say that," Bonnie said. I could practically hear the Cheshire Cat grin spreading across her face. "And that's great for me, too, actually – Peggy's flight gets in tonight and I have a few errands I need to run before she arrives. So we've got exactly enough time to look at three. I've already sorted the list, but you'll want to look through them yourself and choose your own top picks. See you soon."

The phone went silent and I wasted a full minute staring at it and thinking about just how successfully she'd manipulated me. I really needed to beef-up my social engineering skills. I was good, but Bonnie was a master.

But not today. Today I had one hour to figure out who was framing Deb for Stephen's murder.

◆

I had the answer – though I didn't believe it – in thirty seconds.

The Researcher had provided two sets of files, each containing a single file named only with an ID number, together with several companion files named using a combination of the ID number and a date stamp when it was used.

I clicked on the one of the two that only displayed the ID number.

The pass was assigned to Stephen Markham.

I'd have thought the Researcher had finally blown it if the file hadn't also contained an image of the PennCard, complete with Stephen's name, staff ID number, and smiling face looking out at me – sparkling blue eyes not quite hidden beneath a wayward shock of brown hair that I'd long since concluded he'd cultivated as part of his rakish charm.

I left the file open, dragging it to a corner of the monitor, and opened the other non-date stamped file which listed the SEPTA transit system PennPass associated with Stephen's

PennCard. The other files in that set tracked his use of the transit system over the past week.

I skimmed the date stamps on the other files the Researcher had provided, which listed every use of Stephen's PennCard and PennPass for the previous week – beginning on Monday morning – with the most recent use being only a few hours ago.

I pushed away from the desk, got up, and began to pace, my mind racing.

Stephen's PennCard had been used *after* his death – and at least once *before* he died – presumably by the person who killed him, and who I knew wasn't Deb.

Stephen's PennPass was still being used – had been used as recently as this morning.

Stephen's Facebook account was still active, with someone posting on it as him – and someone removing those posts.

Stephen's body was lying dead in the local morgue.

Whatever the hell was going on?

Chapter 13
Present day: Saturday evening

Needless to say, while I'm sure the three houses Bonnie showed me were lovely, and might have appealed to me on any other day, if put to the test, I couldn't describe a single memorable feature of any of them. They were a collective blur of hardwood and tile, wallpaper and paneling, corbels and casements.

Only one feature stood out in my mind – a huge office with a large, antique map of the world on one wall, flanked by built-in bookshelves. Much as I'd liked the effect, I'd have been hard-pressed to say which house the room belonged to.

But it did give me an idea.

"Hey, can we go past the University?" I asked. We were heading back to my house, and the University was only a few blocks out of the way.

"Sure. Thinking of taking another class?" Bonnie asked.

It was a fair question. Since completing my MBA, I'd taken a number of evening, weekend, and online classes through both the University and private institutions – courses in psychology and sociology, costuming and make-up, weapons and security – classes I'd selected as part of my clandestine operations training curriculum. No one thinks twice about someone taking a few random night classes, and the education had served me well.

But that wasn't my goal at the moment.

"Hmm? No. I need a campus map. A big, paper one. Think the student center will have something like that?"

Bonnie gave me a funny look. "You can download a PDF."

"Not big enough, or with enough detail."

"For what?" Bonnie asked.

I didn't answer. I couldn't tell her what I really wanted it for – to track all the places Stephen's PennCard had been used in the last few days – but I didn't have a ready lie, either.

Bonnie was silent for a couple of minutes, but she made the necessary turns to adjust our course so we were headed toward campus before she tried again. "Does this have something to do with Deb?"

"Maybe…," I said, drawing the word out and leaving it hang there, without offering any additional information.

"You can find out how far it is from the Children's Hospital to her ex's office using your phone's mapping app," she said. "I'm not that familiar with the University campus, but it can't be more than a few blocks."

"I'm old school."

"Old school, my ass," Bonnie said, the words almost lost in a laugh. "You're more high-tech than just about anyone else I know."

I couldn't deny that. I shrugged. "Indulge me."

"Oh, I am," she said. We stopped at an intersection and she looked at me as we waited for the light to change. "And when this whole mess is over, you're going to owe me, big time."

I had a suspicion that 'big time' was going to involve serious house-hunting in the not-too-distant future, and a purchase that would leave a sizeable commission in her account.

There were worse things, I suppose.

◆

I wasn't able to get a large paper map at the University, so I ended up having to download a PDF after all. I ordered a pizza – the second of the day, a clear indication of my stress level –

and while I waited for my dinner to arrive, I enlarged the map and printed it across several pages. These I taped together to create the oversized map I wanted, which I then stapled to the back of one of the large, presentation flip charts I sometimes used when talking with clients.

I also printed off a couple of photos of the woman from the security footage, one of her at the door and the other when she was on the stairs, and pinned them to the board.

Then, one by one, I poked a push-pin into the map at each of the locations where the Researcher's files indicated that one of Stephen's cards had been used. I labeled each pin with the date and time, and looped a piece of string around each from one to the next, tracing the chronological path.

I can be totally old-school when I need to be.

My pizza arrived, and I carried it up to my office along with the large Pepsi I'd ordered, and ate two slices while standing there analyzing the pins and strings I'd put on the board.

On Monday, Stephen had used his PennCard's debit feature to purchase lunch at one of the University cafes, but hadn't used it anywhere else on campus. That seemed reasonable – if he'd entered his building through the main front doors during regular hours, he wouldn't have needed the card for secure access.

Similarly, there was no recorded activity for either transit or building access on Tuesday morning. But that afternoon showed him entering just about every building surrounding his own through doors that required the security pass over a two-hour period. That seemed odd to me, but without a full history of his activity, I had no way of knowing if it was a normal pattern – maybe he walked up and down stairs in the nearby buildings during the afternoon instead of heading over to the gym or the track?

On Wednesday, the day he died, the PennCard record showed Stephen entering his building at 6:37 a.m. through the same back door Deb was supposed to have used. That didn't seem right to me – I could have sworn the police report said he'd arrived on campus later that morning. I made a note to check the time, and continued placing pins on the board, growing increasingly puzzled as I went.

11:23 a.m. – A debit purchase was made using Stephen's PennCard at the same campus café where Stephen had gotten lunch on Monday.

12:27 p.m. – The woman I now knew wasn't Deb entered the building using Stephen's PennCard. Had she also been the one to use the card earlier? There was no way to know.

1:02 p.m. – Stephen's PennPass was used to board an eastbound SEPTA train at the 34th Street station, two blocks north of Stephen's building.

1:29 p.m. – The transit pass was used again to board a Route 58 bus at the Frankford Transportation Center, halfway across town from the University.

1:38 p.m. – The PennCard was used to enter a staff-only door at the Children's Hospital, two blocks south of Stephen's building. I noted it down, wondering what sort of access rights the cards granted across the University.

1:46 p.m. – The transit pass was used a third time, to board a second bus – Route 70 – at the intersection of Bustleton & Cottman Avenues. I placed a pin on the intersection, and made a note to look up the bus route to see if it would provide any clue as to where the card-holder had been heading.

The pins and strings formed a strange zig-zag pattern, with events occurring farther and farther apart as the day wore on.

It made no sense.

I traded my Pepsi for a permanent marker and a sticky note, wrote "Est. Time of Death: 11:00a – 2:00p" on it, together with a huge question mark, and stuck it on the board between the University campus and the Frankford Avenue station across town. I then added a second sticky note which I labeled "Two Cards/Two People," at the top of the map, and rearranged the strings connecting the pins to show two separate timelines, running in parallel: one restricted to the campus, the other headed toward the suburbs.

Which card had Stephen been using?

The security footage showed the woman using his PennCard to enter his building. I was reasonably certain she was the same person who had also used the card at the hospital – stashing the bloody scrubs in Deb's locker – and at the café a short time later.

It was possible that Stephen had missed his afternoon classes because he'd left campus unexpectedly and taken the train somewhere. But even if he'd driven back, it would have been after 2:00 by the time he returned, which was after the estimated time of death.

On the other hand, assuming the police were correct, and Stephen died in the early afternoon, the mystery woman remained the prime suspect. But that left the question of who was using his PennPass to ride around town while he was in his office being murdered? Was it even connected, or just a bizarre coincidence? Had Stephen simply lost his pass prior to his death, providing some lucky passer-by the opportunity to take advantage of the free fare?

As much as I disliked the convenience of the coincidence, it seemed a possibility, as the transit pass was still being used – there were several time-stamped files listing travel on Thursday, Friday, and even one from early this morning. I printed off a large version of a SEPTA map and added it to my board, then put pins on it at the various train stations and bus stops where the card had been used, several of which were in the Elkins Park area, about ten miles north of me.

I stepped back from the board and stared at it, my attention divided between the two conflicting stories it was telling.

I felt like I was trying to piece together a jigsaw puzzle without the box-top photograph. There was something there, a pattern I was missing. I just had no idea what it was.

♦

The combination of too much pizza, too much soda, and too many questions left me restless. Sleep eluded me, and I tossed and turned and stared at the clock, noting the passage of time in ten and twenty-minute increments until I finally gave up trying to sleep.

I made myself a mug of tea, liberally dosed with milk and honey, and carried it up to the rooftop patio, snagging a blanket on my way. I snuggled down in an Adirondack chair, tucking the blanket close around me against the cool night air, and sipped at the tea, hoping it would help to settle my stomach as well as my nerves.

It was never truly dark up here, and the glow of city lights cast soft shadows around me. I would need to cover the chairs and prepare for winter soon, but I hoped I might have another week or two before I lost the patio for the season. An airplane winked overhead, and in the middle distance I could hear the traffic passing on the busy street a few blocks away.

My thoughts drifted.

In a bizarre way, I was almost grateful for the turn of events. Trying to figure out who had gone to such lengths to make it look like Deb had killed Stephen had given me something to focus on – and distracted me from the gut-twisting knots that formed in my stomach whenever I thought about Stephen, Eddie, my father, and the common thread that wound them together in my mind.

Work was my escape, my drug of choice.

And I was an addict.

Keeping myself busy – keeping my *mind* busy – was the best way I'd found to keep my personal legion of demons securely locked away. Boredom and I were not good company.

The sudden wail of a fire engine jolted me out of my reverie, and I shifted, muscles stiff from having drifted off in the wooden chair. The blanket had slipped off my foot, and my toes were cold.

It was time to go back to bed.

However it had happened, Stephen had been killed by someone who knew both him and Deb well enough to play on their mutual dislike. I was puzzled. Deb was miserable. For some reason, I had the strangest feeling that Stephen was the only one who would be resting in peace tonight.

Chapter 14
10 years ago

Meg's thoughts were still swimming the next day, so following a casual lunch meeting at the Piazza, she drove around the artsy, Northern Liberties district rather than heading directly back to her office in Center City. She was meandering down the district's narrow, rowhouse-lined streets when an "open house" sign caught her eye. There was an open space along the curb about two houses back, so she parked her Corolla and walked up to the narrow brick rowhouse identified by the balloon-festooned realtor's sandwich board.

A sign on the old-fashioned blue door invited visitors inside. She stepped into the small vestibule, then through the glass inner door... and then stood there for a moment in stunned surprise.

The house was nothing like what she'd expected from its unassuming exterior. The high-ceilinged rooms had been painted a creamy, not-quite yellow that amplified the sun pouring in through the pair of tall, narrow windows that looked out onto the street. Polished hardwood floors drew the eye from the living room and dining area through a wide doorway leading into the kitchen, where French doors at the opposite end of the house provided more light, and a glimpse into a small garden beyond.

Meg had moved into the living room, and was admiring the matching stained glass transom windows above both the entry door and kitchen arch when she heard the distinctive sound of heels clicking down the wooden stairs and a woman's cheerful voice greeted her.

"Hello, and welcome! I am *so* sorry I wasn't downstairs to greet you when you arrived," the woman said, almost leaping off he bottom step in her enthusiasm. Even with her tall heels, she was still shorter than Meg, trim and petite, with wavy blonde hair just brushing her shoulders, and a wide smile on her face. She extended her hand. "Bonnie Kauffman," she said.

There was something familiar about her, Meg thought as she returned the greeting. But before she had a chance to pursue it, Bonnie continued.

"I'm representing this house for the seller. Are you in the market?"

Meg looked around the warm, sunny space, in such contrast to the chill winter day outside. "I wasn't," she said. "Not really. But I am now. This is delightful."

Bonnie beamed, and led Meg through the house, pointing out its vintage details and modern upgrades, and talking about the investment opportunity of purchasing in an up-and-coming neighborhood like NoLibs. Meg barely heard her, filing the relevant details in the business portion of her mind as she settled into how the house *felt*.

It felt like she'd come home.

The third floor was divided into two large bedrooms with a generous bathroom situated between them.

"And this is the master bedroom," Bonnie said, as they entered the rear bedroom. Like the kitchen, two levels down, this room also boasted a pair of French doors, opening onto a rooftop patio. The patio was covered with snow, but still charming, with four-foot brick walls surrounding it and the bare branches of a large maple tree just beyond one corner, swaying gently in the slight breeze, faint shadows dancing on the snow.

"I can sleep anywhere," Meg said, turning back to look at the room, and the odd angles of walls and ceiling where modern ductwork had been hidden behind drywall. She was already visualizing how it would look furnished. "But this would make a wonderful home office."

Bonnie nodded slowly. "Why yes," she said, her blue-green eyes sparkling. "I believe it would."

Meg looked over at the agent. She was sure they'd crossed paths before, though she wasn't sure when. More than that, though – beneath Bonnie's carefree charm lurked a savvy businesswoman, a shark who had just scented the blood in the water and was circling round for the kill. Meg grinned. If the roles had been reversed, she would have done the same.

Bonnie was someone she could work with.

"I'll take it," Meg said.

◆

Meg would never have called her family a close one. After their mother died and her sister had committed suicide, she and her twin brothers had gone to live with their aunt. Aunt Ruthie had tried, but though they all lived in the same house, the prevailing undercurrent of loss and sadness had stunted what little closeness had ever existed between Meg and her siblings.

But her brothers had a share in the Cherry Hill house. And if she was going to give it up, she needed to know what they wanted to do with it.

"An official conference call from the big sister. To what do we owe the honor?" Gary joked once they were all three on the line. Gary was always clowning around.

Thomas was a little more straightforward: "Who died?"

"No one died," Meg said. "Does someone have to die for me to call you guys?"

"Pretty much," Gary said.

"I'm moving out of mom's house," Meg said, refusing to

rise to the bait. "Wanted to know what you two wanted me to do with it."

"Burn it," Gary said.

"Unless you want oversee renting it again," Thomas said, "might be time to sell."

"That's what I was thinking, Meg said.

"I still like the idea of burning it down," Gary said.

Meg and Thomas both ignored him.

"Cherry Hill is a good neighborhood," Meg said. "And the house is in in good condition. I think the renovations will make it very marketable."

"Just make sure Uncle Jim gets his cut," Gary said.

"His cut?" Meg asked.

"We had a betting pool," Thomas explained. "For how long you'd stay in the house. Aunt Ruthie didn't think you'd make more than two months. I gave you six."

"I told them you'd burn it down in three," Gary said.

"And Uncle Jim?" Meg asked.

"He said you were stubborn enough that if you made it past three months, you might stay two or three years," Thomas said, the shrug evident in his voice. "It's been two years, so he wins."

"Tell me you wanted to burn it down," Gary said.

"What's with you and burning it down?" Meg asked.

"I hated that place," Gary said. "Burning it down is too good for it."

"Maybe a new family will have a better time there," Meg said.

"You getting touchy-feely on us?" Thomas asked. "That's not like you."

"No," Meg said. "Just tired. It's a good house. I just don't want to live there any more."

"Where you going?" asked Gary.

"Moving into the city," Meg said, and told them about the rowhouse in NoLibs. "I guess I just thought if I can make a new life in a very old rowhouse, with whatever memories it already holds, maybe someone else can do the same in the Cherry Hill house." Her brothers were silent at that. Even Gary seemed to lack a suitable comeback.

After an awkward silence, the conversation moved on. Gary regaled them with his daughter's latest antics. He'd only been out of high school for a year when she was born, and been terrified at the very idea of being a parent, but Karen, now four, was clearly the light of his life. Meg thought he sounded happy, though he barely mentioned his wife, Janine. Things were clearly as strained there as they had always been, and neither Meg nor Thomas asked after their high-strung sister-in-law.

As for Thomas, he claimed to finally feeling settled in Chicago after being there for nearly a year, but he wouldn't answer Gary's questions about his love life. Meg didn't blame him, and evaded the question when it came to her.

"I'll talk to my realtor, and pull some comps, decide the best price, and get the house listed," she said, turning the conversation back to the original topic. "It's been a buyers' market lately, so it might take a while to sell —"

"It would be sad if it burned down before it sold," Gary cut in.

"—but I'll keep you all in the loop, Meg said, "and see to it that you get your share of the earnings… or insurance money."

Gary laughed, and even Thomas chuckled at that.

"I wonder what normal families talk about," Thomas said.

"Boring stuff like play dates and mortgages and who's got the flu or has to bring cupcakes to the HOA meeting," Gary said. "I have lots of boring friends."

Meg had to admit, arson sounded much more interesting, but she kept her observation to herself. "I'll keep you informed," she said.

"We should talk more often," Thomas said.

Meg thought about that after the conversation was over. Thomas was probably right. She probably should talk to her siblings more often. She just had no idea what they would talk about.

✦

The smell of warm sweat washed over Meg as she pushed through the gym door and made her way down the narrow, dimly-lit hallway. She moved quickly and quietly, her low heels clicking against the well-worn floorboards.

It had been two days since the break-in. She hadn't dared come here obviously injured. But the right makeup could cover a lot, and she wasn't limping any more.

As she emerged from the hallway to the small entry area and paused near the bulletin board, the lingering, appraising glances directed at her from men and women, most of whom she'd never met, sent a wave of déjà vu washing over her.

What did they see?

Most of the women who attended the weekly self-defense class were frightened, in pain, and determined not to feel that way again. Meg had been there once, but not for a long time. Even the man who'd broken into her house hadn't really *frightened* her. Shook her up a little, sure. Pissed her off, mostly.

And shattered her out of her complacency.

She'd learned how to defend herself in the event of an attack – barely. The home invasion had proven that much. But she hadn't pushed herself much beyond the basics, and she'd gotten her ass handed to her as a result. Other than the weekly self-defense class which she went to great pains not to miss, her training regimen for the past few years had been irregular and inconsistent.

If this afternoon went as she hoped, all that would change.

Meg continued on, past the bulletin board and the coat rack and heading toward the small ladies' locker room, noticing that most of the gym rats had gone back to their workouts. If she knew where to change out of her dress slacks and blazer, she'd clearly been here before, even if they didn't recognize her.

She'd nearly made it to the changing room door when a tall, muscular man in shorts and a sweaty t-shirt fell in alongside her, shortening his pace to match hers. "Don't often see you around here during the day," he said.

"Had a hole in my schedule," Meg said, shifting her backpack to her other shoulder. "Thought a workout would be a good way to fill it. How you doing, Ian?"

Ian took two quick steps ahead of her, blocking the door to the changing room with his arm. "Why are you here, Meg?" he asked, his deep voice little more than a rumbling whisper.

Meg looked up at him. No point putting it off. Ian was too good at reading people – or maybe he was just too good at reading *her*.

"I want you to train me," she said.

"Tuesday night, seven p.m., same as always," he said, reaching out with his free hand to press it against her shoulder, trying to turn her away from the locker room.

"That's not what I mean, and you know it," she said, shaking his hand away. "You offered to train me once – *really* train me – I'm ready to take you up on it."

"No." Ian stepped in front of the locker room door, his arms folded across his chest.

"Why not?"

"You don't want it enough."

"It wasn't the right time before. Now it is."

"Why?"

"Priorities change."

"You live in a safe neighborhood, work in a classy one. What's changed?"

"I'm selling the house, moving to NoLibs."

He shrugged. "So, you'll have a shorter commute. Not a good reason to take up Krav Maga."

"You know what I do. It's time to up my game."

He stood there, solid as a rock, staring down at her. Other than the researcher, Ian was the only other person who knew about Meg's clandestine activities, and he kept his opinion about that to himself.

Meg didn't flinch. If she backed down now, he'd send her away. And if she begged, trying to convince him she was sincere, that she was willing to do the work, it would be worse. He'd see it as a sign of weakness. Desperation.

Because it wasn't desperation, it was determination.

She'd trained here for five years. Thought she knew everything she needed to know to protect herself. But like the foreign language student who realizes that they've used up their entire four years' worth of classroom vocabulary during the first ten minutes after actually setting foot in a foreign country, the fight had smacked her in the face in the figurative sense almost harder than the literal hits she'd taken.

And because of it, Meg was ready to go back to school. To immerse herself in her training like she never had before. To learn to fight without thinking about what the next move would be.

Ian was always telling his students that they had to "become the weapon." She'd thought she understood him. Now she knew what he meant.

And she was ready to learn.

But she wanted him to agree to teach her *before* she changed out of her turtleneck sweater and into workout clothes and he saw the bruises encircling her throat and coloring her arms in red and purple blotches. Before he made her wipe the heavy makeup off her face and she had to admit to the battering she'd taken two nights before.

So she waited.

Five years before, when she'd first come to him, all she wanted was to learn to protect herself. The same basic self-defense lessons she now helped him teach. When he offered to teach her actual fighting – street fighting, how to use a weapon, share his covert skills with her along with his bed – she'd turned him down. She'd shared his bed willingly enough, but instead of diving into the world of covert and tactical skills he'd offered, she'd chosen to focus her attention on building her career. They'd remained friends long after they'd stopped sleeping together, but he'd never repeated the offer.

Not taking him up on it had been a mistake, she knew that now, but hindsight had once again proven itself to be 20/20, and all she could do was hope he would agree now.

She didn't know how long they stood there in silence, the fist slaps against punching bags, and grunts of weightlifters in the background the only sound. Finally, Ian's shoulders relaxed and he let out a short puff of air.

"You'll want to cut your hair. I've always liked it long, but it's a tactical disadvantage."

Meg nodded, her thoughts flashing back to the intruder dragging her by her braid like a leash. "Not a problem."

"God, woman. You're gonna be the death of me," Ian said.

"Not likely," Meg said, then grinned. "But I always could out wait you." She shrugged her shoulder, gesturing at her backpack. "Mind if I change now?"

He stepped to one side, and Meg ducked into the locker room, leaning her back against the thin wooden door as it closed behind her. She'd hoped Ian would agree, but hadn't been at all certain that he would. She'd barely stood there for a second, when a hand thwacked the door behind her and she jumped, startled.

"No slacking," Ian's voice called out. "Meet me on the mat in three."

"Be careful what you wish for," Meg muttered. With a grin, she pushed away from the door. If she was going to be on the mat on Ian's timetable, she didn't have any time to waste.

Chapter 15
Present day: Sunday morning

Instead of sleeping in, at seven o'clock Sunday morning I was standing in the middle of my home office, fully dressed in comfortable sweatpants and a mostly faded concert t-shirt, and sipping at my morning coffee. I didn't need to touch my face to feel the beginnings of a frown etching new lines into my forehead as I stared at the improvised map I'd created from Stephen's PennCard and PennPass data. So I'd tracked the cards across the university and then off campus, but now what?

I had no idea *who* I was tracking.

As quests for needles in haystacks went, this was a good one.

I'm not used to playing detective. Sure, there's a certain amount of research involved in my work, whether it's brokering a merger or selling insider secrets. And tracking a target's movement wasn't anything new for me – only rarely did a client choose the site for a hit or a handoff, and even then I preferred to do my own reconnaissance before the job was done.

But this was different.

To clear Deb's name, I had to twist my thinking around and come at the problem like an investigator, a police officer. I had to channel Lieutenant Thackery and find the real killer before he did.

I practically snorted my coffee at the irony, then shrugged as Glau looked up at me, his head bobbing and chin-flap waving – in agreement? Probably.

Feeling like a parody of a television crime drama, I took down a trio of large retro posters from where they hung above a row of low shelves and put them safely in the closet. Then I dug an old paper map of the city out of my files and tacked it to the wall. I hung the University and SEPTA maps I'd marked up the night before, overlapping the city map slightly on the east side. The PennPass data had tracked north, not eastward across the river, so covering that portion of the map didn't matter so much.

I stepped back and looked at my wall. "Well, Glau. What do you think?"

The iguana didn't even deign to look up. He just lay there, basking in the sunshine streaming in through the French doors. I couldn't blame him. As investigative boards went, it was pretty pathetic.

I didn't have photos of either Stephen or Deb, so I wrote their names in big block letters on sticky notes as placeholders and stuck them to the wall. Next, I added a row of sticky notes:

Who benefits from Stephen's death?

Who benefits from getting Deb out of the way?

Who would think to pick Deb as the fall guy?

Who would have access to Stephen's PennCard or PennPass?

Follow the money…

The last one – a quote from some mystery book or show, I couldn't remember – seemed like a good place to start, so I added more notes below it, listing items I would need to research: insurance policies, bank accounts, debts, etc. I already had a decent idea of Stephen's overall financial picture, but putting the numbers on the wall might help me see things in a different way.

Help me spot the clues I normally worked my ass off to conceal.

◆

After two hours, Stephen's side of the wall was covered in sticky notes. I had more questions than answers, but asking them had gotten the wheels turning in my head, which was a good thing.

After a quick trip downstairs to refresh my coffee, check Glau's water, and grab an orange, I returned to my office ready to tackle Deb's side of the wall.

I worked mind-map style, writing names of anyone I thought might have reason to hurt her on sticky notes and putting them on the wall in a random pattern around Deb's name.

Coming up with names – or at least descriptions – wasn't easy, and that wasn't just because she was my friend. Deb Markham is a truly likeable person. Over the years, I'd seen her take complete strangers under her wing and a few minutes later they'd be talking like long-lost friends. But that didn't mean she got along with everyone. Stephen's name was already on the board as a victim, but he'd have easily gone on the "people who don't like Deb" side. I put Malia's name on the wall, Eleanor Markham, and Nathaniel, Stephen's older brother. I didn't know how well Nathaniel knew Deb, but I'd seen no sign that anyone on Stephen's side of the family was friendly toward her, so they all went on the antagonist's side.

I tried to recall if I'd ever noticed any friction between her and anyone at the gym, but came up with a blank. And she'd never mentioned any angry parents of children at the hospital, just sad and worried ones. Even so, both categories deserved further investigation, so I posted sticky notes with large, black question marks for each.

Money-wise, Deb stood to lose financially with Stephen

gone, though she gained when it came to not having to deal with his crap any more. And unless she had a jealous co-worker who wanted her spot on the nursing staff, there was no one who benefitted financially from getting Deb out of the picture.

Which meant the only reason for framing her was to shift blame for Stephen's murder.

Which meant that the murderer was someone who knew Stephen well enough to have found out about Deb, *and* was patient enough to have devised the whole scheme.

The gears in my head were ticking along now, and I smiled as I stepped back and stared at the array of sticky notes covering the wall.

Much as it looked like a crime of passion, the result of an argument gone out of control, Stephen's death had been a cold, calculated murder, planned down to the last detail.

That was a game I knew how to play.

◆

Now that I felt I had a direction worth pursuing, I wanted to continue my brainstorming, but the morning was getting away from me. I'd accepted an invitation to join Uncle Jim and Aunt Maureen for lunch, and needed to shower and dress, make a salad, and get myself across town in the next ninety minutes.

Reluctantly, I left the office and went down the hall to my room, taking a notepad with me in case I thought of anything important. After a quick shower, I dressed and headed down to the kitchen, finger-combing my still wet hair, my mind churning with the challenge of planning Stephen's murder and setting Deb up to take the blame.

I got out a large bowl, then began pulling ingredients from the fridge for the salad I'd planned to take to the lunch. Ever-attentive to the sound of the refrigerator door, Glau scuttled into the kitchen before I'd closed the fridge and climbed up onto the perch I'd built for him against the far wall. The kitchen wasn't large – none of the rooms in the rowhouse were – but once I realized he was going to follow me around like an oversized dog, it had been worth sacrificing the cabinet space for the perch. Since I seldom locked him in his own room when I was home, it was either that or have six and a half feet of lizard constantly underfoot when I was cooking.

I dumped the bag of baby spinach leaves in a colander and rinsed them, then dropped a handful of wet leaves in front of Glau who nosed at them, then turned and looked at me with a baleful stare.

"Yeah, yeah, I know you like kale better, but this is what I've got," I said. "Take it or leave it."

He flicked his tail lazily, and tried one of the leaves, picking at it like a prima donna.

I rolled my eyes at him and dumped the rest of the spinach into the salad bowl, rinsed both the colander and my hands, then grabbed a nylon cutting board and a sharp knife.

"Okay," I said, slicing into a large red onion, "The target, Stephen Markham, is a university professor from a privileged family and thinks the rules don't apply to him." I peeled away the onion's outer skin and began slicing the onion into long, thin slivers. "He conveniently has an ex-wife with whom he has a well-documented, longstanding, strained relationship."

Glau looked over at me, chewing slowly.

"I'm getting into the role," I said, waggling the knife at him. "Don't judge my process." I went back to the onion. "Okay. The ex-wife works within a short distance of Markham's office, so a little surveillance work to establish her habits will allow me to fabricate both motive and opportunity would be simple enough."

I scribbled a note to see if there were any security cameras around either the children's hospital or the English building that had been functional in the weeks prior to Stephen's death. Scanning hours of crappy surveillance footage – assuming the Researcher could get it for me – looking for someone loitering in both areas over the past month or so was going to be tedious, but if it would help clear Deb, they would be hours well-spent.

"As far as means…" I finished with the onion and slid the mound of pinkish-purple slivers into the bowl. "…I wouldn't count on there being something in the office I could use as a weapon, so would probably come prepared. The geode was a good choice – since it was already there, it presented itself as a perfect weapon of opportunity, and avoided questions of how the ex might have come by whatever weapon I might have brought with me. If I'm setting the ex-wife up to take the fall, I don't care if she's charged with premeditated murder or manslaughter, as long as no one is looking for me."

I reached for the container full of fresh strawberries, hesitating just before my hand touched the plastic. Turning away, I pulled out a can of sliced pears from the cupboard near the fridge. Holding the pears in one hand, I picked up the strawberries in the other.

"What do you think, Glau?" I asked. He looked over when I said his name. "Pears?" I extended the can an inch or two toward him. He lay there on the perch like a lump, obviously uninterested in whatever was in the can.

"Or strawberries?" I raised the package of strawberries. Glau grew instantly interested, and began bobbing his head up and down, the dewflap beneath his chin waving with the motion. Strawberries were one of his favorite treats.

I put the can of pears back in the cupboard and popped open the package of strawberries. I dumped most of them into the colander and rinsed them, then grabbed a pair of nice, juicy-looking ones and took them over to Glau.

"Good boy," I said, resting my hand on the back of his head. He raised his head higher, pressing it into the curve of my hand, and I rubbed my wet hand over the knobby scales. "You finished your spinach, now you get a treat." When I set the strawberries on the towel in front of him, he lost all interest in being petted, and chomped down on the first one with gusto.

I patted him one more time, on the shoulder, avoiding the

spikey ridge running down the middle of his back, then went back to the sink, washed my hands, and took the rest of the strawberries over to the cutting board.

I continued with my salad-making, itemizing out the other steps I'd have taken if I'd been planning Stephen's murder while I cut the tops off the strawberries and cut them into quarters.

I'd need to steal his PennCard.

I'd need to get Deb's fingerprints and one of her scrubs without her noticing me. I'd also need to find out where her locker was and how to access it quickly, without anyone else on staff noticing me, so I could hide the bloody scrubs there to incriminate her. And I'd probably want to practice getting in and out of the hospital at least once, just to get the timing right.

Deciding on the day and time of my attack. This would have been critical – and hinged on so many things. Would I have gotten to his office ahead of time, finding the geode and applying Deb's fingerprints in incriminating places while waiting for him to arrive, so I could catch him unawares?

Or would I have become a regular visitor to both the building and the floor where he worked – maybe posed as a student or a colleague – so he wouldn't think anything of it when I came into his office and closed the door behind me.

"Thackery's notes hadn't indicated that Stephen had any defensive wounds," I pointed out to Glau as I tossed a generous amount of feta and the last of a bag of chopped pecans into the bowl. "That suggests that he either knew his killer or was taken completely by surprise."

I looked at my list. My notepad had a half-dozen bullet points – most of which I couldn't answer without more information. I put a lid on the salad and put it in an insulated bag with a bottle of poppy seed dressing, then wiped down the counter.

If I left now, I had just enough time to get across town to the Paoletti's on time. I'd call the Researcher on the way, and ask him to dig up anything else he could – surveillance footage, more PennPass data, the works.

I couldn't put the puzzle together without more pieces.

As I tucked the notepad into my bag, I noticed that the strawberry juice stains that dotted the paper looked very much like blood.

Chapter 16
Present day: Sunday afternoon

It was all I could do to keep from interrogating Uncle Jim over lunch. Not that peppering him with questions about Deb's case would have done me much good. Jim Paoletti has been practicing law since before I can remember, and is a master at deflecting questions. I wouldn't be at all surprised if I first learned the phrase, "you know I can't talk about that" at his knee.

Nonetheless, we were only halfway through our pasta primavera when he casually said, "I got a call from the District Attorney this morning."

I looked up, waiting for him to finish, but he was buttering a dinner roll as nonchalantly as if he'd said nothing of greater interest than making an observation as to the color of the sky.

"On a Sunday? How very interesting. Did he call for a consultation? Have some pressing legal matter that required the voice of experience? Or just call to invite you to his club for a round of golf?"

The corner of Jim's mouth twitched. We could go back and forth like that for several rounds, trading barbs like fly fishermen, each setting our hooks and waiting for the other to bite.

Aunt Eleanor was less patient.

"Oh, just *tell* her, Jim," she said, vigorously ripping her own dinner roll into pieces. "Or I will."

Jim quietly and deliberately placed his buttered roll on its plate, then positioned the butter knife along the edge of the dish. Resting his elbows on the table, to either side of his dinner plate, he steepled his fingers together.

"It's nothing definitive," he said, looking from Eleanor to me. "And certainly not something to get our hopes up over. But in studying the investigating officer's findings, Anthony found some... inconsistencies."

"Poor investigating," Eleanor said.

"Not at all," Jim said. "The officer observed the facts, recorded the data, and drew his conclusions. Anthony came to different conclusions—" he held up his hand, "—but I must caution you. It is much too soon to celebrate. It merely means that the investigation is ongoing. Anthony's call was simply a professional courtesy, nothing more."

I nodded, wondering if the D.A. had seen the same inconsistencies I'd noticed, but unable to ask. So I asked a different question. "What does that mean for Deb?"

"She's still the primary suspect, but I'm glad you and your friend posted her bail so quickly. She's not the type to do well in jail. The Markhams are screaming bloody murder that bail was even allowed. They're a powerful family..." he trailed off, and for a moment I thought he might be finished, but he continued, choosing his words carefully.

"I recommended that the D.A.'s office consider an ankle monitor and regular check-ins as an option to sending her back to jail while they pursue the investigation."

"Would they do that? Send her back to jail?" I asked.

"It's possible," Jim said. "The Markhams have many connections. Anthony agreed to take my suggestion under advisement. If he decides it is warranted, that will let Ms. Markham go back to work at least, and experience minimal disruption to her life."

"*Minimal*," Eleanor huffed, stabbing at her salad like it was alive.

"I'm sure that will come as something of a relief to her," I said. Eleanor did not look the least bit mollified.

I glanced at Jim, but he gave a barely perceptible shake of his head. Clearly this was a topic of some irritation between them, and I was all too happy not to get into it.

I tried again, changing the subject.

"So, I was thinking of looking for a house over in Germantown—" I said, naming the adjacent neighborhood where my Aunt Ruthie lived for no other reason than to tease Eleanor out of her irritation. She and Ruthie were always going at each other about which neighborhood was better, East Falls, where she and Jim lived, or Ruthie's much-beloved Germantown. I had my own opinions – which I kept to myself, in the interest of maintaining the peace.

"Tired of rowhouse living, then?" Jim asked.

"I like rowhouses just fine – and mine in particular. I just thought it might be nice to have a little greenspace of my own, instead of trying to find someplace near a park."

"What a wonderful idea!" Eleanor exclaimed, completely ignoring any mention of Germantown. "Let's see, Mt. Airy is wonderful for parks, but it's much too far for a regular commute into Center City."

Jim and I exchanged glances at that. He'd commuted in from East Falls every day for years, and it was only a few minutes closer than Mt. Airy. But Eleanor was on a roll, naming off all her favorite – and therefore the most desirable – neighborhoods in town and we weren't about to interrupt her.

Suddenly she set down her fork and looked right at me. "I know just the place! I have a friend just a few streets over who is looking to sell her house—"

"Meg doesn't need a large place, Eleanor," Jim chided. "Or a large mortgage."

""Well neither does Sarah, not now that Carlton's passed away," Eleanor said. She turned back to me. "Her children all moved away years ago. I'll just give her a call. It's a short walk over. Even if you decide it's too much house for you—" this said with a sharp look in Uncle Jim's direction "—it's a lovely afternoon. The walk will do us good."

She bustled out of the room before I had a chance to respond.

"She'll have you all moved in before you know it," Jim said, shaking his head at my impending doom.

"I haven't even listed the rowhouse yet," I said. "I only decided to move a couple of days ago."

Jim leaned back in his chair and gave me a long, appraising look. Now, I'm generally considered to be pretty tough in the boardroom, but being the object of James Paoletti's undivided attention always makes me want to squirm like a guilty child who's been sent to the principal's office. There's a small part of me that is just waiting for my uncle – the veteran trial lawyer and former state attorney general – to casually inquire how many insider trades I've made, corporate secrets I've stolen, or people I've killed.

But he never has, and he didn't ask then.

Instead he said, "She reminds you of your mother, doesn't she? Deborah Markham, I mean."

I sipped at my iced tea, grateful for the moment that gave me to collect my thoughts.

"Yes... and no," I said, setting the glass down, but not letting go of it. I ran my thumb up and down, tracing patterns in the water droplets that had condensed on the lower part of the glass. "Less now than she once did." I shrugged. "Times are different. Deb's managed better than Mother did in the same circumstances."

"But those shared circumstances still connect them."

"They do."

"Do you think she killed her ex-husband?"

The question caught me off-guard, and I jerked my head up so hard to look at him that I nearly pinched a nerve. He met my startled gaze with his own steady one, and I understood why he'd always been so successful in court.

"No," I said. "I don't think she did. Sure, she had plenty of reasons to want him out of her life, but that's been the case for years. Why would she snap now, when she has nothing to gain by it?"

"People do all sorts of strange things."

"True, but killing him? No. She's just not a violent person. Even in our self-defense class, she spends more time helping the other women than hitting anyone."

Jim raised an eyebrow at that. "She's in your self-defense class?"

I groaned inwardly, hoping I hadn't just said something that would somehow hurt Deb's case. But outwardly, I nodded. "Yes. It's almost all women who have been attacked, or abused in some way. We teach them how to protect themselves – nothing lethal, just how to block a punch, get out of a hold, fall without getting hurt so they can get up and run away. That kind of thing. We help them stop being victims, and learn how to recognize predators and avoid them. We don't teach them to go on the offensive."

"But someone who was a victim once might go farther, yes? Become a vigilante?"

I needed to tread lightly here. Jim didn't know it, but we were talking about me now, and not Deb.

"I suppose that's possible, but they'd need skills our class doesn't teach," I said. "We're strictly self-defense. Empowerment. Someone to call if you end up stuck somewhere late and don't want to take an Uber alone."

Jim leaned back in his chair, his expression somber as he studied me. I met his gaze without flinching. I knew what he wanted to ask, but didn't dare – what had driven me to a class like the one I'd just described to him? And if he'd asked, I'd have told him the same thing I tell anyone who asks: That I'm a single woman living in the city. That answer satisfies most people.

It wouldn't have satisfied Jim. Of that much, I was certain.

Fortunately, I was spared from having to put it to the test. Aunt Maureen came back into the dining room, with the news that her friend – Sarah? – would be only too happy to show me her house, and a set of photos on her cell phone to tempt me.

As Maureen scrolled through the photos, occasionally stopping to show me a particularly lovely view, Jim and I exchanged a glance over her head.

Our conversation was over for now, but if I knew Uncle Jim, it was far from finished.

◆

It was well into the middle of the afternoon by the time I finally extricated myself from Aunt Maureen and her good intentions. On any other day, I'd have been glad to stay, but Stephen's murder had been skulking around in the back of my mind all afternoon, and much as I'd enjoyed both the visit and the house Maureen had dragged me to, I was impatient to get back to work.

It's a pretty straight shot across town from East Falls to NoLibs, but instead of heading directly home, when I got to the Henry and Hunting Park intersection, I turned to the northeast, following the road until it dumped me onto Roosevelt and from there, on to the expressway. I hadn't planned it, but once I realized where I was heading, I asked my phone's GPS to guide me to the last place I knew Stephen's PennPass had been used: the Frankford Transportation Center.

I was seldom in that part of the city, and had no idea what I was expecting to find – more than likely one of the many small interchanges where passengers could transfer from a train to a handful of buses. But as I drew closer, I realized that I was completely mistaken. Frankford Center was a full-on *terminal*, a large brick and glass building capable of serving hundreds of passengers per day as they arrived on elevated trains and made their way down to the numerous bus pickups, or vice-versa.

I would need to know exactly who I was looking for to have even the slightest chance of spotting them in this facility, and even then, it wasn't likely.

I cruised on, passing under a maze of bridges at the station's northern end and then cruised slowly past the front of the building while I tried to decide what to do next. Above me, a train slid into the station, while on the cross street a small swarm of riders on motorcycles showed off, revving their engines and popping wheelies as they crossed the intersection.

I drove for a few blocks, the tracks that had been off to my right now running directly overhead. I had no idea where I was going, other than that I needed to head generally south and east. Even on a Sunday afternoon, there was enough traffic to keep me moving along and I'd gone several blocks before a traffic light finally gave me an opportunity to reset my GPS to provide a more direct route home.

Twenty minutes later, as I parked my car in the small space at the back of my rowhouse, I congratulated myself on having had the foresight to ask the Researcher for additional data on Stephen's PennPass. If it was still being used, there might be a record of which bus the user was taking to and from the Frankford station, and when they usually traveled. There would be no record of where they got on or off the bus, of course, but knowing the route to follow would be a starting place.

I grabbed my things and headed into the house. It had been a long day, full of mixed results, and as much as I'd wanted to get back to work all afternoon, now I just wanted to kick back and relax for the evening.

But before I could do that, I had to make the toughest call of all. I had to tell Bonnie I'd found the house I wanted to buy.

And it wasn't one of her listings.

♦

I managed to find enough to do to keep me busy for about an hour – feeding Glau, running the vacuum, tossing some things into the laundry. I was putting off the call, and I knew it.

When the only choices left to me were to clean the bathroom, mop the kitchen floor, or call Bonnie and confess my infidelity to my realtor, I reached for my phone.

"Hey, I was hoping to hear from you," she said. "Have you thought any more about the houses we looked at the other day?"

"Yeah…," I said. "None of them really work for me…"

"I thought as much. That's fine. I'll go through the listings tomorrow, and see if I can find—"

"I had lunch at my uncle's today, over in East Falls," I said. She knew Uncle Jim was representing Deb, and I half-hoped she'd ask how the case was. I couldn't tell her much, but it would buy a few extra minutes. I knew she wasn't going to be happy about me finding a house without her.

"It's nice over there," she said.

"Yes, it is."

"If you want, I can look that direction. I don't know what we'll find – people tend to stay put once they buy there."

Time to bite the bullet

"No need," I said. "I already found a house."

There was silence on the phone for a good three seconds before Bonnie said, "I see," the icicles dripping from my headset as her words reached my ear.

"Don't take it that way," I said.

"Tell me about the house."

"It's in East Falls," I said, "a few streets over from my aunt and uncle's. A friend of theirs is downsizing. It's a big house, nice yard, and it's all been very well maintained. It's a great opportunity."

"Who's representing it?"

"That's the thing," I said. "Nobody. She wants to do it herself – signed up with one of those services that helps you with the paperwork—"

"Oh. My. God." Bonnie said, finally sounding more like herself. "Please promise me you'll at least let me look over the papers before you sign anything."

"Of course I will," I said. "I know better that to do a real estate deal without you."

That wasn't entirely true, of course. I'd invested my ill-gotten gains in properties all over the country – and a few foreign countries – to spread the money around, all without Bonnie's help. I'd actually gotten rather good at the nuances of real estate contracts. But that was irrelevant to this conversation. I don't have many close friends, and I was willing to do quite a bit to keep our friendship healthy.

"And I'll want you to handle selling the rowhouse for me," I added.

"Small consolation," she grumbled. "So are you committed?

"As in 'should I be committed?' or 'have I made any binding promises yet?'"

"We already know the former to be true," she said drily. "So that leaves the latter."

"Cute. And no, nothing binding. I did tell her I was very interested and would like to come back when I had a little more time. Want to come along? I'd love your opinion on the place. They turned the family room into a conservatory-style space right in the heart of the house – it will be perfect for Glau—"

"I'd better come see it, then," Bonnie said with exaggerated patience. "If for no other reason than to protect you from yourself."

Chapter 17
Present day: Sunday evening

Lunch had been substantial enough that I wasn't hungry, so I settled down with a glass of wine, a small plate of cheese and crackers, a good book, and the intention of unwinding for the evening. But I couldn't concentrate. My mind kept going back to what uncle Jim had said earlier about the district attorney's reaction to Deb's case file. After reading the same paragraph three times and still not being sure what it said, I gave up the pretense.

I needed to know what else was in Thackery's notes.

"I'm going out," I told Glau. He blinked at me, and followed reluctantly as I led him to his room. By the time I'd checked the room's temperature and made sure there was plenty of water in the humidifier, he'd climbed up to his perch among the broad-leafed potted plants that filled the room.

"You'd like a conservatory of your own, wouldn't you?" I asked him. "Filled with lots of green, and maybe even a fountain."

Glau bobbed his head at me, then moved further up onto the perch, settling himself under the heat lamp.

Since I never knew why he bobbed his head, I generally chose to take it as an affirmative response. The East Falls house really did have a lot of features I liked, but the two-story conservatory – which sat between the living and sleeping wings of the house like an enclosed courtyard – was definitely a selling point.

I changed into jeans and T-shirt and a light hoodie, then donned a wig and pair of dark-rimmed glasses – it may have been overly cautious on my part, but in my experience, you can't be too careful. I didn't want anyone in the area to notice me and remember that they'd also seen me in the area only a few days before. The shoulder-length, light brown wig was a favorite of mine for times like this, when I just wanted to blend in with the crowd. And for some reason, people tended to focus on glasses frames, rather than the face behind them, making non-prescription glasses a Clark Kent-worthy part of my disguise.

I returned to the same family restaurant across the street from Lieutenant Thackery's precinct, driving most of the way this time, because I didn't want to spend the time making train and bus connections. I parked on the side of the road about a block down, slung my bag onto my shoulder, and walked to the restaurant.

Hacking the case file database a second time was no more difficult than it had been the first, and I had the updated records saved to my iPad before the waitress brought me my milkshake. I sipped at the creamy chocolate, reading a steamy romance novel I'd downloaded as part of my cover, and when I finished the shake left a couple of dollars for the waitress. On my way out, I flashed a shy smile at the cop who had been trying to flirt with me for several minutes from his seat at the diner's counter.

I don't date cops. I don't care how cute they are.

♦

There are a number of reasons why someone might be fingerprinted that have nothing whatsoever to do with breaking the law. Many banks keep fingerprints on file for check-cashing purposes. Some employers use fingerprints as part of running a background check. Others use them as part of biometric security access to sensitive areas.

However, it turned out that Stephen Markham had never been officially fingerprinted. So with his facial features half-destroyed – including significant damage to his teeth that would make identification by dental records problematic – and no official fingerprints on file, the police had relied on other identifying factors: hair color, his wallet, his wedding ring, all of which were confirmed by his wife, who swore up and down that the man in the morgue was her husband.

The odd thing was, when the forensics unit processed Stephen's office – which was how they found Deb's partial fingerprints – they found numerous fingerprints belonging to other people, but not a single one that matched the deceased. Thackery had considered that unusual enough that he'd requested a warrant to search Stephen's home, and hoped to collect matching fingerprints there, but was waiting for a judge's approval.

He'd also added a few lines below the photo of the woman on the stairs:

Identity of female captured on stairwell footage: unknown.

D. Markham's alibi partially verified: suspect's ID was not used on campus on the day of the murder, and she did not report for work that day or the previous/following. Family members assert she was at home sick all week. Confirm medication prescribed, purchased.

Actual whereabouts on the day of remain inconclusive.

Investigation ongoing.

I read that again, then pushed away from the computer, my mind filled with the same questions that Thackery had noted and the D.A. had referred to as inconsistencies:

Who was the woman on the stairs?

Was the dead man actually Stephen Markham?

If not, whose body was lying in the morgue – and who killed him?

◆

I was far too wound up now to do anything other than work, so I spent the next couple of hours rearranging the notes I had pinned to my wall and adding new ones. There was more to this murder than any of us had seen at the beginning.

I'd printed out copies of pictures I'd found online of both Deb and Stephen, and hung them on the wall, one to either side of the map, which still took center stage.

But now, I pinned a blank sheet of paper just above the top of the map. At the top, I used a black marker to write "Stephen Markham, murdered by Deb Markham" in large letters, and then I drew a line through it with a red marker.

On the next line I wrote "Stephen killed by someone else who framed Deb" – again in black marker, and again, drew a red line through it.

Then I wrote "John Doe killed, made to look like Stephen, by Jane Doe, who framed Deb." This time, I used the red marker to underline the names – or placeholders – for the four players involved.

I stood back and looked at the list, shaking my head. I was glad there was room on the page for another scenario – and half afraid I was going to have to use it.

I'd run into nothing but dead-ends trying to figure out who the mystery woman who had impersonated Deb was – even sharpened to the best of my photo-manipulation ability, the hazy image I'd printed out from the security camera feed was no help at all. And I had no image – fuzzy or not – to represent the fake-Stephen. So I pinned a generic silhouette of a male head to the wall and began skimming through the police records I'd downloaded, looking for someone who closely matched the real Stephen in height, weight, and general appearance. It was a long shot, but it was a place to start.

The one thing I knew for certain was that there was definitely a dead body. I wanted to know who it belonged to.

Between my two hacks into the police records, I'd pulled about two weeks' worth of files. I sifted out other murders, assaults, robberies, and the like, and focused exclusively on missing persons reports. The reports skewed heavily toward female; eliminating those together with cases that had been open for more than a month brought the list to a manageable size. I next filtered by race, because even with his artificial rich-boy tan, there was no way either Stephen or his dead body-double could be mistaken for a person of color.

That left me with six men, ranging in age from their late thirties to mid-seventies – this last one being an Alzheimer's patient who had gotten away from his caregiver earlier in the day and was being sought by friends and family. I'd seen the report on the morning livestream of the news, and while I wished the family well, he was clearly not a candidate for being mistaken for Stephen Markham. I crossed him off the list.

Another, who was of the right general build, had been seen at a party by several witnesses the night before, but had never made it home. I hoped he was sleeping it off with the wrong person and crossed him off my list.

That left four.

But before I could take a closer look at them, *Here Comes the Sun* started playing on my phone.

"Hey, Deb," I said. "How are you?"

"What's your morning look like tomorrow?" she asked, not answering my question.

"Just another Monday," I said. "Some paperwork, a couple of calls. I have a big client meeting tomorrow afternoon, but the morning is pretty flexible. Why?"

"Can you do me a huge favor?"

"Name it."

"Will you take me to the police station? They want..." her voice, already low, dropped to barely a whisper. "They want to put an ankle bracelet on me. Track my movements."

"I'm so sorry," I said. "Of course I'll take you. Did they say why?"

"It was that or go back to jail," Deb said. "Mr. Paoletti says it's for the best, and I believe him, but I just don't think I can do it alone."

I ground my teeth, trying not to scream. I'd seen the same evidence the police had. If Jim had told her she needed to do this, that meant the Markham family – namely, Malia – was having a hissy fit about Deb having been freed on bail, and was trying to pull strings to get her tossed back into a cell.

There was no way Deb could know – and I couldn't tell her – that Jim had pulled strings of his own to keep her out.

Chapter 18
7 years ago

If anyone had asked her what she wanted to be when she grew up, Meg would not have answered, "a corporate espionage agent." It just wasn't something most high school guidance counselors suggested as a possible career path.

But time and opportunities had put themselves together in such a way that by the time she was thirty-one years old, Meg could very easily have listed that profession on her resume.

She didn't of course.

Publicly, she was one of the top mergers and acquisitions executives in Philadelphia, a position that provided her with access to information that was valuable to both her legitimate and her less-than-savory clients. Her association and training with the Researcher had both expanded her skills and given her access to the dark web database where high-paying clients advertised for skilled agents to assist them in less than legal enterprises.

It wasn't like she needed the money, but the challenge, the intrigue the work provided kept her mind from going to dark places, and Meg regularly reviewed the listings for jobs that would satisfy that craving.

It was an interesting tightrope to walk.

Both sides of her life had rules and consequences for breaking them, and Meg was extremely careful to avoid uncomfortable entanglements that might cause problems.

The one thing all her training and contacts had not been able to do for her, was help her locate her father. He had vanished more thoroughly than even her rapidly developing skills could track, and had a twenty-year head start before she'd even begun looking in any serious way. And while Meg never wanted to admit that finding him might be a lost cause, she never stopped looking, even though each time she thought she'd found a clue, the trail went cold.

It was at those times she turned to her favorite surrogate punching bag, Stephen Markham, and took out her frustrations on him.

"What are you up to today, Stephen?" Meg said, tapping a few keys to access the report provided by the skip tracing service she had invested some of her ill-gotten gains heavily into a few years back.

"Oh no, no, no," she said, looking at the passport record that had recently been updated to the system. "Are you planning a trip, Stephen? Well, we can't have that, can we?"

He'd managed to work his way off the no-fly list she'd put him on, and while it would be easy enough to pull the same stunt a second time, where was the fun in doing the same old thing?

Meg stared at the screen, tapping her fingers on the desk.

She had already messed with his credit, and initiated a foreclosure on one of his vacation homes. What could she do today that would be an appropriate punishment for a man who had all but abandoned his children and fought his ex-wife for every penny of child support he provided? There was just no way she could excuse that.

Her father hadn't even done that much, leaving her mother with nothing.

Meg stood and walked to the window, taking a deep breath to calm her racing heart. She wondered where her father was, what he was doing, what kind of life he was living. Her mother was long dead – it was possible her father was dead, too, though she hoped not. She wanted to find him. She wanted him to know the damage he had done, the pain he had caused.

She wanted to kill him herself.

But until she found him, she would have to settle for hounding Stephen in his place. She returned to her computer, and in a few minutes had settled into the calming flow state that only airbrushing his face into a series of compromising photos could provide.

◆

There were some things even Meg's photomanipulation skills couldn't fix.

Aunt Ruthie had found a box in her garage – things that had come from the Cherry Hill house where Meg had grown up that she thought Meg might want. Meg didn't want anything from the Cherry Hill house, but she dutifully brought the box home and set it in a corner where it resided for several weeks before she finally opened it up and started going through things.

It was one of those boxes of memorabilia, the kind of thing people liked to keep but don't know what to do with later. There were crayon pictures drawn by young hands that had probably hung on the refrigerator or been taped to the bedroom wall, craft projects made for a long-forgotten Mother's Day, and a few books.

Meg picked up one of the books. It was one of the ubiquitous collections of children stories her mother had liked to read to her and her siblings at night before bed. As she opened it and began to flip through the pages, a photo fluttered to the floor. She reached down for it and froze, her hand momentarily hovering over the picture before she slowly picked it up.

It was a five-by-seven glossy of the entire family, clearly a studio portrait, though Meg had no recollection of it being taken.

Her mother sat center-stage with the twins, Gary and Thomas, looked to be about seven years old at the time, standing proudly on either side, bright smiles on their freckled faces. Eddie stood behind her mother, his usual grin on his face.

Meg stood to Eddie's left. She was Maggie then, only about 12 years old, and had moved as far as Eddie's hand on her shoulder, fingers wound in her long, blonde hair, would allow. She wouldn't call the expression on her face a smile – it was more of a grimace.

Then her eyes tracked over to Sheila. Eddie's right hand was around her waist, and it was obvious to anyone who really looked at the picture that he was pulling her closer to him, even as she was clearly angling her upper body in the opposite direction, her face a rigid mask.

"My god, Mother," Meg murmured. "Were you really that blind? How could you see this and not have known?"

Meg scooped up the picture and tore it into pieces. She tossed the scraps along with the book and the other memorabilia back in the box and threw it all in the garbage.

Some things were better not remembered.

◆

Meg paced around the rowhouse, almost jogging up and down the stairs, the memories threatening to drown her.

When she finally couldn't stand it any further, she went to the dark web and logged in to the covert listings bulletin board. She sat there staring at the letters scrolling by, green text on a black screen, greedy, desperate people willing to pay for information, for assorted services, for murder.

Meg was feeling murderous.

She normally filtered the listings that she viewed to those looking for information to buy or to sell. But this time she adjusted that filter.

A businessman wanted an associate who had been stealing from him punished.

A wife wanted a cheating husband out of the way in such a way that the life insurance would not be lost.

There were so many reasons and so many ways people wanted other people killed. Oddly, Meg felt no guilt, no revulsion at the thought of murder for hire.

She leaned back in her chair, watching the listings scroll by. Could she do it? She thought she could. The real question was could she do it and get away with it?

The idea of walking up to someone and just shooting them seemed crass, it lacked finesse – and it would have law enforcement looking for the perpetrator. No, if she was going to expand her services to include assassination, she was going to do it in subtle ways, kill using methods that were much less obvious.

The very idea sent a frisson of excitement down her spine, and lifted her spirits.

It probably said something about her that she found the idea so very intriguing, but Meg had stopped caring about what people thought about her a long time ago. She was the person her father had made her – he was to blame. All she'd done was figure out a way to benefit from his inattention and if anyone wanted to judge her for that, she'd happily add them to her list of people who deserved to be punished.

It would be a new project, a new course of study to add to the multifaceted curriculum she had assigned herself when she began working with the Researcher. Ian had taught her how to shoot, how to fight. And while those skills would definitely be part of an assassin's repertoire. Meg knew she had to expand her skillset well beyond the obvious if she wanted to stay off the radar.

Ian had warned her when he trained her, cautioned her about letting a fight go too far. "The skills you're learning can protect a life or take one," he'd said in his ever patient, Zen-master way. "And once you take a life, it changes you. There's no going back. It can never be undone."

There's no going back.

There were many things in life that changed you, Meg thought, returning her attention to the dark web and the future that scrolled past her eyes. Green letters on the black screen.

So many things that could never be undone.

At least this one was her choice.

Chapter 19
Present day: Monday morning

I picked Deb up at seven.

"Thank you for doing this," she said as we pulled away from her house. "I couldn't ask Mom or Cassie to come with me. It will be hard enough to explain why I have to wear the tracker…"

"You haven't told them?"

"I couldn't," Deb said, her voice trembling. "I just didn't know how. This is all so horrible."

I reached over and gave her hand a squeeze. We said very little else on the ride to the station. Deb was lost in thought, and I've never been good at meaningless small talk. So we drove in silence.

I was surprised when they let me go back with Deb when she was fitted for the tracker.

"It uses a GPS signal," the officer told her, "which allows us to see where you are at all times."

"It monitors constantly?" I asked.

"The old ones used a monitoring unit that would call out periodically to tell us where you were. This one has both the transmitter and receiver incorporated into the unit, and sends a ping to the nearest cell tower every 10 seconds," the officer replied. "If it fails to send or receive the signal three times in a row, an officer is dispatched. You'll want to be sure to keep it charged up."

"I work in a hospital," Deb said. "I don't know if the signal will get through there."

"You'll have to discuss that with your probation officer," the officer said with a shrug. "I just hand them out. Sign here."

I was glad to get out of there, and didn't regret the sigh of relief that escaped my lips as the doors closed behind us an hour – and a great deal of paperwork – later. But Deb was moving like a zombie, barely lifting her feet, her eyes not really tracking, her skin pale and a little clammy.

"Hey," I said, stepping in front of her and taking hold of both of her arms. "Deb. Look at me."

She looked up, her eyes not focusing, in that deer in the headlights sort of way.

"We're going to get you through this," I said.

"Mm-hmm."

She was going shocky, stress sending her fight or flight response into a tailspin and causing her to freeze up. I glanced around. Where we were standing was halfway between the station doors and the parking structure. Across the street was the family restaurant I had twice visited.

Even factoring in crossing the street at the intersection, the restaurant was closer than my car was. And my car didn't have orange juice or coffee or a sugary pastry that might help kickstart Deb's brain – or at least her body. I didn't want her having a total meltdown or passing out on me.

I tucked her arm in mine, and began to walk her toward the corner. She went along, compliant, surfacing briefly to look around in confusion as we crossed the street.

"Where are we going?" she murmured.

"I thought we'd get a cup of coffee," I said.

"Oh, okay."

We didn't talk, what was there to say? Instead we sipped at

coffee, nibbled at surprisingly good cinnamon rolls, and sat in silence until the color returned to Deb's face and the look in her eyes had gone from empty to something that bordered on normal.

"Ready to head home?" I asked her.

"Yes," she whispered, nodding slightly.

I finished my coffee, and paid the bill, then we left the restaurant and headed to the car. It was a nice day, though I doubted Deb noticed. She walked with her head tilted down, as though afraid anyone who made eye contact with her suspected her of murder.

Frankly, she was pissing me off, just giving up like that. Yes, what was happening was demoralizing, but *she* knew she hadn't killed Stephen. I guess I expected her to be stronger, more hopeful, or at least not collapse in on herself. Seeing her like this… she *looked* guilty. And with all the circumstantial evidence pointing at her, if it came to trial, there's no way a jury would believe in her innocence.

But rather than give her a pep talk and try to encourage her out of victimhood, I held my tongue. I was here to be her friend, to support her. Not to make promises about everything working out for the best when we both knew there were no guarantees of that, and certainly not to judge her when she was down for falling short of my expectations.

As I eased into traffic, I glanced over. Deb was staring down at the bulge around her ankle, just visible under her pant leg, tears sliding silently down her face.

♦

When you do the kind of work that I do. It's important to compartmentalize.

As stressful as the first part of the morning had been, when I finally got to the office and dove into my morning tasks, things went quite smoothly – for a Monday. I returned phone calls, replied to emails, and groaned inwardly when I received the notification that my afternoon client had indeed booked our meeting for an indoor shooting range.

Apparently, some trendy influencer had decreed that shooting range meetings were all the rage these days. Not that I preferred golf, but it was definitely easier to talk while walking a course than to have any thing remotely resembling a conversation over the thunder of gunfire echoing through a cement warehouse.

"Jessica," I called out.

My assistant appeared in my door almost instantly. "Yeah?"

"What? Were you standing right there?"

"Was about to get a refill on my coffee," she admitted

"Bring me one too, please?" I asked, raising my own empty mug.

She came and got it. "This isn't what you called me for," she said, grinning. "What did you really need?"

"Herriman Industries…" I said, raising my eyebrow by way of a question mark.

"The shooting range. I know. I'm sorry," she said. "Mr. Herriman called twice this morning while you were out. He said not meeting at the range would be 'a deal-breaker.' And later, when his assistant called to confirm the time, she sounded like she thought she'd be fired if you didn't take the meeting."

"And what makes you think *I* won't fire *you*?"

"I know how you like your coffee!" Clutching my mug in her hands, Jessica spun around and fled. She was out of sight, heading downstairs to the coffee shop in the building's lobby before I finished laughing.

"In all seriousness, though," I said when she returned with the steaming cup. "I don't like doing these. It's all about the men trying to show how macho they are."

"Like they think *they* can intimidate *you*," Jessica said, settling into one of the two visitor's chairs in front of my desk and taking a sip of her own coffee.

"They can't, but that doesn't stop them from trying," I said raising my own mug in salute. "Next time someone tries to badger you into one of these oddball meetings, tell them I prefer to conduct business in the boardroom. If they insist, it will be reflected in my bill."

"That will get them," Jessica said.

"Maybe. But probably not."

"Hey, at least. It's only the gun range. His assistant said he wanted to go out on a paintball course."

"That's a hard no," I said, looking at her over the rim of my mug. "Should it ever come up again."

"A deal-breaker?"

"Oh, yes."

We sipped at our coffee, and once again I reflected on the importance of compartmentalization, of not letting my two businesses overlap, and of setting boundaries with my clients. If I'm going to go out into the woods with a rifle, it's going to be loaded with bullets, not with paint.

And that would definitely be a deal-breaker.

♦

There was no way I was going to the shooting range in the pastel silk blouse and plum-colored, mid-calf length skirt and heels I'd worn to the police station.

I'd chosen the outfit with the idea that less formal attire would make Deb feel more comfortable in a stressful situation. But even with the black blazer I'd added when I arrived at the office, the combination of colors and soft fabrics that had been perfectly appropriate this morning would just add fuel to Herriman's power trip.

Because that's all this afternoon's last-minute change of venue was – a power-play. And a shooting range? He was clearly trying to intimidate me. Women may have cracked the glass ceiling – and broken through it in many places – but men like Herriman still thought they were in charge.

We'd only met by conference call to this point, but it was clear that he wanted our first in-person meeting to establish his position as the power player in the negotiations between Herriman Industries and my client, Southern Coast Holdings, a conglomerate out of North Carolina. I'd brokered a half-dozen deals for SCH over the past few years, scooping up small-time entities like Herriman's that thought they were worth more than they really were, and turning them into some real money.

My job was to keep Herriman happy enough to not blow the deal, but not offer more than SCH was willing to pay in dollars, options, and other concessions. It was a tricky balancing act – but one I seemed to have a knack for, if my track record and bank account were to be believed.

So I left the office a little early, and stopped by the rowhouse to change before heading to the shooting range. Ten minutes later, I headed out in jeans, a scoop-neck t-shirt, lightweight, three-quarter sleeve black leather blazer, and low suede boots.

It was a don't mess with me, business-casual wardrobe that said I was more than ready to play with the boys – on my terms.

Chapter 20
Present day: Monday afternoon

I got to the range about ten minutes before the scheduled meeting with Herriman, and used the time to get registered and rent a weapon. Even thought I had a concealed carry permit, and often carry a gun in a locked safe mounted inside my car, I had no intention of bringing my own weapon to my first meeting with a client.

Instead, I selected a 9mm Beretta 92FS from the range's rental options. Similar to the military issue, I had used the model many times in the past. It fit well in my hand, and I like the action.

I was stepping away from the counter with my weapon, ammo, eye and ear protection, when Herriman came in, flanked by two of his aides. All three of them were wearing dark suits.

"Mr. Herriman?" I said, stepping forward. I shifted my bundle to my left hand and extended my right.

"Ms. Harrison," he said, taking my hand in a firm grip. "Thank you for joining us."

He was an older man, with graying hair and a military bearing. I knew from the company precis that he'd retired from the Marines some fifteen years before, but ran his organization like a military squadron. He looked me up and down as we shook hands, frowning slightly at my casual attire.

"What are you shooting?" he asked, nodding toward the gun bag as he released my hand.

"Beretta 92FS," I told him.

"An acceptable choice."

"I like it well enough," I said.

He turned to one of his aides. "Kyle, see to our weapons," he said.

Kyle – a younger man who looked to be close to my age – stepped past me to the counter and began speaking with the attendant. The second aid remained quietly to one side, almost at attention, like some sort of security guard.

"This is an interesting choice of venue for a business meeting," I said.

"Yes. I apologize," he said. "I had no idea there were so many homeless in the area. I hope it did not make you feel uncomfortable."

"That's not what I meant," I said. "Only that we'll not be able to discuss much business here."

"I'm not here to discuss anything," Herriman said brusquely.

"Then what are we doing here?" I asked.

"How a man – or a woman – handles themself on the shooting range, tells me a great deal about our future business dealings," he said. "Your choice of weapon tells me you think you know what you're doing. We shall see."

I raised an eyebrow at that. "So someone skilled in business, but new to the gun range...?" I left the question open-ended.

Herriman did not respond.

This was going to be interesting.

After everyone had their gear and weapons, we listened to a brief safety lecture from one of the range staffers. Herriman chafed visibly at the indignity of being lectured by someone barely more than a teenager. His two aides were stoic, but as I put on my protective glasses, it was all I could do to stifle a grin.

Finally, we were allowed to go into the range and take our assigned positions. We had the range to ourselves, but stood in adjacent lanes, with Kyle in the lane to my left, Herriman to my right, and the second aide at the far end of our little group.

It had originally been my intention to let Herriman shoot first, to see what his skill level was. I would then take my own turn, doing well enough to impress, but letting him have the better grouping on at least one of the target sheets.

I wasn't so sure I wanted to let him win now.

Showing up with his security detail and treating me like I had to earn the right to do business with him. What was it with guys like him, anyway? Yeah, he was pushing my buttons, but I've never liked bullies, and that's all he was, really. I was actually grateful for the calming routine of setting up my station. Removing the gun from the bag and clearing it – removing the magazine, ensuring the chamber was empty – and setting it out on the bench gave me something else to focus on.

"Ladies first?" asked Kyle.

I shook my head as I spoke, not looking over to see if he was looking at me through the tinted barrier.

"No," I said. "That's not necessary. Mr. Herriman, you are the guest. Please, go ahead."

"As you say, Ms. Harrison, there is no need to stand on formality." He looked back at the range officer, who nodded, then turned to the aide to his right. "Anton, you may fire when ready."

I settled my earmuffs over my ears as Anton sent his target out. The shots followed a moment later in fast, muffled "pops." He emptied his Glock 17 in about ten seconds, and as the target slid back toward him it showed two primary groupings – in the head and the center mass.

Herriman's target slid out next. Like me, he was shooting a Beretta 92FS, and emptied it in a series of smooth, controlled shots. Every shot was in the target's center mass.

I was up next.

I pushed the button to send my target out and stepped back to the bench, my feet automatically assuming a stable, comfortable stance as I picked up the Beretta. I slid the magazine in, feeling it click into place, then raised the gun, holding it with both hands. Looking along the barrel at the front sight, I flipped off the safety, leaning slightly forward as I slid my finger down off the side of the gun and onto the trigger.

Time is strange on the range. It only takes a few seconds to squeeze off fifteen rounds, but as I stared down the line, my finger pressing again and again on the trigger in a smooth, relentless rhythm, arms absorbing the recoil as the rounds left the chamber one after another, it was hard to tell if my heartbeat was keeping pace with each explosion, or vice-versa.

And then the last round flew.

I drew my arms back to my body, lowering the Beretta toward the bench. When it was about an inch from the bench, I hit the release, letting the empty magazine fall into my hands. I set it aside, checked the weapon chamber, and set the gun on the bench, then turned and pressed the button to recall my target.

The grouping was nearly a duplicate of Herriman's.

I resisted the impulse to grin, shout, or even smirk, but did glance Herriman's way. I honestly couldn't tell from his expression whether he was pleased or furious.

There was something satisfying in that.

Kyle was shooting a Sig Sauer P226, and made quick work of it, emptying it into his target in a center mass grouping that, while neat, wasn't quite as tight as either mine or Herriman's.

"Well done," I told him when he pulled the target back.

He shrugged, but there was a hint of a smile around the edges of his mouth. Breaking that stoic façade was oddly satisfying. I wondered if I'd manage to get a smile from Anton as well.

I turned back to Herriman. "Another round?"

He stared at me for several seconds before answering. "No, that won't be necessary," he said. Then he turned to the range officer. "We're done here."

Leaving Anton to clean up his weapon, Herriman pulled off his earmuffs and protective eyewear and walked out of the range.

I turned to Kyle. "What was that all about?"

Kyle tucked his Sig into the gun bag, then looked over at me, a full grin on his face now. "Grandfather doesn't like to be shown up. Especially not by a woman, if you'll forgive me for saying so. I keep telling him he needs to catch up to this century…" he shrugged.

"Grandfather?"

Kyle nodded.

This day was just getting more and more interesting.

♦

I sat in my car, watching, as Herriman and Kyle paused near the back of their rented sedan and had what appeared to be a one-sided discussion – though while Herriman doing the bulk of the talking, it didn't seem as though Kyle was backing down from his position. Anton did not participate, standing silently near the driver's side door, as though awaiting instructions.

After a few minutes of this, Anton and Herriman got into the car, while Kyle retrieved a briefcase from the back seat but did not get in. Then the sedan backed out and drove away leaving Kyle standing in the parking lot, looking at his cell phone.

More curious than I should have been, I slowly pulled up alongside him and put the window down.

"Need a lift?" I asked.

He startled, and looked over at me.

"Oh, it's you. I was just scheduling an Uber," he said.

"I set aside the entire afternoon for your grandfather," I said. "The least I can do is give you a ride. Where you headed?"

"Actually," Kyle said, "I was going to your office – if that's not an imposition."

I shrugged. "Hop in."

I wasn't sure what to make of Kyle. Or why he was planning to head to my office. I could have asked, but thought I'd let him volunteer the information. After all, in a negotiation it's usually the person who can't stand the silence most who loses ground.

Besides, for all I knew, sending Kyle to my office was just another part of Herriman's "test."

We drove in silence for seven-and-a-half minutes before Kyle broke

"So, I suppose you're wondering what that was all about," he said.

"Family dynamics can be weird," I said, "especially in business, but I'll give you points for creativity."

I stole a glance. He was nodding, a slight smile on his face. He wasn't bad looking anyway, but the smile suited him far better than the stern, bodyguard-face.

"Grandfather built the business," Kyle said, resting his hands flat on his legs as he spoke. "But he doesn't participate as much as he would like to anymore. It irks him."

"Is that why he's selling?"

"Is that why *I'm* selling you mean."

I looked over at him again. "Maybe you should start at the beginning," I said, "I've been dealing with your grandfather for three weeks now. This is the first I've ever heard of you."

Kyle was grinning broadly now. "And that's where you would be wrong," he said.

I shook my head, and then the recognition dawned on me.

K.H., Kenneth Herriman.

K.H., *Kyle* Herriman.

"You're K.H.," I said.

He nodded. "Grandfather just signs using his last name. Herriman. It's a military thing he never let go of. It confuses a lot of people."

"Why didn't you show up in the company paperwork? What is your role?" I was annoyed and embarrassed. I'd been working on this deal for three weeks and didn't even know who I'd been talking to. Served me right for thinking I was on top of everything.

"Grandfather had a heart attack three years ago," Kyle said. "We were on the verge of going public, and he was afraid that letting anyone know about his health might affect the stock price."

"So you kept it quiet."

"We kept it quiet. I've been running the day-to-day operations ever since. His name is on the books, but all the paperwork is in place. Either one of us can sign."

"K. Herriman."

"Yes."

I said nothing, tapping my nails on the steering wheel as I negotiated a busy intersection.

"It doesn't change the value of the company," he said.

"That will be up to SCH to decide," I said. "They're looking to acquire a fully functional operation. Not one being run by a shadow puppet."

Kyle bristled.

"Don't say you didn't anticipate the reaction," I said.

"No, you're right, of course."

"Yes, I am. So why are you telling me this now?"

"Because you were going to find out anyway, and if you – and SCH – had found out at the wrong time, the deal would have fallen through. I told grandfather that we needed to tell you now, so we could get ahead of it."

"Is that why he left you back there?"

"You could say that," he said with an embarrassed shrug. "He's a proud man, and hates to admit to any kind of weakness."

"Well I suppose it's a good thing then that I have some free time this afternoon. I need to look over everything and see how we need to spin the situation and still keep SCH happy." I looked over at him. "I'm assuming you want this deal to go through?"

"I do."

"Then we've got our work cut out for us."

"We came to you because we heard you were the best."

"I don't work for you. I work for SCH."

"You're still the best," he said, a smile spreading across his face.

"Flattery won't lower my commission."

"How about dinner?

"Ask me again after deal is done. Right now, we've got work to do."

When we got to the office – and after she stopped making heart-throb gestures and dreamy eyes behind Kyle's back – I had Jessica set up the conference room with water and coffee. I had an appointment to take Bonnie to see the East Falls house right after work, and just hoped I'd be able to sort things out with Kyle in time to not have to reschedule the visit.

"How long have you been working for the company?" I asked flipping through the folio he'd handed me. I was pleased to see that other than the insertion of Kyle's name replacing the generic "K. Herriman" in several key positions, little else was changed. This might not be the disaster I'd feared.

"I started working in the mailroom when I was sixteen," Kyle said, pacing around the room while I studied the papers. "Stayed on through college and grad school, working my way up. Grandfather and my father were running the business as partners, but Grandfather never really took me seriously."

"Why not?"

"He'd been career Army, signed up straight out of high school, and started the business after he retired. My father served for ten years, then joined him in the business when I was in elementary school. I never served – and getting an MBA didn't impress Grandfather."

He'd stopped pacing, and was standing at the window, looking out at the skyline.

"So, how'd you end up running the place?"

"Like I said, I'd been moving up. When Father died, I got his job. The stockholders approved, but Grandfather mostly just ignored me, treated me like a nobody, like some homeless guy who was just going to disappear one day—"

I looked up from the papers I'd been studying. "What did you say?"

Kyle flushed, backpedaling. "That a homeless person could go missing and no one would notice. Not that I think that's right or anything…"

But I was only half-listening, my mind racing in the opposite direction.

I'd been looking in the wrong place, checking the missing persons reports. The dead man in the morgue wasn't someone whose family or employer would be searching for him. He was one of the city's unwanted. Expendable. Someone the killer had viewed as valuable only because he had the right physical build to pass for Stephen – once his face had been bashed in.

"Meg?"

I blinked, bringing the office back into focus. Kyle was staring at me, a puzzled expression on his face. "You haven't heard a word I've said, have you?"

"Sorry, no. I guess I got distracted."

The pieces were falling into place. The Herriman's switch wasn't that different from the one Stephen Markham had engineered: find someone else to fill the public role – someone no one would notice missing – while the other walked away quietly, with no one the wiser.

I shoved Stephen's twisted murder scheme into one of the compartments in my mind and locked the lid on it while I finished sorting out the best way to present K. Herriman-the-younger as a viable option to SCH. But like a body buried before it was cold, Stephen had begun tapping at the lid.

I knew that when I finally dug it all up, it was going to be a nasty, smelly mess.

◆

Bonnie tapped at my office door precisely at five o'clock.

"You ready?" she asked.

"Almost. Just dotting the last i's and crossing the last t's," I said. I gestured down the short hallway. "You know where the kitchen is. Grab yourself a drink. I'll be ready in a minute."

Kyle had left about 20 minutes earlier – much to Jessica's dismay – but with the promise of stopping by the office again the following day with some additional paperwork. We had made excellent progress. It had mostly been a matter of figuring out the best marketing spin to present Kyle to the conservative SCH board as the head of Herriman Industries and his grandfather as their public face. Kyle's "public face" was photogenic enough that I was certain SCH would soon abandon the grandfather in favor of the young, new CEO.

I shut down my laptop and was just putting the Herriman Industries file into the filing cabinet, when Bonnie came back into the room and handed me a water bottle.

"It's a nice space you have here," Bonnie said.

"But?"

"But it's a little cramped, don't you think?" Bonnie glanced around.

I followed her gaze, puzzled. "I have reception, kitchen, and conference room, and a spare office for when I have a guest client in. There's plenty of seating, ample parking, and a prime Center City location. What more do I need?"

"The building is old."

"It's historic."

"I could get you something that looks as high class as your reputation."

"Probably – and it would have a high-class price attached,"

I said. "No thank you."

I locked up and pointed out the large window at the end of the hall. "I have a great view from my office, too," I said.

"Not as nice of you, as you'd have from higher up."

"Maybe," I said. "But I'm high enough - and if the elevator ever goes out, I don't mind climbing the stairs."

Bonnie laughed as we got onto said elevator.

"Your car or mine?" I asked.

"Yours. I've been driving all day."

I punched the button, and we rode down to the second level, then crossed the enclosed bridge to the adjacent parking structure. A few minutes later we jumped into the rush-hour traffic and headed toward East Falls.

"You realize you're going to be dealing with this traffic every day," Bonnie said.

"Your point?"

"Only that you're used to living downtown. Being out on the edge is going to be like going back to the suburbs."

"I lived in the suburbs for quite a while before I met you."

"Yes, and then you wisely moved to the city."

"And now I'm moving back to the not-quite suburbs. I like the house. You'll like the house."

"I won't like the house, and I will never visit you," Bonnie said with a defiant grin.

"You're going to love the house."

Bonnie loved the house.

"Oh. My. God," she said as we turned onto the drive. "I hardly ever get to sell houses with any property."

"That's what you get for focusing on all those city folk," I said.

The driveway curved up and around through a wooded lot, no more than a hundred feet, but that was more than twice as long as my entire rowhouse, so I considered it something of a luxury.

Then we came around a massive oak and the house itself,

which had been mostly hidden from view from the street by mature trees and shrubbery, came into view. Two stories of fitted gray stonework, slate tiles, and large windows with dark shutters, and a third floor identified by a row of gabled windows, the house nestled into the grounds, surrounded by a small, manicured lawn and bordered by low mounds of brightly-colored flowers.

"I give up," Bonnie said as she got her first glimpse of the house. "It better have an extra room for me. I'll be spending a lot of time here."

"I shouldn't say 'I told you so,'" I said, "but I told you so."

"It's gorgeous, is it really is. Is it as nice inside? Tell me it's as nice inside."

"Nicer."

"It looks like something out of a magazine..." Bonnie said, twisting around to see as we pulled up in front of the garage.

"Actually, Sarah said it was one of several houses featured in a write-up of historic home restorations a few years ago, just after they finished the renovation."

"Of course it was," Bonnie said. "How much is she asking?"

"Let's walk through the house," I said. "Then you guess, and I'll tell you if you're right."

Bonnie looked at me, an eyebrow raised. "You're being cagey."

"No, I want your expert opinion."

Sarah had given me a key the day before, and told me she would be out for the evening, so we had free run of the house for as long as we wished. As I unlocked the door, gestured for Bonnie to enter, and watched her mouth fall open, I realized I already felt a sense of ownership and pride. I took that as a good sign.

The front door opened onto a large entry hall, which was nothing unusual for a house of this size. But the entry hall itself which led right and left to the two wings of the house, was practically an afterthought. Directly in front of the doors was the conservatory – a glass enclosed, octagonal space rising two stories in height and filled with trees and vines. A small fountain splashed gently in the center of the room, with a chaise lounge to on one side.

Opposite a pair of comfortable lounging chairs flanked a small table. The four straight walls featured French doors, leading to the dining room on one side, the bedroom wing on the other, and out to the yard at the back, while the late afternoon sky shone blue through the leaded glass ceiling panels. It was a perfect indoor courtyard.

"I see what caught your attention," Bonnie said, walking straight into the conservatory just like I had when I first visited the house the day before.

"Oh, yes, this is definitely a selling point."

"Or a buying point, from my point of view," I said.

"Touché."

The rest of the house was also lovely. The rooms had been decorated in a very traditional style that made it feel open and spacious, yet warm and inviting at the same time.

"What are you going to do with six bedrooms?" Bonnie asked.

"Host sleepovers?" I said. "I don't know. I'm sure I will figure out something. This is too nice to pass up." Bonnie agreed. Six bedrooms, four bathrooms, a large kitchen that had been updated only a few years before. Even a library I was already looking at as a future office.

"All right," she said. "I'll let you live here."

"I appreciate that."

"Well you weren't planning to buy it without my approval, were you?"

"Certainly not," I said, grinning.

"I just wish you'd told me you wanted to buy out here," Bonnie said as we headed back downstairs. "I'd have found you a great place."

"Not this great," I said.

"No, not this great. Probably not that great at all," Bonnie acknowledged. "After you told me you'd found a house, I actually looked at the listings for this area. Nobody's selling here. There was only one place that wasn't a condo, and you wouldn't have liked it."

"What was wrong with it?"

"It was a repo, in bad shape."

"Bad shape can be fixed up. I've done it before."

"Yes, but why go to the trouble of fixing someplace up, when you can have this?" She gestured around the living room at the series of multi-pane windows, a pair of French doors at the center that opened onto a view of the large yard and one of the house's three patios.

"That's what I was thinking," I said.

"You weren't thinking anything," Bonnie said. "You fell in love with it at first sight."

"Yeah, pretty much," I agreed. "Still, I wanted you to see it."

"You just wanted me to forgive you for cheating on me," she said, dropping onto the couch.

"There's no other realtor, so it's not really cheating on you." I took a seat in one of the matched Queen Anne chairs opposite.

"So, how much is she asking?" she asked.

"How much do you think it's worth?"

She told me and I told her what Sarah was asking. Her eyes got huge. "You're stealing this house from her"

"I'm making a full price offer," I said. "And will cover the points. I'll probably even offer extra for whatever furniture she's not taking with her. And she won't have to pay any realtor fees, so she won't lose as much of the asking price as she would on a traditional sale."

"There is that," Bonnie said. She gave me a stern look.

"You better treat her fair."

"I will," I said. "I might be a cutthroat negotiator, but I don't take advantage of elderly widows."

We relaxed, enjoying the view as the sky beyond the windows turned to twilight over the tops of the trees and the lightning bugs lit up, twinkling against the darkening shrubbery at the edges of the back lawn.

"We're going to love this place," Bonnie said.

"We?"

"I'm claiming the guestroom at the end of the hall for myself and Peggy," Bonnie said with a matter-of-fact nod. "The one with the big bay window and claw-footed tub in the bathroom."

"I suppose I'll have to let you decorate it," I said, looking at her skinny jeans and plaid flannel shirt. "It better not clash with the rest of the house."

We raised imaginary glasses in a toast.

Chapter 21
Present day: Monday evening

It was after eight o'clock when I finally got home, tired, but generally satisfied with how the day had gone.

Except for the taking Deb to get an ankle monitor part.

And the trip to the shooting range had just been weird. Why couldn't the Herrimans – older and younger – have come to the office, instead of insisting on all that tough-guy nonsense?

But the rest of the day had gone well. Kyle had a good head for business, and was either oblivious to or deliberately ignored Jessica's goggling over him. Poor girl. In his early-forties, he was four years older than me. The odds of him being interested in a twenty-something girl were slim, though probably not outside the realm of possibility. But as long as she didn't embarrass herself or the office, I wasn't going to do more than give her the occasional hard stare.

I was glad Bonnie had liked the house. Not that I would have passed on it if she hadn't, but we've been friends for a long time, and her opinion mattered.

I was thinking about all these things – in more or less chronological order – when I parked my car and headed to my back door, and saw the large, white express-mail envelope that had been tucked between the screen door and the door frame.

Icing on the cake. The Researcher was as good as his word.

I snatched the packet and went inside. I could feel the flash drive through the lightweight cardboard, but the envelope was heavy, like it was filled with papers, too. I wondered at that. The Researcher almost never sent hard copy of anything.

I managed to resist opening the envelope until after I had kicked off my boots, gotten something to drink, made a snack for Glau, and sat down at my desk. In addition to the flash drive, which I immediately plugged into my laptop and set to running the decryption sequence, the Researcher had included a collection of SEPTA bus route maps and schedules, each with particular segments of the routes highlighted.

Curious.

While I waited for the files to open, I spread the SEPTA maps out on the floor, then stepped back and studied them, looking for the pattern the Researcher had clearly intended me to see.

Some of the highlighted segments were long, others short, all just a random stretch along a particular route. But if I overlapped the maps, matching up intersections as closely as the varied scale of the maps allowed, patterns began to emerge fanning out in a variety of directions from Cheltenham, Elkins Park, and Stenton, neighboring suburbs a few miles to the northwest of the Frankford Center terminal.

I went to the wall and looked at the original PennPass data. The Researcher hadn't provided me with a route map for the Route 58 bus from the Frankford Center. But he had given me a map for the Route 70 bus that had been used on the day of the murder, though the highlighted segments of the route did not run all the way down to the Bustleton and Cottman intersection where the person using the card had changed buses.

Very curious.

Someone – the real killer? I thought that more likely than a random, opportunistic thief using the card – had taken a train north from the University, then headed northwest by bus, ending up in in the suburbs.

I could hardly wait for the data, so I could match up the times and routes to the highlighted maps. It was the first real clue I had. If the PennPass user was following any sort of a pattern, there was a chance – albeit a slim one – that I could find them.

If it would clear Deb, I'd take that chance.

♦

As I studied the data the Researcher had sent, I glanced at the flash drive, half-expecting it to transmute itself into gold as I watched.

The data was everything I'd hoped for, and more.

The murder had taken place on Wednesday afternoon. In the five days since then, the unidentified PennPass user had stayed in the same general area, coming and going on a *very* regular basis, and using multiple bus routes to obscure their travel.

I plotted the days, times, and routes on the wall.

Two trips utilizing multiple routes going to and from the shopping plaza at Adams and Whitaker. If I hadn't been plotting the dates and times and coordinating them to the maps, I wouldn't have seen that pattern. They'd ridden one bus a good distance south, then walked a few blocks to another stop, taken a second bus east, then walked a few more blocks before taking a third bus north that dropped them off near the plaza. The route back was similarly circuitous, utilizing four routes instead of three, but the timestamps on the PennPass card drew the map as clearly as if they'd been wearing a tracking device.

Afternoons north to Fox Chase or south to Oak Lane, on an irregular schedule.

Mornings from Ashbourne Road to Lawndale and back. Every day. Regular as clockwork.

I knew where he would be and when.

Now I just needed to catch him.

♦

The Researcher had been able to get two days' footage from the camera mounted over the same staff-only door at the Children's Hospital where Stephen's PennCard had been used on the day of the murder. I took my laptop downstairs and started the video, displaying it on the large flat screen television in the living room.

Convinced as I now was, from both my own research and Thackery's, that the dead man was not Stephen Markham but an unidentified homeless man, I found myself speculating on the PennPass user's identity while I scanned the footage. The door saw little traffic, so I bumped the speed up to double-time, taking a good look at anyone who passed by the camera.

Was Stephen Markham really clever enough to pull off a stunt like this, and then be stupid enough to stay in town?

I put the question to Glau, who had come to join me, climbing on the couch and quietly munching on a slice of apple I'd shared with him. He bobbed his head vigorously in reply.

"Yeah," I agreed. "It's possible."

The townships and neighborhoods where the bus had taken him were only suburbs — by my definition — by virtue of being away from the city center. In my admittedly limited experience, I didn't recall them being the tract-house variety suburb that might appear in a television show. Lots tended to be large, houses spacious, and the whole area was peppered with parks and golf courses. So while he might be away from the prying eyes of neighbors, there was a good chance he might run into someone who recognized him. Why take the risk?

What was he waiting for?

And who was helping him?

The soundless video played on. Sometime later, I woke with Glau on my lap, his tail dangling down my leg, the tip twitching against my foot. I shifted the lizard, shut down the video, and went up to bed.

There had to be a better way to do this.

Chapter 22
7 years ago

Meg walked into the crowded auditorium and looked around for Deb's family, smiling and waving as she saw Josh bouncing up and down and gesturing her over to where he and his sister had saved a seat for her with their grandparents.

Josh and Cassie had grown in the five years she'd known them, from the bashful five and seven year-olds who had peeked at her from the safety of the hallway the first time she'd visited Deb at her parents' home, to the confident ten and twelve year-olds bursting with pride as they waited for their mother to walk across the stage and receive her nursing degree.

Deb had grown more self-assured as well, Meg thought, thinking back to the quiet woman she'd first met. While always reserved, Deb laughed more now than she did before. And earning her nursing degree had been a major part of that growth.

"You should be proud of yourself," Meg told her later. She'd gone back to their house with them, for a celebratory dinner, and now the children chattered over ice cream sundaes in their cozy kitchen. Deb's father had taken up his customary position in the old leather recliner that dominated one corner of the living room, a football game occupying most of his attention, and her mother monitored the children while she cleaned up the supper dishes.

"I am proud," Deb said, raising her hand to touch her cheek as her face flushed ever so slightly. "I really am — and I'm not ashamed to admit it."

"You worked hard, girl," her father said, extending a hand to her, but not looking away from the game. "You deserve every bit of good this brings you."

"Thanks, Papa," Deb said taking his hand in both of hers.

He did look at her then, and though he was smiling, Meg saw the glint of tears in his eyes.

Deb jumped up and hugged her father tightly.

"Okay, okay," the older man said. "You two skedaddle on out of here and let me watch my game in peace, now." But he was smiling as he said it, and he gave Deb an extra hug before releasing her.

Meg followed Deb out onto the old Craftsman's wide front porch, and they dropped into the pair of large Adirondack chairs.

"So," Meg said, "I don't know anything at all about nursing. I'm assuming the degree will help you get a better job — or at least better pay?"

Deb laughed. "When there are jobs to be had, yes, it should. I've been hoping to get on at the University Children's Hospital, but they're not hiring right now."

"Why not?"

"No budget. They've actually had to let a few people go. Who would think there could be too many nurses?"

"Thank you, recession," Meg said. "What will you do?"

"I still have the job at Mercy," Deb said. "I don't expect a raise or a promotion, but a paycheck is a paycheck."

"And the child support? Is that still coming in?"

"Stephen's contesting it — claiming I submitted fraudulent paperwork. So no, no payments while it's being reviewed. I got the notice a couple of days ago."

Meg frowned. "What kind of fraud?"

"How much I earn. I have no idea what he's using to support his claim, but he's saying my proof of income was incomplete, that I actually earn more than I do, and that he's been overpaying."

"Really?"

"Oh, it gets better. He wants the support amount recalculated all the way back to when we very first divorced. If he gets his way, I'll have to repay him."

"He can't do that," Meg said, shocked.

"Maybe not, but he's trying," Deb said, shaking her head.

"Do you have the paperwork to prove him wrong?"

"Oh, yes. It makes me feel like a hoarder, but one thing I learned long before the divorce was to keep extremely careful records – especially when it comes to Stephen," Deb said. "I called my lawyer and I'm sure he'll sort it all out, but that's just more lost money. Between that and Malia's nasty phone calls, I'm just glad I'm finally done with school. It's been almost more than I can handle."

"What's his wife got to do with it?"

"She calls every so often, just to tell me what a horrible person I am." Deb said. She laid the back of her hand on her forehead as she dramatized Malia's melodramatic demeanor. "And how my demands for money are hurting her children, who get nothing from their father."

"I don't understand," Meg said.

"Neither do I," Deb said. "I guess her ex is a deadbeat, too. I told her that was no excuse for Stephen not to fulfil his responsibilities. She had a few choice to things to say about that." She laughed, but it was bitter, and without humor.

"Enough of them," Meg said, practically jumping up from the chair and grabbing Deb's hand. "Today is for celebrating. Do you suppose the kids left us any ice cream?"

They went inside and rejoined the party, but in the back of her mine, Meg decided that perhaps it was time she looked a little more closely into Malia Markham. From what little Deb had said, it sounded like she was just as much a piece of work as her husband.

Clearly, they both needed watching.

◆

Maybe it was the conversation with Deb, maybe the second helping of ice cream drowning in hot fudge that Josh had plunked down in front of her, and which she'd dutifully eaten as much as she could of. Whatever the cause, Meg had a restless night, drifting into dreams she couldn't easily wander out of.

Eddie rested his hand on twelve year-old Maggie's shoulder, sliding his long, mean fingers forward and giving her small breast a squeeze as he leaned over her to set a salad bowl on the table in front of her. "Growing up so nicely," he whispered in her ear.

Maggie sat there, frozen. Her little brothers were playing swords with their forks, and Shelia was playing tug-of-war with the dog for her napkin. Eddie had never touched her when anyone else was around before. She didn't know what to do.

And then her mother came in from the kitchen carrying a casserole. "Coming through – it's hot!" she called out.

Eddie stepped to the side, moving out of her way, brushing his hand across the back of Maggie's neck.

She avoided looking at him all through dinner. She knew it was rude, but just couldn't look over and see him looking at her like… like something he wanted to eat.

"Are you all right, Maggie?" her mother asked. "You're not eating."

"I'm not very hungry," she murmured, pushing the food around on her plate.

"Maybe you should go up to bed early."

Eddie was going to be upset with her.

"I'm not sleepy," Maggie said, wrapping her arms across

her belly.

Eddie could be mean when he was upset.

Maggie shuddered, wishing she could wrap her arms around her whole body, knowing that even if she could, it wouldn't do any good. Eddie would come to her room that night, and places nobody was ever supposed to touch were already beginning to hurt in anticipation.

♦

Among other regular charges on Malia Markham's credit card statements were weekly visits to both the spa and tea room at the Rittenhouse, one of downtown Philadelphia's crown gems. It was a place one went to be pampered.

To be *seen*.

Malia liked to think of herself as a socialite – and in many ways she was – but in truth, she was more of a social *climber*. After leaving behind a rural background, and achieving some visibility as a model, she had married Stephen for the money she thought he had, and traded on the family name in lieu of a fortune ever since.

With that in mind, Meg added High Tea at the Rittenhouse to her regular Tuesday afternoon calendar. Sometimes she would take a client, other times she would go alone, but she always made a point of noticing where Malia Markham was seated and getting a table that put her where she could watch Stephen's social-climbing wife.

And where she could be seen in return.

It took a few weeks, but eventually they happened to be leaving the Tea Room at the same time.

"I've seen you here before," Malia said, her voice almost a purr as their paths converged near the Tea Room door. Malia was rail-thin – almost anorexically so – and a few inches shorter than Meg, but made up for it with high, stiletto heels. Meg was wearing low-heels, so when she turned toward the voice, the two were eye-to-eye.

"Margaret Harrison," she said, holding out her hand.

Malia took it, her grip stronger than Meg would have expected. True socialites, the ones born to money, raised to privilege, and educated in private schools, generally employed a fragile, weak grip that they thought made them seem like delicate, hothouse flowers. Malia's was the solid grip of someone with more down-to-earth roots that she had obviously failed to obscure entirely.

"Malia Markham," she purred in return, with just a touch of emphasis on her last name.

She was watching for a reaction. Meg obliged and gave her one, widening her eyes slightly as if impressed. "My mother, may she rest in peace, was a friend of Eleanor Markham's, though I've never had the privilege. You're her daughter, then?"

"Her daughter-*in-law*," Malia said, withdrawing her hand. But she stayed at Meg's side, matching her stride as they crossed the elegant lobby toward the elevator leading to the parking garage.

Invoking Eleanor Markham's name had been a tactical move on Meg's part. She thought it highly unlikely that Eleanor would have mentioned their brief acquaintance five years before to anyone, especially not to Malia. For as much as Malia presented herself as a Markham in society, it was common knowledge that Eleanor only tolerated her daughter-in-law for her youngest son's benefit.

Meg had studied Malia, watched her closely over the previous few weeks. And while she had used her repeated presence at the Tea Room as a lure to get Malia's attention, establishing a connection, however tenuous, to her mother-in-law was the bait. She was almost certain that Malia would take advantage of the opportunity to attach herself to the daughter of one of Eleanor's friends in the hopes that it would put her one step closer to being accepted into the Markham's inner circle.

In Malia's world, appearances were everything.

"I'm here for High Tea every Tuesday," Malia said as they waited for the elevator. "I'd like it very much if you joined me at my table next week. It would be wonderful to get to know you better."

"I'd love to," Meg said, with a truly genuine smile.

Malia had taken the bait, just as Meg had thought she would. Hook, line, and sinker.

The rest was just a matter of time.

Chapter 23
Present day: Tuesday

I've met Malia Markham for High Tea at the Rittenhouse nearly every Tuesday for the past seven years. Over time, that ritual has expanded to include myself and two other well-connected women – Julia Norris and Cynthia Delacorte – gathering for a leisurely morning swim in the hotel pool followed by a massage or manicure or some other necessary spa treatment. After all, in Malia's world, we must be suitably pampered prior to our afternoon tea.

Many people in our social circle think of us as great friends – for all I know, Malia does, too.

I don't.

Being friends with her has one rule: it's all about Malia. We do what Malia wants to do, we talk about what Malia wants to talk about – which means we listen while she holds court. Whether we are volunteering at a charity event, attending an art auction, sitting at tea, or lounging by the pool at the Rittenhouse spa, Malia graciously allows us to bask in the glory of her presence, listen to her talk about her accomplishments, her disappointments, her tragedies.

We nod in agreement, sing her praises, extol her virtues, and lament her difficulties like a modern Greek chorus. Acolytes to our goddess.

In truth, I've always viewed Malia as a resource. Another way to monitor Stephen's weaknesses. The social connections I've gained through her a bonus.

I almost didn't go to tea the Tuesday after Stephen's death, but then thought better of it. It was slightly ghoulish, and entirely voyeuristic, but I wanted to see how the new widow was faring.

When I arrived at the Rittenhouse, Julia and Cynthia were waiting in the lobby.

Julia saw me and rushed over, pulling me into the circle of chairs where they'd been standing. "Have you heard," she whispered.

"Heard what?" I asked.

"Malia's husband was murdered!"

"No," I gasped, putting a hand to my mouth and taking a half-step back, as though in surprise. "When?"

Julia nodded. "Last week."

"That can't be – nothing has hit my newsfeed. And certainly Malia would have called *us*—" I began, feigning a combination of shock and skepticism.

"Malia told me herself – *in confidence* – when I called to confirm our spa appointments this morning," Cynthia said, preening slightly at being the only one of the three of us who had heard the news directly from the source. "She swore me to secrecy – the police are keeping it very hush-hush for the moment, out of respect for the family, while they investigate. They think his ex-wife did it. Can you imagine?"

It didn't take long for word to get around, I thought. While Cynthia was talking, Julia kept craning her neck around, like she was trying to look past us. I turned to look behind me, but saw nothing out of the ordinary.

"Who are you looking for?" I asked.

"Malia, of course," she said, as though I should have known. "We can't let her hear us talking about it – it's sure to upset her."

"But they haven't even had the funeral. Surely she won't come—"

"Oh, yes," Cynthia said. "She told me so herself. Said she needed to fortify herself for the ordeal—"

"Shh!" hissed Julia. "There she is!"

I turned to look.

Malia Markham was always talking about her glory days as a model, and how she longed to go back out on the runway. And today she was finally making her comeback.

She stood in the open doorway for just a moment too long, ostensibly letting her eyes adjust to the interior light, but in reality, giving everyone present the opportunity to notice her. Dressed in mourning, she was an eye-catching silhouette, a slim line of black against the brilliant, foaming white column of the fountain outside.

Then she stepped into the foyer. She was wearing a long, black sheath dress, slit to well above the knee, with a black shawl of Spanish lace draped loosely over her pale arms. Her chestnut hair was piled up on her head, which was crowned with a small pillbox-style hat trimmed with large side bow made of black netting, and more netting that covered the upper half of her face.

Leave it to Malia to make a fashion statement of the moment.

When she saw us, she swept forward, stiletto heels clicking on the tile floor, stopping in the center of the lobby waiting for us to come to her. We rushed to her side, of course, expressing our sympathies and support in a flurry of inanities.

"God, I could use a drink." she said after a moment. "Do you suppose the bar is open yet?"

♦

It occurred to me, as the morning slid over into afternoon and we flowed through our weekly ritual of swimming, relaxing, and on toward tea, that Malia didn't strike me as a grieving widow.

Oh, she spoke of her husband's death, almost in passing, and of Deb in the same pejorative terms she always had, but there was no more passion in her voice than there had been last week or the week before or the months or years before that. In fact, there had been many instances in the past when she'd been far more passionate in her hatred of Deb and the ongoing burden of the child support Stephen was obliged to pay than she was expressing now, when she believed Deb to have actually killed Stephen.

It was only when she spoke of the upcoming funeral, which was scheduled for later in the week, and 'her tremendous loss' that I got any sense of her emotions – and they weren't of grief. She hadn't said anything specific, but Stephen's death had thrust her into the spotlight, and I had the strongest sense that she relished it. She was savoring the moment. Basking in the glow of our attention. No longer relegated to being in her husband's shadow.

"It's horrible of me to say, I know," she said as we lounged on the divans near the indoor pool, "but it will be a relief to finally be rid of that woman. She's been leaching off Stephen for over a decade. I never got a penny of child support for my boys and we did just fine; what makes her think she's so special?"

"What will happen with the child support?" Julia asked.

"Oh, that," Malia said, staring down her long nose at Julia as though she'd mentioned something distasteful. "It's over. They don't garnish the dead."

"Bonus money for you," Cynthia chirped.

Malia snorted – a sound we all judiciously chose to ignore. "The pittance she was getting wasn't enough to keep me in shoes. Besides, it was coming from Stephen's salary – which he's no longer earning."

"No… no, of course not…" Cynthia stammered her face coloring at her gaffe. "I just meant that she won't get any of the life insurance, or anything like that."

"Of course not. He left everything to me; nothing for the bitch or her precious children – and she screwed them over herself, by killing him."

"What do you mean?" I asked, almost feeling my ears swivel, radar-like, toward her at this tidbit.

"Insurance companies don't pay you for killing the person you have a policy on. Dear, sweet Deb just flushed ten years of premium payments down the drain."

We all sat there, stunned. Malia leaned back, laying a cloth across her eyes, a cruel, smug smile twisting her lips.

I had no idea Deb had an insurance policy on Stephen. She'd mentioned the idea once, ages ago, and the court had approved it – but she'd run into no end of challenges trying to find a carrier that would actually let her cover her ex.

I didn't know anything had ever come of it.

I'd tormented Stephen for ten years, but never did him any direct harm because I didn't want to hurt Deb and her children; I'd always believed he was worth more to them alive.

My stomach churned.

Was it possible that Deb really *had* been involved somehow? Could the woman in the video footage actually have been her? That she'd finally reached the end of her patience and gone to confront him?

The body in the morgue wasn't Stephen – I was certain of that – but had Deb actually visited Stephen's office that day? And if she had, was it before or after the murder?

My mind was reeling, trying to figure out how to fit this new piece into the puzzle I'd been building.

If she'd argued with Stephen, actually touched the geode, setting her up for the murder hadn't been the carefully thought-out plan I'd been working to sort out. It would have been hastily thrown together…

The pieces didn't fit.

But I could see quite clearly how the family was trying to spin the story.

I reached for a bottled water, choking back the bile that rose in my throat when I thought of Deb languishing in a jail cell while Malia chattered inanities with her acolytes, sipping her white wine and trying to choose between a rejuvenating facial or an airbrushed tan.

I had been right to come, to maintain the charade of friendship with Malia that I had built so carefully over the years. Once again, the deception had provided me with potentially useful information. But now I chafed to leave.

Instead, I rose from the divan where I'd been reclining with the others and dove into the pool.

It took three laps before my mind cleared enough for me to think logically. With Stephen technically out of the picture, I realized, I no longer needed to keep up the pretense.

I reached the end of the pool, flipped, and started back toward the opposite end, my strokes smooth and regular. I'd have to back out of the association gradually — scheduling conflicts, travel, client meetings, things of that sort — but it wouldn't take long before Malia tired of my excuses and replaced me. My days as an acolyte were numbered.

I was almost smiling when I pulled myself out of the pool.

And then I saw everyone staring at me.

Malia was holding a phone – my phone, I realized as I came closer the theme from the *Godfather* still playing as I approached.

"Why is James Paoletti calling *you*?" she asked. It was obvious from her reaction that she knew he was representing Deb. I could only imagine the shock on her face when she saw his name on my Caller ID.

"Did he leave a message?" I asked, ignoring the implied accusation as I took the now-silent phone from her.

I made a show of checking my phone for messages as I

continued, the lie coming easy. "I've been trying to reach him for several days, and all I ever get is his assistant… Oh, and once again: 'he's out of the office for the rest of the day, but I'm welcome to try back next week.'" I tossed the phone into my open bag, noticing as I did that one corner of my iPad was peeking up from the inner pocket where it was stowed.

The bag hadn't been open when I went for my swim. I didn't say anything, but I was glad both the phone and tablet required a security code. It wasn't like she could actually read anything on either – I routinely used multiple layers of encryption – but it was the principle of the thing.

To the best of my knowledge, Malia didn't have principles.

"Well, that's just too bad for you," Malia snapped. "But that doesn't explain *why* he is calling you. Or why you've set a customized ringtone for him."

"Hmmm? Oh, one of my clients listed him as a reference," I said nonchalantly, scooping up a towel. "I've been trying to confirm it. Can't be too careful – not with that much money at stake. I set the ringtone so I'd know when Mr. Paoletti's office was calling – the *Godfather* theme. Pretty good choice, no?"

Julia and Cynthia murmured their agreement, falling into silence when Malia shot them a withering glare. Then she turned that glare on me.

I met her eyes and didn't look away, as I drew the towel along my arms and across my shoulders, my unspoken reply one of simple, calm assurance that was neither confrontational nor subservient. She broke the contact first, her breath escaping in a slight huff when I raised my foot to the divan and began to dry my leg.

"What do you say, ladies?" I said as I rubbed the towel across my calf. "We have just enough time for a detox massage before tea."

"That sounds wonderful," said Julia, poking her ebook reader into her bag.

"Delicious," agreed Cynthia, almost leaping to her feet.

"Malia, are you coming? You *must* come!"

Malia favored me with one last glare before turning a megawatt-bright smile on the others. "You go ahead, if you like. I think I'll touch up my tan."

The deer-in-the-headlights looks on Julia and Cynthia's faces was priceless. Malia had put them in the predicament of having to choose whether would they go with her, or follow me, the insolent acolyte who had clearly fallen from grace.

I wanted to throw back my head and laugh out loud.

Fortunately, I was saved by the bell in the form of Patsy Cline belting out Bonnie's ringtone. Keeping my expression carefully neutral, I answered the call in as businesslike a manner as I could muster.

"I take it, you're with someone you're trying to impress," Bonnie said dryly.

"How good of you to return my call," I replied, my response deliberately vague for Malia's benefit.

With an apologetic shrug to Julia and Cynthia who were just slipping into the plush robes provided by the spa after our post-swim showers, I pressed my phone to the towel as though I thought it would really muffle the sound. "I have to go," I said in a stage whisper. "Call me later, and we'll get together."

They wouldn't call me, nor I either of them, but it was the polite thing to say – and my entire association with them had always been about the social niceties, after all. Besides, Philadelphia was only so big, and it was likely our paths would cross again down the road. There was no reason to burn bridges.

I dropped my own robe on the bench then, and turned away, thanking Bonnie for her oh-so-timely intervention as I went back to the locker and my clothes.

It looked like I was going to miss the High Tea after all.

◆

About halfway between downtown Philadelphia and my rowhouse in NoLibs was a little hole-in-the-wall electronics shop where I've picked up more than a few useful gadgets.

I stopped there that evening on my way home.

Malia had been just enough herself that day that it bothered me. I knew her to be cold and self-centered, but her attitude toward Stephen's death was off-putting. It went farther than denial – she almost acted as though she knew he hadn't died.

The woman in Thackery's photo wasn't Deb, but it hadn't looked like Malia, either – though I had to acknowledge that her modeling background might have given her the skills to alter her appearance enough to pass for Deb on a grainy surveillance cam image. But while Malia was a possibility, I'd never given her credit for being all that bright. Certainly not as having the skills needed to plan out something as complicated – or messy – as this.

Malia was the "what's in it for me?" sort. Anything that suggested getting her hands dirty or, heaven forbid, breaking a nail was beneath her.

Then again…

Combined with the weird PennPass use and the odd message Josh had received, and it just had the hairs on the back of my neck tingling. As clichéd as it all felt, I needed to follow up on it.

Hence my visit to the electronics shop.

The shop was small, little more than a closet, but it was packed floor to ceiling with every imaginable electronic device, and the elderly proprietor, Charlie Johnson seemed to have an encyclopedic memory. He knew where every item was in his store. I respected that.

"Well, hello Miss Maggie," he called out when I entered the shop.

I looked up, following the sound of his voice to see the wiry little man up on a tall ladder, arranging small boxes on one of the high shelves. His close-cropped hair seemed a little grayer, contrasting more and more with his dark skin each time I saw him. I realized with a pang that the day would come when I'd come into the shop and Charlie wouldn't be there.

"Should you be up there, Charlie?" I asked.

"These boxes don't put themselves away," he said, pulling another small box from the lumpy pocket of his apron and tucking it into its assigned space on the shelf. "What can I do you for?"

"I need to put a tracker on my car," I said.

"That teenage boy of yours starting to drive, eh?"

As far as Charlie knew, I was Maggie Jones, a suburban housewife with a husband, a dog, and two children. I'd listened in on my supposed husband's phone calls using devices Charlie had sold me, installed nursery monitors in my young daughter's room to keep tabs on the babysitter, chipped the dog using a DIY kit of his devising, and now wanted to keep tabs on a teenage son. It was a convenient persona.

"Can't be too safe," I said with a smile. "Do you have something he won't notice? It would need to have a good battery – and I'd have to be able to track it on my own phone, not just on a laptop."

"I've got just the thing for ya," he said. "Give me just a sec to finish up here."

I browsed around the shop for a few minutes while Charlie finished emptying his pockets onto the shelf and then climbed slowly down the ladder. He led me deeper into the shop to a shelf of gadgets that looked to me just like every other shelf of gadgets in the shop. But Charlie knew exactly what he was looking for, and pulled a small box from the shelf and handed it to me.

"Here's what you need," he said.

"And this will transmit to my phone?"

"It will. It operates on a motion sensor, so it's only on when the car is moving. Makes for decent battery life. When it's tracking, it will send notifications straight to your phone every few seconds. There's a small monthly fee for the service – all the information's inside the box."

"And it's easy to install?"

"Oh, sure. Boys being boys, you'll probably want to tuck it under the seat where he won't notice. I'd stay away from attaching it to the undercarriage like they do in the movies – he and his buddies will probably end up tinkering around down there at some point, and he'll be on to you."

"Can't have that," I said. I turned the box in my hand, trying to read the microscopic print in the not-too-bright light.

He looked up and gave me a smile. "If you have any trouble setting it up, just give me a call. I'll be happy to walk you through it."

I thanked him, and made my way forward, looking around the shop with the same sense of wonder I got every time I came in. The seemingly infinite combinations of wires and circuits and other bits of tech that surrounded us always left me feeling a little out of my depth. Not that I was a technophobe, by any means, just that I wasn't as adept as someone like Charlie. Put him in a locked room with a shelf of electronics, and he'd reassemble them into a dozen useful items before I'd manage just to take an inventory of the component bits.

But knowing I needed his help was a skill of a sort, I told myself as I counted out the bills to pay for my purchase. I never used plastic in Charlie's shop. And, assuming – correctly, though for the wrong reasons – that I didn't want to create a paper trail, Charlie never questioned my cash payments.

I suspected I wasn't the only customer who paid in cash. It was that kind of shop.

"You have a grandson or someone who can help you out around here, Charlie?" I asked as I headed for the door.

"A grandson," Charlie said. "He's in college. Comes in on Saturdays. Why? You think I'm too old to run this place by myself?" He said it with a grin, but there was an underlying challenge to his tone.

"Not yet," I said. "But it's probably time to start training him up for it. It'll take him at least ten years to be half as good as you. Might as well get him started."

He laughed. "Send your boy in. I'll keep him out of trouble for you."

I shook my head at the thought of Charlie waiting for my imaginary son to show up. "It's a little far for him to be driving just yet," I said. "But I'll keep it in mind."

Chapter 24
Present day: Wednesday

I get what most people would probably consider an unhealthy pleasure sneaking around in the middle of the night. The challenge of staying out of sight – both from other people as well as the increasingly ubiquitous street cameras – and bypassing security systems is an adrenaline rush like no other.

I'd been tempted to go further into Malia and Stephen's posh Rittenhouse townhome, to plant a few bugs in the house itself, but decided against it. I was less interested in who she entertained or what she did at home than in where she was going.

I hoped she would lead me to Stephen.

I had a search running on Deb's finances, looking for any indication that she actually did have a life insurance policy on Stephen, but I didn't expect to find anything. She'd have said something. Or Thackery would have found it and added it to her list of motives. But since the possibility had been raised, I needed to verify it, just to be sure.

And I had a set a second search running on Malia's finances.

I'd only done random spot-checks on her and Stephen for the last couple of years, seeing less of a need to constantly monitor them as Deb's children got older and the child support payments drew closer to ending. It had been almost two years since Cassie had turned eighteen, and Josh was getting close to his birthday.

So, I was curious to see what a deep look at Malia's finances for the previous year would reveal.

But for the moment, I had to focus.

Rittenhouse is a trendy neighborhood, filled with high-end apartments, a wide variety of restaurants, and bars that tend to stay open until the wee hours. There's always someone about, which makes it both harder and easier to sneak around, unobserved.

That meant that the best way to get into Malia's building was through the front door, right after the trendiest bars finally managed to shoo the latecomers out so they could clean up for the next day.

There are a few ways I could have done this, but I opted to try the one that required the least face-to-face interaction first. It was taking a chance – hanging out in the shadows dressed like a party-girl closer to Jessica's age than my own, and watching for someone making a wobbly beeline toward her building – but the fates were with me. As soon as I saw a promising group of late-night partyers, laughing and talking as they headed toward the lobby doors, I fluffed my shoulder-length brown wig just enough to fit in, and caught up with them as they headed up the steps.

When two of them got into a small tiff over whose key fob to use, I took advantage of the opportunity to relieve the more inebriated of the two of his and slip it into my pocket. Rather than try to convince them I'd been with them all evening – which I've been known to do in similar circumstances – I then reached past them and used the pilfered fob to select a lower floor than the one the revelers were headed to.

In a high-end building like this one, it's generally best to assume there are cameras everywhere, even when they're not obvious. It's annoying, but that's just the way it is these days, and I prefer to be safe rather than sorry. That's where a little play-acting comes in handy.

I left the elevator and headed down the hall, presumably toward my apartment. But before I reached whatever door I was going to, I stopped and made a bit of a show of digging through the overly large handbag I was carrying, being annoyed, and heading back to the elevator.

Anyone watching the security camera would assume I'd lost something.

They'd also get a decent view of pushed-up cleavage, but not much of my face, with the long hair messed up to hang down over about half of my face in a ratty snarl.

Once in the elevator, I held the key fob up to the scanner, then pressed the button for the garage level where, according to my research, Stephen and Malia's assigned parking places were located.

When the doors opened, I headed toward Malia's car, with just enough wobble in my walk to keep the bored security guard watching me wander through the building both entertained and unconcerned. I was just another tipsy resident with long legs and a short skirt who'd left something in her car.

I wanted them to watch me. To see what I wanted them to see, instead of worry about what I was actually doing.

To play up the "lost item" scenario, I continued to paw through my bag while I walked, with the added benefit of palming the tracking device with the magnetic side out, ready to go. I'd charged up the battery, and even tested it on my own car as I'd headed across town to make sure it was both tracking and transmitting correctly.

Then, before I reached "my" car – but just as I reached Malia's – I let the big raffia handles on my bag slide off my shoulder. I "tried" to catch it as it fell, but succeeded only in dumping several items to the ground, which of course I had to chase after – giving me the opportunity to reach under Malia's car for an errant tube of lipstick and settle the tracker in place under the edge of the rear fender using the hand I was "supporting" myself with.

All perfectly innocent.

And, thanks to a triple coating of clear nail polish on the pads of my fingers, fingerprint-free.

◆

Planting the tracker on Malia's car and tying the account to a burner phone and throwaway credit card was only the first part of my plan. I needed to give her a good reason to go to wherever it was Stephen was hiding. And I knew just how to get her attention.

It's pitifully easy to hack into a social media account if you know anything at all about a person. And when the person routinely takes those silly quizzes that encourage them to share details about themselves? Child's play.

Both Stephen and Malia were all over social media. You name it, one or the other was constantly posting a photo or a meme or had something – usually irrelevant – to say about something someone else posted. They thought it made them 'influencers.' Most of the time, it just showed how self-centered they were.

But all that digital data had given me everything I needed to easily figure out their account passwords – which were also super weak and which neither of them had updated since setting up the accounts.

So it was no trouble at all to hack into Stephen's accounts, one after another, and set a different application to monitor and record any activity on them.

With a brief apology to Josh and Chrissie, who I knew would probably see some of my posts and be upset by them, I started by changing Stephen's profile photos. Whatever photos he'd used before had all been replaced shortly after the murder by the somber image of him in a dark suit– another indication that I wasn't the only one haunting his accounts, though whether it was Stephen himself, his wife, or as Josh had guessed, his teaching assistant who had made the change, I had no idea. For what I was doing, it didn't matter.

I sorted through his past photos, and found a handful of him in happy, vacation poses – at the beach wearing snorkeling gear and holding a crab by one claw, at what looked like a Mexican restaurant with a drink in each hand, and so forth. On every account, I chose the happiest, brightest photo I could find to use as his new profile photo, tagging them with inane, silly comments.

Social media is all about sharing personal stuff, and that's never been something I've ever been very good at. Jessica usually handles what little internet outreach the business requires, and I could just imagine her laughing at my rather pitiful efforts. But I did my best.

Under my less-than-skilled hand, Stephen wished everyone well, said he'd missed seeing them, couldn't wait to hit the beach again, and proclaimed his boredom with just 'hanging out and doing nothing.'

And then he said how much he was looking forward to seeing all of his friends again, very soon.

I didn't know which post Malia would see first, but she was going to go ballistic.

Sometimes my job is just too much fun.

♦

Following my late-night adventures, I slept in the following morning. When I did get up, I messaged Jessica that I'd be there in a couple of hours, and then went online to check Stephen's social media.

Perhaps it speaks to my unfamiliarity with the medium, but I had half expected Malia to chew him out online for the inappropriate posts. Or at the very least say something semi-incriminating. She'd done neither. Instead, all of my posts had been deleted, the profile pictures once again displayed sedate images – though not the same ones as the night before – and the passwords had been changed.

I had to say I was disappointed.

Then again, it had been a cheap shot. And in some ways, I would have been more disappointed if they'd taken the bait.

For form's sake, I logged in to the car tracking app. There was no tracking data yet, not that I expected Malia to have gone anywhere in the few hours since I attached it to her car. It was only ten a.m., after all, and I'd never known Malia to be out and about early.

The financial scans on both Deb and Malia had finished running sometime during the night. I skimmed through Deb's quickly, looking for any indication that her financial status wasn't exactly what I had thought it was – stretched almost to the limit, punctuated with support payments arriving and going directly to her lawyer as she had said, tuition for Cassie, and the usual home and family expenses. Health, life, and disability coverage was paid through payroll deductions. Auto insurance was made through automatic withdrawal from her bank account.

But going back a full year, there was no separate life insurance payment made to any carrier. Malia had been wrong. Deb did not have a policy on Stephen. And while that was unfortunate, because she could have used the money, it did remove one more motive for murder from whatever case Thackery might try to build against her.

On the other hand, Malia's report was most enlightening.

She not only stood to gain a small fortune – to the tune of $1.5 million – from her husband's death, but four months ago had had also purchased two tickets for Vienna for travel… I checked the calendar… ten days from now.

As I looked at the data, I glanced over at the wall and the sticky note that read, "follow the money," and heard another piece of the puzzle fell into place with a satisfying *cha-ching*.

Malia and Stephen had decided to cash in on the insurance and then disappear, leaving Deb to take the blame.

And they'd been planning it for at least four months.

An hour later, I was heading to the office when Jessica called.

"I'll be there in ten minutes," I said.

"Mr. Herriman called."

I sighed. "Which one?"

"The gorgeous one," Jessica said, her voice going all dreamy. "Kyle."

"Stop that. He's a client."

"Most of our clients aren't anywhere near as hot as Kyle—"

"What did Mr. Herriman want?" I asked.

"Lunch."

"Excuse me?"

"He wanted to set up a lunch meeting with you. For Friday."

"And this couldn't have waited until I got there? I'm eight minutes out."

"He's on the other line. Waiting for you to say yes, so he can make the reservation. I didn't tell him you weren't in yet. Didn't want to give you a bad rep."

"Thanks, I think. Wouldn't want a bad rep with a client you're hot for."

"My thinking exactly," she said, laughing.

"Okay. Did he say where this lunch meeting will be? Or when? And what's my Friday schedule look like?"

"Let me check."

"Six minutes, if the lights like me."

"You have lousy luck with lights," Jessica said. I heard her tapping at the keyboard as she checked my schedule. "Seven or eight minutes at least. Lunch at the Philadelphia Cricket Club. You've blocked off from seven to ten on Friday morning, but the rest of the day is unscheduled at the moment."

"I hate Center City traffic," I growled, I'd hit the last two lights just as they turned red. "Tell Mr. Herriman I'll be happy to meet him for lunch, and accept any time he suggests between eleven-thirty and one-thirty. The Cricket Club… isn't that in Stenton? Not far from the Herriman Industries offices?"

"Chestnut Hill," Jessica said. "But yes, it's close. Only a few blocks away. Are you here yet?"

"No. I'm not, and at this rate, I don't know when I will be. There's an accident up ahead and the road's blocked off. If you look out the window, you'll see the lights."

"I heard the sirens. Didn't think to look."

"They're routing everyone around who-knows-where. I'll see you when I see you."

"I told you. The traffic gods are not your friends."

"Only in Center City. I don't have these problems anywhere else."

"You shouldn't tempt fate," Jessica warned.

"Good point. Figure out what sort of offerings I have to make to get the gods on my side," I said, turning away from my office – I could see the building two blocks ahead – as the traffic cop waved us all down a side street. I was tempted to just park along the curb and walk. I would have, had there been an open spot. "And don't gush when you talk to Mr. Herriman."

"I am the soul of professionalism," Jessica said, her manner perfectly proper.

I snorted, and clicked away from the call.

Philadelphia is a city of narrow, one-way streets, and when you're in a hurry, none of the streets are going in the one way you want to go. I've learned to cope with it by keeping myself busy – usually with a podcast or a phone call – and just going along with the traffic. I do not need to give in to road rage.

So instead of churn about the inconvenience of the detour – which was further re-routed due to construction on one of the connecting streets – I made another call.

Bonnie picked up on the second ring.

"What do you know about Stenton?" I asked without preamble.

"A lot of single-family homes, on decent lots," she said. "You getting cold feet about the East Falls house? I don't have anything in Stenton, but I just took on a new listing in Elkins Park, which is practically next door. I've only seen it on paper, but the owners are motivated—"

"No," I said, cutting her off before she could get the sales pitch going. "Still totally enthralled with the East Falls house. One of my clients wants to meet at a cricket club up that way, that's all."

"Up by Stenton? That would be Philadelphia Cricket Club," she said. "Nice place, from what I hear. I think it's in Mt. Airy, but who knows where the township borders are without a map?"

"Yes, that's the one. And it's in Chestnut Hill. Jessica looked it up."

"That's what I said. You need a map." Bonnie laughed.

We chatted a bit more as I crawled toward my office, but in the back of my mind I was thinking about another map - one showing Elkins Park at its center.

A map that just happened to be pinned to my office wall.

Chapter 25
Present day: Thursday, one week after the murder

In some very small, very naïve part of my brain, I thought I'd simply be an invisible bystander at Stephen's funeral, one of many black-clad attendees sitting quietly at the back of the chapel. Watching Malia. Slipping unobtrusively away after the interment.

It didn't happen that way.

I arrived at the funeral home about halfway through the viewing, in the hopes of offering my condolences and finding a seat before things got too crowded. As I pulled into the parking lot, I saw a cluster of people standing near the doors. I paid no particular attention to them – there's not that much to do while waiting for a funeral to begin, once you've paid the obligatory respects to the family in the viewing room, and it was a pleasant autumn day.

But after I parked and was walking towards the building, I realized that something was going on. The people I'd seen outside the building were separated into two distinct groups of people facing off against each other. Closer to me, about halfway down the main sidewalk between the building and the parking lot, were Deb, her two children, and her mother Barbara. Standing in front of the doors – and blocking the way, it appeared – were several men I did not recognize.

I approached cautiously, trying to observe before getting involved, but Cassie saw me. She ran up to me, grabbed my hand, and began tugging me toward her mother. "They won't let us in," she said, breathless. "Josh checked the other doors — they've got them blocked, too. Mom's trying to stay calm, but Grandma's beside herself."

"What do you mean, they won't let you in?" I asked her. "It's your father's funeral, for God's sake."

"Those men at the door, there?" she said, indicating the group of dark-suited men clustered directly in front of the door. "They're Malia's brothers or cousins or something. They say we're not invited. But I know we were — Dad's brother, Uncle Nat, called and told Mom when and where it was going to be. She said he was very nice about it."

"They announced it in the paper," I said, pulling my hand away from Cassie's and took a step back. "Date, time, place. That's all the invitation you need. I'll talk to them."

"Thank—" she began, but I cut her off.

"No," I said sharply, holding up a hand to stop her from saying anything else. I shook my head, speaking softly so only Cassie could hear me. "It can't look like we're friends, Cassie, or they won't listen to anything I say."

Cassie's a bright girl and caught on quick. She moved away from me with a look of despair I was sure wasn't entirely feigned. As I passed, she turned, her face in full view of the men blocking the door, reaching one hand toward me as she called out, "Please…?"

I ignored her, schooling my features into the cool, emotionless mask I routinely wore when dissecting a corporate client.

And as I walked past Deb and the rest of the family, I ignored them, too. They had apparently only seen the last moments of my exchange with Cassie, because they all watched in stunned silence as I passed them, none of them — not even the usually too-vocal Barbara — saying a word.

The men at the door rearranged themselves as I approached, forming a blockade. They were large men, a half-dozen linebackers in ill-fitting, off-the-rack suits, arms folded across their chests.

I strode purposefully toward them, scanning them as I drew near. The one at the center was several inches taller than me, broad-shouldered, with shaggy blond hair that looked like he'd run fingers through it, and stubbly patches along his jawline. He watched me with eyes that were as ice-blue as Malia's.

This would be her brother, Roger, and the others flanking him, her cousins.

In all honestly, I was surprised that Malia had allowed them to come. As part of the background check I'd done on her, I'd also learned several things about her extended family. Nothing major, just small things like bar brawls, money troubles, family squabbles – but all part of the rocky past she'd tried to put securely behind her when she married into the Markham name and fortune.

Yet here they were, bouncers at her husband's funeral.

Was keeping Deb away from the service really so important to her that it was worth jeopardizing the high-society image she'd worked so hard to build?

Did she think Deb would recognize the fake Stephen for what he really was?

I filed the question away for later. More cars were arriving, and other people were heading up the walk from the parking lot.

I halted about two feet from Malia's brother. "Excuse me," I said pleasantly.

"Who are you?" Malia's brother asked.

"A friend of the family," I replied. "And you?"

He glanced past me, toward Deb and her children, and then back. "Which family?"

"The Markham family," I said evenly. "Is there some problem? I came to pay my respects. Are you interrogating everyone? This is most inappropriate."

One of the cousins cleared his throat. "We're just tryin' to make sure the wrong people don't disturb the family, is all," he said. "She's okay, Roger. Let her in."

Roger shifted, turning slightly to create a small space between himself and his cousin through which I could squeeze past to get to the door.

"Really?" I said, not moving.

Large men, like Roger, often use their size to intimidate women, and all too often they get away with it. That was one of the many reasons I'd joined Ian's self-defense class, and why I still help teach it – to give the women in the class the confidence to stand up to them.

Roger was asking to be taken down, and I was itching to do it – could probably even have been excused for accidentally landing a well-placed heel right through the top of his cheap dress shoes as I pushed my way toward the door. Sadly, this was neither the time nor the place to teach him a much-needed lesson.

But I wasn't about to shimmy through the opening either.

I met his glare with an icy stare of my own.

After several seconds, he finally caved, stepping to one side and actually opening the door for me. I walked through, not bothering to thank him for the courtesy.

The blockade had reformed before the door clicked shut behind me.

◆

There were several dozen people waiting in the viewing line to extend their condolences. Under normal circumstances, I would have joined them, but I'd left Deb's family waiting outside, and they took priority.

I bypassed the line and went in search of the minister, identified as a 'Hon. Rev. Lawson' on the small program I picked up from where it had been left on the table displaying the visitor's guest book. If the blockade was truly Malia's idea, any appeal I might make to her would fall on deaf ears. I hoped the minister might be able to persuade her to let Deb's family come in.

The line of mourners wound through the foyer and through a pair of double doors into an anteroom where Stephen's body now lay. People were exiting the room through a second pair of double doors, further down the hallway, and crossing to take their seats in the large chapel where the funeral service would be held.

The minister – or someone I assumed to be a minister – stood in the chapel doorway, shaking hands with many of the mourners as though familiar with them.

I went up to him and introduced myself during a gap in the mourners.

"You're Reverend Lawson?" I asked. "You'll be conducting the service?"

"Yes," he replied. He was of medium height and build, and probably about ten years older than me. He wore wire-rimmed glasses, and his dark hair was still thick, cut short, with just a touch of gray at the temples. "You're a friend of the family?" he asked. "I'm sorry for your loss."

"I am, and thank you. I wanted to ask you something. Did you know that Stephen's children – his natural children – and their mother are being prevented from entering the building?"

His eyes widened, looking almost owl-like behind the thick lenses of his glasses. Before he could say anything, another pair of mourners arrived, and I stepped to one side of the doorway to let them pass. He nodded toward them, then touched my arm and asked me to wait before turning back to the new couple.

I wasn't going anywhere.

A moment later, Reverend Lawson joined me in the hallway, and we walked a few steps from the chapel door where we could talk undisturbed.

"Now what is this you're saying about Stephen's children being kept out of the building?"

I told him about Malia's brother and the blockade, omitting the part about how they'd harassed me personally.

To his credit, he seemed genuinely surprised. He shook his head. "People react in strange ways when a loved one passes," he said, a sad expression on his face. "I've seen people – good people – say and do things they would never do under normal circumstances."

"That may well be," I said. "But right here, right now, there are two young people who should be allowed to mourn the loss of their father. Malia is understandably distraught, and not herself. I was hoping *you* might be able to intercede on their behalf."

He seemed to withdraw into himself at that, as though recoiling from the idea of a confrontation. "Well…" he began, letting the sentence trail off, unfinished.

He was weak. Whether it was a part of his nature, or whether he had simply been intimidated by Malia as had so many of her acolytes, it didn't matter. Weak or not, he was the only tool I had.

"You know it's wrong, keeping them out," I said.

He nodded, almost imperceptibly.

"Then you'll talk to her?"

He nodded again, his gaze focused on his shoes.

I stood there for a moment, waiting. When he neither spoke nor moved, I pressed further.

"*Now*, Reverend? So Stephen's children have time to come inside before the service begins?" I touched his arm.

He flinched, then looked up at me, not quite meeting my eyes. "Yes, yes, of course, you're right," he said. "The children should be allowed to come in."

We walked back down the hall together, entering the viewing room through the door the mourners were exiting.

The room was mostly rectangular, the two sets of doors on one long wall. The opposite long wall was slightly curved, with a raised platform at the center for the casket. While most of the room was dimly lit by tasteful wall sconces, the area where the casket lay seemed bright by contrast. Three overhead lights shone down on Stephen, who lay in state, dressed in a dark suit, the glowing white satin of the coffin lining surrounding him like heavenly clouds.

Or such was the impression I got as Reverend Lawson and I entered the room and crossed to where Malia sat with other members of Stephen's family. Her mother-in-law, Eleanor Markham, was seated next to her, on her right, and Nathaniel Markham, Stephen's oldest brother, the one Cassie said had called Deb, was on Malia's left. Their chairs were on the same raised platform with the casket, allowing them to receive the mourners without having to rise. Large floral arrangements, heavy with lilies and scarlet roses, sat to either side of the coffin, their scent almost overwhelming in confines of the room.

Reverend Lawson waited until a break in the line, then he approached Malia bending toward her and speaking softly in private conversation. I held back, not wanting to aggravate the situation, instead taking advantage of the opportunity to pay my respects to the deceased – whoever he was.

Considering what I knew about the murder, I was surprised they'd gone with an open casket. For that matter, if, as I was coming to believe, Stephen and Malia had arranged the entire scheme, why hadn't Malia insisted on having the body cremated, rather than risk the chance that anyone might realize the man laying there wasn't really Stephen? I had no way of knowing, but speculated at the battle of wills that had raged between Malia and Mother Markham over that decision.

From where I stood, I was close enough to the casket to see the waxy pallor of the man's face. While I'd never been to a viewing yet where I thought the deceased looked like anything other than a wax figure slathered in stage makeup, I had to admit that the morticians had done an excellent job of repairing the damage and covering up the bruising.

If anything, the anonymous homeless man looked more

like Stephen than the real Stephen had in life. As though the morticians had rebuilt the face from a photograph, forcing the face to take on the features not his own...

"Of course I know she's out there," Malia said, the haughtiness in her shrill voice catching my attention. I looked away from the casket and moved closer, staying behind the minister. "We've called the police already. They'll take care of her."

"I invited her—" said Nathaniel.

"Stephen would want—" Reverend Lawson began at the same time.

Malia cut them both off with both words and a sharp gesture. "Stephen would *want* to be alive. *She* killed him. She's already *seen* his dead body. Why should I let her see him now?"

"His children should be allowed to say goodbye to their father," I supplied, finally stepping from the shadows behind the minister and into the lighted area beside him.

Malia glared at me. "Taking her side now?"

"I'm not taking anyone's side, Malia," I replied, keeping my voice low. "I'm just saying that his children should be allowed to mourn their father's passing."

Malia raked us all with a scathing glare – Nathaniel, Reverend Lawson, me, and even Eleanor, who hadn't said anything, but was simply sitting there looking so stunned at the loss of her youngest son that I wondered if she'd been medicated. Even the nearest mourners, only steps away and standing next to the casket, received the benefit of Malia's wrathful gaze, and turned away with apologetic murmurs.

"You're hateful, all of you," Malia hissed, "ganging up on me like this when *I'm* the one who's been wronged."

"You know that's not—" Nathaniel began.

"I know nothing of the sort," she snapped, cutting him off again. "Fine. Let the brats in. Let them see their precious mother's handiwork. But I will not have *her* in this room."

"Of course," said Reverend Lawson, nodding and stepping back, as though prepared to flee before Malia either changed her mind or turned the full force of her fury on him. "I'll notify your brother that the police are no longer required, and he's to let them come in," he said as he inched away from her. He caught my arm, pulling me with him. "And Miss…" he looked at me, then frowned. "I'm sorry, I seem to have forgotten your name."

"Judas," Malia sneered.

"Margaret Harrison," I supplied.

"Yes," Reverend Lawson said, nodding. "Miss Harrison will stay with the former Mrs. Markham, and ensure that she doesn't come into the viewing salon."

I must have looked as surprised as I felt, because when I looked up at Reverend Lawson, his expression was pleading. "Of course," I murmured. "Anything I can do to make this day easier for everyone."

"Sit at the back," said Malia. "I don't want to see either of you."

She looked away then, dismissing us, and Reverend Lawson and I left the viewing room.

♦

Reverend Lawson spoke to Roger, pulling him aside as we came out of the building. I left them to their conversation, continuing on to Deb and her family.

A uniformed police officer was standing with them. The tension surrounding the little group was so thick, coming up to them was like walking through fog.

"I wouldn't exactly say you've won the day," I said when I reached them, putting on my best professional manner, "but Malia has agreed to let you attend the funeral." I extended my hand to the officer. "Margaret Harrison. I'm a friend of the Markham family. Mrs. Markham has asked me to accompany the former Mrs. Markham and her children into the building."

I gestured behind me toward Rev. Lawson and Roger. "The minister is explaining the situation to Mrs. Markham's brother. I believe he is the one who called you."

Reverend Lawson joined us a moment later, and it took only a few minutes to explain things to the officer's satisfaction.

Before he left, the officer graciously offered his condolences to Deb and her family. Then he shook his head and said, "Family situations are awkward for everyone – we're called out to weddings, graduations, and funerals more often than anyone would probably imagine."

He offered Deb his card. "If you need anything, don't hesitate to call me."

"Well, at least you have one cop who likes you," I said to Deb as the officer walked away.

"This is wrong," Josh said. I looked over to see what he was talking about. I'd given him the program I'd picked up, and now he was clutching it so tightly it was crumpling in his hand.

"What's the matter?" Deb asked.

"We're not listed as pall bearers," he said, raising the crushed program. "She's put down *her* sons, *her* brothers, and Uncle Nat, but not *us.*"

"I'm sure it was an oversight," Reverend Lawson said.

Josh fixed him with a level gaze, but he was shaking all over and his voice trembled when he spoke. "It was no more of an oversight than her calling the cops on my mom," he said. "She doesn't like it that we even *exist.* She did this on purpose."

"It's okay," Cassie said. "At least we can go in now."

"It's *not* okay," Josh said. "He might not have been the greatest father, but he was our father. It's our responsibility... no, it's our *right* to carry him to his grave."

I looked at Reverend Lawson and shook my head. "Malia will never allow it," I told him. "Talk to Nathaniel – he's more rational than she is. Since he's already one of the pallbearers, he might be able to help sort things out."

I put a hand on Josh's arm. "There's nothing at all 'right' about this day," I told him. "Just stay calm, and things will work out as well as they can."

Josh and Reverend Lawson walked away, passing Malia's relatives without giving them a second glance.

I turned then to Deb, Cassie, and Barbara. "Are you ready?"

They looked at each other, then back at me, and nodded. Then we walked through the gauntlet of Malia's cousins, and into the funeral home.

Chapter 26
5 years ago

"I know, I know. 'Don't think about it, just throw the damn knife,'" Meg muttered, echoing Ian's repeated admonition before he had a chance to say it.

She'd hesitated, *again*, looking at the target and calculating before taking the throw.

Ian walked over to the table and pulled the knife from the block of ballistic gel, then studied the blade as he carried it back to her.

"Your aim is good," he said as he drew within easy speaking range. They were in the training portion of his long, narrow backyard, with the target about twelve feet from where Meg was standing. "And the throw was stronger this time—" he held up the knife, showing her the bead of red-tinted corn syrup that clung to the tip. "You weren't sinking the blade deep enough to hit the blood packs a month ago."

"So that's good, right?" Meg asked, feeling like an unruly student hoping to avoid the scolding she knew was coming.

"Yes, that's good," Ian agreed. "Of course, if you stopped thinking about what you're doing and just threw—" he spun, threw the knife, and turned back to her, still speaking, as the blade sank hilt-deep into the block of gel, "—you might manage to hit your target before he has time to pull his weapon and shoot you."

She deflated as he took the last two steps, closing the distance between them, stopping only an arm's length from her. While she'd been practicing, Ian had been picking herbs from the narrow planters that ran along one side of the yard, and now the scent of crushed basil wafted on the breeze to her along with the slightly sharp hint of sweat.

She needed to focus... On what he was teaching her... Not on how he smelled... On the way the muscles rippled under his t-shirt... Or the way the lines of the tattoo snaking around his upper arm disappeared under the hem of his shirt sleeve...

Just being around the man sometimes made her think she'd been a fool to let them drift apart.

But she couldn't study, couldn't train, couldn't crawl around in the underworld of espionage and assassinations, and pull herself up the corporate ladder at the same time if she let a great body distract her. It had only been three months since she'd left the mergers and acquisitions firm that had recruited her when she was fresh out of grad school and gone out on her own, and even with her reputation, building up a stable clientele was taking all of her time. Maybe later, after she was better established...

She gave herself a mental slap. Business before pleasure.

"I'll get the knife," Meg said, ducking past him and sprinting to the end of the yard. The air helped – the hot, humid, gritty air that was Philadelphia in the height of summer. Who'd have thought she'd have chosen air pollution over the prospect of dragging Ian back to her bed?

She was insane.

But she was also driven. And there was no way in hell she was going to let Ian know what he did to her.

Meg reached for the knife, surprised when it didn't slide free easily. The cube of warm ballistic gel sucked at the metal, clinging to it like hot flesh, making it tougher to pull it out than seemed right. She shifted her grip on the knife's tape-wrapped handle, made sure she was holding it at the correct angle, and pulled again.

The blade slid along the cut, a line of their corn syrup artificial blood following it. When she finally pulled it out of the gel – which released the blade with a squishy, sucking sound – the line of the fake blood ran down the front of the wobbly cube.

"One summer a buddy and I practiced in his uncle's butcher shop," Ian said, coming up behind her. "We'd sneak in at night and throw knives at the hogs and sides of beef before they were cut and wrapped for sale."

"I bet that made for some interesting steaks," Meg said. "Pre-tenderized. No extra charge."

Ian laughed, scooping the cube into a bucket along with the globby chunks they'd cut from it during their practice. "Yeah. If we'd only done it once in a while, we'd probably have gotten away with it all summer. But we were having a blast – and weren't too bright, I'll admit it." He grabbed a rag and wiped the rest of the stray bits of gel off the table and into the bucket.

"We got caught. Spent two weeks cleaning the shop after hours. Now there's a smell for you." He turned and headed toward the house, then looked over his shoulder at Meg. "You coming?"

Meg was puzzled. "It's only been an hour," she said.

Ian gestured with the bucket. "Gel's getting too warm, losing integrity. Don't worry. You're not done yet."

Near the rowhouse, the narrow yard split into two sections – a ground-level patio just off the kitchen, and a small, sunken courtyard that led into Ian's basement. Ian led Meg down the short flight of stairs toward the basement, then gestured for her to go inside.

Meg took only a few steps in, and stopped. It was cool and dim in the basement, with only a trace of the humidity of the outdoors. But as soon as her eyes adapted to the lower lighting,

226 • Lauryn Christopher

she realized she was looking at a very elaborate model train setup. Tracks curved and looped around in seemingly random patterns, often climbing inclines or passing under bridges.

"I didn't know you were into model trains," she said.

"I'm not," Ian said. He carried the bucket across the room, stepping over the crisscrossing levels of track, and set it on a sturdy worktable in a far corner of the room.

"Um... That's a pretty complicated setup for someone who isn't into it."

"That's for you," he said. "I told you practice wasn't over." He picked up a laptop and a bundle wrapped in a small towel, circled over to the foot of the stairs to switch on the overhead lights, then crossed back through the train yard to where Meg stood.

"What's this?" she asked as he handed her the bundle.

He didn't bother to answer, just left her with the packet and went over to the freestanding bar that stood in the corner near the door to the courtyard.

Meg opened the bundle, juggling the throwing knife in her hand, and found four ordinary kitchen knives of different sizes and styles — a serrated steak knife, a wide, heavy butcher knife, a small, short-bladed paring knife, and a knife with a long, skinny blade and sharp tip.

"Care to explain?" she asked.

"It's all well and good to learn with a proper throwing knife," Ian said, powering up the laptop and connecting it to some sort of console while he spoke. "But life isn't like the movies. Nobody has an inexhaustible set of their favorite knives to get all fussy about. If you're in a bad situation, you've got to be able to use what's at hand. And that could be just about anything."

"I'm glad you didn't give me a butter knife or pair of scissors," Meg said. It would have been just like him — start her training with the traditional weapon, then move to using ordinary items for the same purpose. He'd done the same thing when he taught her how to wield a baton – just as she was beginning to feel proficient with it, he switched it out for a crowbar, an umbrella, a broken stick, a tightly-rolled newspaper, and a set of salad tongs, and made her learn how to defend herself with each.

Honestly, she loved the challenge.

Ian looked up from where he sat, half-perched on a barstool behind the bar. "I didn't?" he said, a wicked grin forming. "I'll have to remember those for next time." He dug in his pocket, then held out his hand. "Here."

Meg went over and held out her hand.

Ian dropped a pocketknife in it.

"Really?" she asked.

"Really." He flipped a few switches, and from three different directions, the big engines – each well over a foot long – pulled out of the shadows and onto the track. And when she saw what they were pulling, Meg burst into laughter.

Each engine towed behind it a flatbed car loaded with a large block of ballistic gel.

"How did you do that?" she asked.

"It wasn't hard," Ian said, grinning. "Just needed to find the right sized container and set it up with a couple of anchor bolts to attach the gel block to the car so it doesn't fall off on the hills or the curves."

"Impressive."

"What will be impressive," he said, "is to see if you can hit the blocks with the knives I've given you."

"While the trains are moving?"

"Try not to damage the engines."

"You're an evil man, Ian Mitchell." Meg said.

"I do my best," he said. "Why are you just standing there? Grab a knife and throw it. And no more thinking about it."

She threw the steak knife at the first train – and missed. The knife clattered harmlessly to the floor as the train cruised by, tooting its whistle.

This was going to take some practice.

Meg threw the next knife.

♦

Meg set her phone on the end table and curled up into the corner of the couch, holding one of the cushions close to her chest. Gary's little girl, Karen, wasn't doing well. The leukemia she'd been diagnosed with only a few weeks before was burning through her little body like a brushfire, and it was tearing Gary up to watch his precious child suffer.

His wife was no help. Meg had always thought Janine was a little odd, but she'd chalked that up to the differences between her corporate world and Janine's pride at being a stay-at-home mother. The two hours she'd just spent listening to her brother alternately rant or cry over his wife's anti-medical establishment attitudes – and her faith in 'natural remedies' even in the face of their daughter's rapidly failing health – had left her stunned.

Nine-year old Karen was heading down the same road their mother had gone, and Gary was terrified for her. Meg was afraid, too, and promised to sit with her whenever her parents needed to be away, needed to sleep…

A child needed love and comfort to help them face their fears. Needed to know that the adults caring for them would hold them and keep them as safe as they could when they were tired or sick, and wouldn't use their weakness as an opportunity to poke and prod and touch and hurt. But she couldn't breathe without coughing. And she was cold, so very cold that she was too weak to push the hands away…

Meg jolted to wakefulness, a cold sweat leaving her shivering. She'd slipped back into her own memories in the dream, the line between nine year-old Karen and eleven year-old Maggie blurring along the very different, very real fears both girls shared.

♦

Meg always made healthy – and anonymous – donations out of her illicit funds to charities supporting drug rehabilitation programs. And when the pink ribbons heralded the annual appeal to support breast cancer research, another round of anonymous donations went to both local and national charities.

Besides being a way to honor her sister and mother – and possibly have some good come from her activities – it was also a good use of the money.

But other than wire the funds, she never personally participated in the fundraising efforts or attended the charity events.

So when the embossed invitation to the annual Pink Tie Ball arrived, Meg tossed it. But when it was followed up later that same day with a call inviting her to be a special guest at the Young Professionals party being held in conjunction with the Ball, she groaned inwardly, accepted graciously – and then enlisted Jessica's aid to locate the discarded invitation.

At barely six months old, her private consulting business was still too new to pass up on the kind of visibility her attendance – and the recognition – would generate. At least the only "angel investors" she had to answer to were her own alternate identities.

And that was how she ended up at the party, dressed in a chic black designer gown with beadwork on the bodice and running down one sheer sleeve in a pattern of reds, golds, and yellows that caught the light like shimmering flames. Pink looked awful on her, and she'd seen no point in wasting money on a gown in a shade she would never wear again. The few lines of pink beading in the design, echoed in the rose-gold setting of her ruby earrings were her sole concessions to the event's color-coordinated theme.

She was standing at the bar, tapping her nails on the counter while she waited for her third cocktail, hoping it would make the evening pass more quickly. The music was excellent, the ambiance everything the hosts had promised, but she didn't want to be here, had no reason to be here other than to smile for photos that had yet to be taken, and couldn't wait to kick off the four-inch stilettos that were part of the evening's uniform.

"Having that much fun?" a male voice asked as one of the ubiquitous black tuxedos prowling the party joined her at the bar.

Meg turned her head and found herself staring directly into a pair of bright blue eyes, that crinkled slightly as the man smiled. That her stilettos made them the same height put him at about an inch shy of six-feet. He was trim, and clearly came from money — his tailored tuxedo, and hot pink vest were superbly cut and fit him like a glove. And unlike so many of the pink-trimmed men at the party, the matching tie and handkerchief peeking out of his breast pocket did nothing to diminish his masculinity. His features were more refined than strong, but the smile and slight dimple in his chin gave him a slightly roguish air.

Meg wasn't in the mood to be hit on.

"I wouldn't go that far," she said. "It was a long day to start with. The shoes don't help."

"I can understand that," he said. "My wife's sick, but she insisted I come. Wants me to outbid all challengers for a couple of the auction items she has her eye on."

"Good luck."

The bartender set Meg's drink in front of her and took the man's order. Thinking the polite small-talk was over, Meg dropped a few bills into the tip jar, tilted her glass in salute to the man, and turned to go. She was only a step away from the bar when he caught up to her, laying his hand on her arm.

Meg paused, turning her head to look over her shoulder at him.

"Wait," he said. "Don't go so soon. We only just met."

"We haven't met," Meg said coolly. She glanced meaningfully down at her arm. "Please?"

The man hastily withdrew his hand. "I'm sorry," he said. He had the grace to look embarrassed, which was probably the only reason Meg didn't just walk away. While she was more than happy to donate to the charity, attending a function with a malignant disease as its central raison d'être while her niece lay dying in a hospital bed from a version of that illness was more stressful than she'd anticipated. Add to that the fact that she didn't like being touched by strangers, and the handsome man in the pink vest was lucky she'd given him the chance to remove his hand rather her removing it for him.

"Let me start over," he said. He gestured toward the ballroom, where the orchestra was playing a lively selection of big-band music. "You're one of the only women here who doesn't look like a peacock. I'd like to dance with you – that is, if you're not here with someone else."

"Hmmm," Meg said. "'Not a peacock…' I suppose that's a compliment?" She took a sip of her drink. He wasn't her type – even if he weren't married, there was too much about him that said 'born to money and used to privilege' for her liking – but she had to admit that she was finding the encounter amusing, at the very least. "Do you have a name?"

He switched his glass to his left hand and held out his right. "I'm Stephen Markham."

As Meg reached out her hand to take his, it seemed for just a fraction of a second as though the party had come to a stop around them. The music held a single note, and the black and pink swirl of people froze into a faceless blur.

In the seven years since she'd first met Deb and decided to champion her cause, Meg had never felt any need to actually meet Stephen. Why should she? He was the target. The person who was continually annoying her friend. A driver's license photo she'd never bothered to enlarge. A passport photo come to life.

He was the man who had abandoned his children.

Meeting him wouldn't change that. Nor would it change her attitude toward him.

So, despite the handful of occasions on which their paths had potential to cross, Meg had never gone out of her way to orchestrate a meeting. Which was what made meeting him completely by accident all the more interesting.

Her hand connected with his, the music swelled like a movie score, and time resumed. "I'm Margaret Harrison," she said, hoping her smile didn't look *too* feral. "I would be happy to dance with you."

Suddenly, her shoes didn't bother her at all.

Chapter 27
Present day: Friday, eight days after the murder

After the debacle at the funeral, I was sorely tempted to haul Malia's skinny ass to an empty warehouse and beat the truth – and Stephen's whereabouts – out of her.

Thank goodness for Glau. His calm gaze as I paced back and forth ranting not only brought me back to my senses, but spoke eloquently about just how much I was letting this job get to me.

I needed to focus.

A bodyweight workout – running the stairs, doing squats, lunges, planks, and pushups – helped me burn off the anger.

A chilly hour of Tai Chi out on the roof deck helped me ground.

A review of my murder-board helped me plan.

And after a good night's sleep, I was sitting in my car, refreshed, focused, and sipping very slowly at a latte, while watching to see if Stephen Markham boarded his usual morning bus.

I was actually rather surprised at how many people were already at the bus stop when I pulled to the curb on the opposite side of the street a few car-lengths down. Then again, it was just before eight on a Friday morning. This and the next several buses would probably be busy with commuters.

The small pair of binoculars I usually kept in the car's glove box were missing – I'd probably stuck them in a jacket pocket and would find them when I got home. I tried using my phone's camera instead, but the distance meant that the facial features were blurred just enough that I couldn't clearly identify Stephen.

I took the photos anyway.

By the time the bus arrived, I'd decided that four of the dozen men at the stop were of the right height and build and looked similar enough from a distance that any one of them could be Stephen. I cataloged their similarities and differences in a small notepad.

One wearing a light blue nylon jacket, similar to my darker blue windbreaker, a dark ball cap, and carrying a backpack.

Three wearing dark hoodies, one with a light-colored ball cap but no backpack. The other two both carried backpacks, one wearing his hood up, the last with his hood down.

All wore jeans or dark slacks – I couldn't tell – and dark shoes, which may have been sneakers or dress shoes, though I thought the latter unlikely.

The bus arrived, everyone boarded, and I turned away as it drove by. I hadn't seen Stephen in a couple of years, but didn't want to risk him recognizing me.

When the bus was out of sight, I eased the car forward a little and set my phone's alarm for Stephen's return, forty minutes later. If he was the creature of habit his PennPass use had shown him to be, I should be able to spot him when he got off the bus.

Since I had some time to kill, I pulled the burner phone out of a zipper pocket in my bag and launched the app connected to the tracking device on Malia's car. It had been forty-eight hours. I was curious to see where she'd gotten to.

The app traced out her route on the map, showing the path she'd traveled, and putting a marker at any point where she'd lingered. I had to switch between the tracking app and my GPS to identify those addresses, but in a little over a half hour, I had a good picture of her activities, as predictable as they were.

In anticipation of the funeral, Malia had spent most of Wednesday shopping for her widow's weeds, with a brief stop at a liquor store on her way back to her apartment. She'd spent two hours at her favorite salon on Thursday morning, before going to the funeral home and then to her in-laws' home. And, of course, it was still too early for her to be out yet this morning.

The tracker was clearly as good as Charlie had promised, but at this rate it was going to be tedious trying to catch her doing anything incriminating. I was pondering this when my phone alarm went off and the bus pulled up to the stop, and three people – two men and a woman – got off. Jacket-and-cap man headed northeast, down a walking path into the heavily wooded neighborhood, carrying a coffee to-go cup and small paper bag. Hoodie-and-backpack man went off down the sidewalk to the south, swinging a plastic grocery bag.

Again, I didn't get a good look at either man's face.

I was reasonably sure that jacket-and-cap man was the same one who had gotten on the bus, but now that I was closer, I could see that he was a little thicker in the midsection than I remembered Stephen being. I wasn't certain about the second man. His hoodie was so ubiquitous that he could have been one of the earlier passengers or a completely different person.

Time to choose.

I watched for an opening in the traffic, flipped a U-turn, and followed the man in the hoodie, hoping to catch a glimpse of his face as I cruised by.

◆

I passed hoodie-and-backpack man, timing it so that I was pulling into a strip-mall parking lot just as he reached the spot. I glanced over, ostensibly watching out for the pedestrian's safety, and getting a good look at his face as I drove into the lot.

From a distance, sure, there was enough of a similarity to warrant following him, but looking him full in the face for two full seconds was all the confirmation I needed.

I'd followed the wrong man.

To maintain the illusion of being a normal, everyday executive, I pulled into a parking space, then called the office to check in with Jessica.

"Appointment go well?" she asked.

"Rather disappointing," I said, watching the man continue on his way down the sidewalk. "Unlikely we'll be doing business together."

"Sorry about that," Jessica said.

"Can't win 'em all," I replied, trying to put a nonchalant shrug into my voice. "Besides the lunch meeting with Mr. Herriman, what else is on my calendar for today?" I asked.

While I was completely aware of my schedule, confirming details of meetings both real and fictitious was a long-standing routine. I never knew when one of my illicit jobs was going to require additional time or travel, and often scheduled random blocks of out-of-office time – even if I was just holed-up in my home office.

Having Jessica view the erratic nature of my comings and goings as normal was better than having her question my occasional disappearances.

"You have a conference call with Davis Meyer this afternoon," she said, "and..."

"Did he finally get his documentation sent over, or is he still stalling?"

"Messenger brought it about a half hour ago," Jessica said. "The packet is on your desk. And he called himself to make sure it had arrived and set the meeting."

"It's about time." I tapped my fingers on the steering wheel, acting like I was trying to make a decision – one I'd already made. I was never going to find Stephen and learn how they'd set up Deb as long as my time and attention was as divided as they'd been for the past week. Just as I'd needed bring my mind and body into focus the night before, I also needed to focus my time.

"I'd like to have more time to review it, but pinning him down has been such a bear, I'm not about to try to reschedule. How flexible is next week?"

I heard her tapping on her keyboard to bring up the schedule, but she started answering my question even as she typed.

"You have an eight o'clock with James at SCH on Monday," she said. "But he was open to pushing it off to Tuesday afternoon…"

"All right," I said. I'd been expecting a call from SCH, so that came as no surprise. "Monday at eight is good," I said. "What else?"

There was a pause as she clicked through the calendar. "Back-to-back meetings with Erick Mann and Kamiko Tsuda on Wednesday."

"I can't do either of those," I said. "Something has come up and I need to be out of town, and probably out-of-pocket, most of next week. Reschedule both of them for early the following week, at their convenience. I'll make it work."

"Is everything all right?" Jessica was used to me rescheduling meetings or needing to travel at the drop of a hat, and sounded only slightly concerned.

"Yes. Just juggling time. What time is the meeting with Davis this afternoon?"

"Three o'clock."

There was a clatter as Jessica's fingers flew over the keyboard. I made a mental note to look for a quieter one for her. "You can synchronize your smartphone to your schedule, you know," she said as she typed.

"Yeah, I know. I just keep forgetting to do it," I lied, tucking the burner phone in the glove box and locking it away for safekeeping.

On the other end of the line, I could practically hear Jessica roll her eyes, clearly aghast at my overwhelming display of Luddite tendencies. I glanced at the glove box and smiled.

If she only knew.

◆

I've always found it easy to compartmentalize multiple projects, and generally move from one to another without giving it much thought, sort of like taking one book off the shelf and putting another one back in its place. So, while I didn't know why Kyle had asked for a meeting, the country club was convenient to both my early morning excursion and his office, so I figured I'd go ahead and see what he wanted.

Northeastern Philadelphia is beautiful at any time of year, and even with the autumn leaves beginning to fade and fall, the drive to the Cricket Club was still lovely. Mature trees in shades of fading reds, oranges, purples, gold lined the road, and a scattering of leaves dusted the still green lawns. It was a nice change of pace from the concrete canyons of Center City.

Kyle must have been waiting just inside the doors, because he met me as I came up the walk to the Cricket Club.

"I hope I haven't kept you waiting," I said

"Not at all," he said, pressing my hand in a firm handshake.

We went through the pleasantries of greeting and seating, ordering food and drink. Finally, after we'd both commented on how fortunate we were that the weather was nice enough to eat on the patio overlooking the sparsely populated tennis courts, and a waiter had brought our drinks, it seemed like time to get down to business.

"I suppose you want an update on the progress with SCH," I said. "I sent over the new paperwork, and have a meeting with them Monday. I don't anticipate any problem…"

"But you never know," Kyle finished the sentence for me.

I shrugged. "That's the business," I said with a smile.

"Then will just take it as it comes," Kyle said. "But that wasn't why I asked you to lunch."

I waited, curious, but said nothing.

He glanced away, out across the tennis courts, and I noticed a hint of color rising just above his collar. A moment later he turned back to me.

"I thought it would be nice to re-set," he said. "After the whole shooting-gallery thing, I mean. I'm not my grandfather, and I don't do business the way he did—"

"Don't give it another thought," I said, cutting him off before he could launch into an apology that would only serve to embarrass us both.

"—and I thought you might like a tour of Herriman Industries."

A few years ago, at a party where some very attractive man was hitting on me and I was apparently oblivious to it, Bonnie rightly pointed out that I could be about as aware as a brick when it came to certain social interactions – meaning that men flirt with me all the time, and I seldom realize it until after well after the fact.

And while nothing Kyle had said had been the least bit inappropriate, or even suggestive. I was suddenly uncertain.

"It was my understanding that SCH already sent their division heads out to tour the facilities," I said, deciding the best response was to stick to a business focus. "I don't know what I could add to their evaluation."

"They trust you," Kyle said. "And you're vouching for me. It couldn't hurt for you to see what I've done with the place."

"Okay, that's fair," I said. "I've got a couple hours."

The waiter brought our food then, and our conversation drifted, wandering off onto a variety of topics that had nothing to do with either the food, the weather, or the merger.

As we were walking across the parking lot to our cars, I glanced over at him. He was enough taller than me that I had to tilt my head to look up at him. It was a nice height.

"You know, I could have simply met you there, at your office," I said. "You didn't have to buy me lunch."

"We both needed to eat," he said. The response was casual, almost a verbal shrug. But the telltale flush creeping up from his collar was the real response.

Kyle Herriman was definitely flirting with me.

I barely give a second thought to juggling the complexities of a corporate merger and the intricacy of an assassination. They're like two sides of the same coin – coin I happily accepted, regardless of the client.

I just wasn't sure if there was any place in my life for something as complicated – and unpredictable – as a relationship.

Chapter 28
Present day: Saturday, nine days after the murder

I don't usually go armed.

While I have a concealed-carry permit and a couple of legally registered handguns in a safe in my closet, and a portable gun safe bolted to the underside of the driver's seat in my car, most of the time there's just no need for me to carry a gun. There are so many other ways to kill a person without attracting so much attention as shooting them.

But today I wanted to be doubly prepared.

I was hunting a murderer.

The forecast was for partly cloudy weather, cooling toward the end of the day, with the likelihood of rain increasing as the weekend progressed. So I dressed appropriately – jeans, comfortable sneakers, and a snug t-shirt with built-in holsters along both right and left ribs. I topped it with a windbreaker that would allow easy access to my holstered weapon without calling attention to it, and tucked a pair of lightweight knit gloves into my jacket pockets. No sense leaving any stray fingerprints.

I dithered between covering my too-noticeable blonde hair with a hat or a wig, finally deciding on the wig, pulling the long, light-brown locks back into a ponytail. If the weather had been cooler, or already raining, the hat would have been the obvious choice – other people would also be wearing them, so it would be unremarkable. But just as I'd noticed the men wearing hats or hoods at the bus stop the previous morning, I didn't want to call attention to myself because I'd worn a hat on a day that didn't really warrant it.

I had my ID, a credit card, and some cash in a stretchy wallet around my ankle. In my jeans pockets I carried a slim leather sheaf of lock-picking tools and my cell phone, set to silent mode.

It was time to choose my weapon.

But instead of going to the gun safe in my closet, I went into Glau's room.

"Excuse me," I said, moving his tail from where it dangled down over the side of his perch and gently nudging it up onto the cushion. He shifted at the movement, turning his head to watch me.

Glau's perch was a long, padded shelf that sat on top of a cabinet where I stored his vitamins, leashes, cleaning supplies, extra food and water dishes, and so forth. I opened the cabinet, moved a few things out of the way, and then pressed at a spot at the top of the inner wall, opening a panel that provided access to the space under the ramp leading to the top of the perch.

And the gun safe under the ramp.

I'd made it difficult to get to for a reason. This was where I stored my unlicensed, unregistered handguns. I always had at least one, and usually two or three.

If I had a pattern, this was it: I never used the same gun twice.

They were just too easy to come by to be worth the risk. On those occasions when I decided a gun was the best choice for the job, I always found that it was better to use it, then disassemble it and discard the pieces.

There were always more guns.

I keyed in the code to unlock the safe. Two guns lay on the foam-covered shelves: a Glock 17 semi-automatic, and an older

Smith & Wesson model 42 compact, five-shot, .38 Special revolver.

Both were excellent weapons, but I was going hunting in the suburbs and decided the revolver was the better choice for the situation. It was lightweight, and had an enclosed hammer, which made it nice to carry. I'd tested it when I first picked it up, shooting off several rounds one night at a rock quarry about an hour outside of the city, and liked the action. And while there's no such thing as a quiet gun, it seemed to me like the revolver wasn't quite as loud as the Glock and the recoil was a little less.

Choice made, I pulled it from the safe and double-checked to make sure it wasn't loaded. That was a habit Ian had drilled into my head – even when I'd put it away myself, and made sure it was empty first, I always check every weapon when I pick it up.

I tucked the revolver into my holster. It was a nice, comfortable fit, and drew clean, with no hitches on the fabric. I'd clean and load it when I got downstairs, but for the moment I re-holstered it, then filled a small coin-pouch with fifteen rounds from the partial ammo box on the shelf where the revolver had sat and tucked it into my pocket. Since I didn't have a registered weapon that used the .38 rounds, I left the box in the safe when I locked it, then closed up the panel.

"Good thing you can't talk," I said, looking up at Glau as I restored the cabinet to order. "I'd hate to have you go blabbing all my secrets."

He just blinked in response, then stretched out his head for an under-chin scratch. I obliged, then went downstairs to clean and load the revolver, wiping it clean of fingerprints before tucking it into my holster. I wouldn't touch it again without gloves.

A short time later I was in my car, and on the way to watch for Stephen at the bus stop.

♦

I parked as close as I could get to the walking path the man in the blue jacket and cap had taken the previous morning.

The road paralleled the path for at least a couple of blocks before hitting a T-intersection. While I waited, I launched my GPS app, but all that showed was the circuitous route the road took as it wound through the neighborhood – I had no idea if the path was the Elkins Park version of a sidewalk, or if it provided joggers a scenic route through the woodland.

I checked my watch. The bus was running late. Only by a couple of minutes, but the four people waiting at the bus stop were checking their watches and phones, as well.

Nothing to do but wait for it.

I switched to a browser-based map, to take a look at the neighborhood from an aerial view. Lots of rooftops peeking through a heavy canopy of trees, but even the roads were difficult to spot. Of the walking path, there was no sign.

So much for technology. I was going to have tail him the old-fashioned way.

It's one thing to tail someone on a crowded street, in a shopping mall, or even a busy office building. As long as you're paying attention, you can blend into the surroundings pretty well. But whether you're in a vehicle or on foot, the fewer other people there are between you and your target, the more likely they are to spot you.

Tailing someone through a residential neighborhood is doubly challenging, because you have no way of knowing who is watching from the safety and comfort of their home and taking note of the stranger passing by – a stranger they'll remember having seen if something untoward subsequently happens in the neighborhood.

The only way to become invisible in that sort of situation is to become a regular sight. A jogger who runs the same route every day, a new neighbor who walks their dog around the block each morning. But that kind of setup takes time, and time was one thing I didn't have – their flight to Vienna was now only a week away.

It would take another couple of months, at least, for the life insurance to be paid out, but Malia could use the time to find a tidy apartment with a nice view of the Danube or something and get herself settled into her new life, making it look like it was all perfectly normal for a grieving widow to go abroad rather than stay in the city where her husband had been killed.

It's how I'd have planned it, anyway.

I peeled an orange, the sharp citrus scent filling the car as I waited. The bus was now seven minutes late. Two of the people at the stop – a man and a woman – had given up on it, and were climbing into a car I assumed was an Uber while the remaining two women watched. One looked annoyed, the other simply resigned to the delay.

Either of them could have been me, depending on the day.

Most of the time, I want things to keep moving along, in some semblance of an orderly fashion. I'm open to variations in a schedule, the need to regroup when a plan doesn't go as expected, as long as things keep moving, even if the movement is backward. I reevaluate, adjust, and keep going, like a shark that can never stop swimming, as the saying goes.

It's when things stall that I start to get antsy. Too long without some sort of movement, and it's like a pond whose surface is mirror-still. I don't do well when the only thing that surface is reflecting back at me is coming from the inside. Still waters grow stagnant, and the darkness oozes up from the depths.

So I stay busy. Like that shark.

I had nearly finished my orange by the time the bus finally arrived. I set the last of the fruit aside and started the car, so I would be ready when Stephen passed by.

A woman with a young child got off the bus, followed by an elderly man taking the steps slowly and cautiously. Then two women who had been waiting at the stop got on, and the bus drove away.

There was no sign of Stephen.

Well, shit.

I had no way of knowing if he'd missed the bus or taken another – or if he'd even gone out that morning. If he'd taken the convoluted route up to the shopping plaza for supplies as his PennPass data showed he'd done before, or gone someplace else altogether, there was no telling where he was or when he would return. And short of sitting here, watching the bus stop all day – which was pointless, since he'd only used this route for what I'd decided must be his morning coffee run – there was a whole lot of nothing I could do to find him.

Time to regroup.

I was reasonably certain that he was hiding out in a house within a ten- to fifteen-minute walk of the bus stop. I didn't know Stephen well – and hadn't seen him in over a year – but he'd never struck me as the sort to go out of his way when there was an easier way to do something. Just taking the bus was so far out of line with the arrogant, self-important man I knew and loathed, that I didn't think he'd have agreed to walking any noticeable distance on top of it.

Not even for $1.5 million.

I eased away from the curb and drove slowly down the street, turning to the left when I came to the intersection. The walking path crossed the street and headed along what looked like a park – though may have just been a large back yard. I followed the street as it wound around through the neighborhood, catching only occasional glimpses of the footpath between the houses.

This was no cookie-cutter tract neighborhood. These were older homes, no two alike, and probably built at least twenty years ago, if not more, judging by the age of the trees and general lack of both fences and sidewalks. Many of the houses were set well back from the street, several partially obscured by that canopy of foliage the aerial map had been unable to photograph through.

Occasionally, two or three houses were clustered together, but even then it was nothing like being in the city, where the rowhouses actually shared walls. Here, I rarely saw a house that was closer than a literal stone's throw from its nearest neighbor.

I'd been driving around for a little over half an hour when I took a right turn at an intersection with a house on the corner. I hoped to find my way back to the walking path which I'd lost sight of a few turns back, and thought the corner house – I'd encountered very few – would be a good landmark. It was a large, two-story Craftsman that looked to be in exceptionally good repair. It had been painted in a soft creamy, not-quite yellow, with the trim work in a deep burgundy, which made a striking combination against the foliage. It had a deep porch, and sat sideways on the lot, facing the intersection. From the porch, which wrapped partway around both sides of the building, it had a commanding view of the neighboring houses – a pair of ramblers that looked like they'd probably been built in the seventies – that flanked it on either side.

I wondered if the trio had been some version of a single-family compound, with the parents occupying the central home and the children – grown but not entirely independent – living nearby, under the watchful eye. It was the kind of arrangement Aunt Ruthie would have reveled in, if we had let her. I smiled at the thought. She'd tried to do her best by us after our mother died, she really had, but we hadn't made things easy for her.

All thoughts of Ruthie faded along with my smile when I saw the "For Sale" sign next to the Craftsman's mailbox near the mouth of the driveway – and Bonnie's face smiling out from the hanging board.

◆

"'Of all the bars in all the world,'" I muttered, cruising past the house and its neighbor. Yes, Bonnie had said that she was representing a house in Elkins Park. And true, it wasn't like the community was all that big – it couldn't have been more than three or four miles across at its widest point.

But that didn't mean I wasn't unreasonably annoyed to find her working in the same neighborhood where I was hunting. The last thing I needed was to worry about running into her, or her somehow managing to end up caught in the crossfire when I finally found Stephen. Because I knew that if Bonnie spotted my car, she'd have to see if it was mine or just another navy blue Altima. Even if she decided it was someone else's, her curiosity could put us both in jeopardy.

Friendships could be so damn inconvenient.

There's a reason I never take jobs from the dark web if they're within a couple hours' drive from Philadelphia. The closer you are to home, the harder you have to work to avoid running into someone you know. It's just too easy to get caught.

I'd broken my own rule, and now was facing the very challenge it was intended to help me avoid.

The road curved a couple of blocks down. When I could no longer see the big house on the corner in my rear-view, I pulled over to the shoulder of the road. The walking path was about fifty yards to my left, running along a greenbelt that may have been a park, may have part of some other homeowner's yard, I had no idea. If there were any other houses on that side of the road, I couldn't see them.

Ahead of me, on my side of the road, was a cluster of mailboxes – maybe three, maybe five, it was hard to tell from this angle. So while I couldn't see them, I knew there were houses hiding in the woods.

And people in the houses, who might have a better view of me than the no-view-at-all I had of them.

I busied myself with my GPS unit, only half-pretending to be lost in these backroads. They really did all look very much the same, and with the clouds coming in and blocking any direct sunshine, I didn't even have much in the way of shadows to go on to tell me which direction I was going.

I had no idea where Stephen was. No desire to cross paths with Bonnie.

I've killed people before for no other reason than because they were in the wrong place at the wrong time. Collateral damage happens in this business. And when it's a choice of them or me… let's just say I have a well-developed survival instinct.

But I didn't want to kill a friend if I could help it.

Bonnie had just made my job a lot more complicated. Because short of locking her in a dark room with a bag over her head, I was now going to be looking over my shoulder until this was all over.

And if she got in my way, I was probably going to kill her.

Probably.

Chapter 29
Present day: Sunday, ten days after the murder

For the third morning in a row, I headed to Elkins Park.

It was a gray day, the kind that promised to be drizzly later. I'd worn the wig again, still pulled back in a ponytail, and had the revolver tucked neatly into my underarm holster. I'd traded in the windbreaker for a slightly heavier zippered sweatshirt, and found the missing binoculars in the pocket. I still needed to blend into the sparsely populated neighborhood, but it was too chilly for the lighter jacket.

When I reached Elkins Park, I waited in the same place I had the previous morning, within sight of the bus stop, at the point where the walking path and the street diverged. I'd printed out a map of the area the night before, noting several places where the walking path came close to one of the neighborhood streets.

I didn't want to lose him. I also did not want to get lost in the convoluted streets of the neighborhood again.

The bus was on time.

I grabbed the little binoculars and watched as each person stepped of the bus. Woman with child. Older man. Teenager of unknown gender. Man in a blue jacket and ball cap.

There was no mistaking his face. It was Stephen Markham.

I was almost surprised. I'd been sure he was still alive, but there was a tiny – very tiny – portion of my mind that was still clinging to the belief that the man I'd seen buried three days before might possibly have been him. Watching him step down off the bus and then turn to help the elderly woman descending behind him snuffed out that last flickering belief.

I traded the binoculars for my phone and pretended to talk, watching in the rearview as he approached. As before, he carried a to go cup and small paper bag. I wondered what coffee/pastry shop he had found that was worth such dedication, or if he just really didn't like the isolation of hiding out in a quiet house in the woods.

If he glanced over as he walked past my car, it was as surreptitiously as I watched him. I continued my pretend phone call until he was a good two or three car lengths down the path. Then I shoved my phone in my pocket, got out of the car, stepped to the rear of the vehicle, and did some warm-up stretches, as though preparing to go for a run.

While I stretched, I kept an eye on Stephen. He continued down the path, showing no signs of turning off into any of the unfenced yards between where I was parked and the next place where the path and the neighborhood streets connected. Rather than follow him on foot, once I was confident he was staying on the path, I hopped back into my car and drove to the next spot I had identified on my map and parked, pulling on my gloves while I waited.

My new vantage point was far enough back from the path to not call attention to my vehicle, but let me see up and down the path for about fifty yards in either direction. If Stephen didn't show up within about five minutes, that would tell me that his hiding place was in one of the dozen homes between where I'd last parked and here. It wasn't a perfect way to find him – and honestly, I didn't like it a bit – but it was a way of narrowing the search grid.

At four minutes forty-five seconds, I saw Stephen approaching.

I checked my map, then drove to the next parking spot, reset my phone's timer, and once again settled into wait. I did not anticipate having to do this more than three or four times – there were enough other bus routes that would have been more convenient to locations farther down the walking trail than the one he repeatedly used. I was certain his hiding place was somewhere in this neighborhood.

He came into sight just when I expected him, and I moved to the next location.

My third waiting spot was along a section of the walking path that paralleled the road for a good distance. When I had driven down this road the previous day, there had been three or four cars parked along the shoulder. I had hoped to simply be able to join the line. But whatever they had all been here for then, there were no other cars to hide among today. Hoping no one would arrive while I was waiting, I backed into the partially obscured mouth of a driveway, and watched for Stephen.

As before, he appeared right on schedule.

I sank low in my seat before he got to me, and watched as he passed by, as casual as anyone out on a morning stroll. Stephen walked as though he owned the world. There was nothing to suggest that he was a man in hiding, who had murdered a look-alike in an insurance fraud scheme. His expression showed no guilt, no remorse.

I was going to enjoy killing him.

About two hundred yards to my left, there was a T-intersection. When he reached that point, Stephen left the walking path, jogged across the road, and continued down the intersecting street. That was my cue. I pulled out of the driveway, drove up to the intersection, and turned onto the street.

Stephen was about halfway up the block. I'd barely completed the turn, when he abruptly left the shoulder of the road where he had been walking, and disappeared into the trees.

It was all I could do to refrain from gunning the car's engine, and leaping noisily ahead to the point where Stephen had disappeared. Thankfully, the Altima accelerates quietly, and only a moment after I lost sight of him, I pulled off onto the shoulder on the opposite side of the street.

I slipped out of the car, closing the door softly, and peered over the roof to see where he had gone.

There were only two houses on this section of road – a long, low rambler about three car lengths to the left, and a large, cream-and burgundy Craftsman sitting at an angle to the corner at the end of the street.

The house Bonnie was representing.

With a muttered curse, I raced across the street and into the woods after Stephen.

I've gone camping, and been dragged out into the woods for the occasional corporate retreat, but when it comes right down to it, I'm a city girl and not ashamed to say it. I have virtually no woodcraft or tracking skills to speak of, but the narrow path marked with the occasional footprint outlined in dried mud was obvious even to me.

I tried to move quietly, hyper-aware of every twig that brushed past me, any leaf that crunched under my shoes. Every few steps I stopped, scanning to the right and the left, listening and looking for any sign of movement.

Then I caught a glimpse of blue off to the right.

I stayed on the path, looking between the ground and the blue patch, hoping the path would change direction before I had to leave it to follow him. Even with my lack of woodcraft, I knew I could move more quietly along the packed earth of the path than if I had to plow through the underbrush on my own.

Thankfully, about ten feet further on, the path altered course. Looking back, I could no longer see my car behind me. Ahead, Stephen was heading toward patches of white, which resolved into one of the long white ramblers as I got closer.

Stephen crossed through the yard to the back door. I followed, ducking from tree to tree, trying to stay out of sight both from him and from anyone who might be in the large Craftsman next door. As far as I could tell, there were no lights on in the big house, and I hadn't seen Bonnie's car in the drive as I crept through the yards – or any other car, for that matter – but that didn't mean a thing. I wasn't taking any more chances than necessary.

Inside the rambler, a light went on in the window near the door – presumably the kitchen. A moment later, a second light went on, shining from a small window set high in the wall about halfway down the length of the house. A bathroom.

Taking advantage of the opportunity, I jogged across the lawn to the back door. In a matter of seconds, I'd finessed the cheap lock.

I pulled my gun and let myself into the house.

◆

The back door opened directly into the kitchen. Directly in front of me was an archway leading to a hallway that split in two directions, straight ahead and to the right, like an "L". To my left was a long counter with the sink positioned beneath a window along the back wall that ended in a high bar separating the kitchen and dining room. Stephen's to-go cup and paper bag sat on the counter between the door and the sink.

I heard the swish of a toilet flushing from down the hallway to the right.

I followed the sound.

There were four bedrooms, doors open, two on either side of the hall. The bathroom – a thin strip of light shining beneath the bottom of the closed door, the sound of running water muffled by the hum of a ceiling fan – was between the two bedrooms on the back side of the house.

Stephen was taller than me. And he would be coming out of the bathroom facing me. So there would be no sneaking up on him from behind. Challenging him head-on would be pointless, because he would just close the door in my face, giving him time to brainstorm a defense in the time it took me to get into the room.

He didn't know I was there – that was my biggest advantage.

A direct assault was my best option.

I positioned myself in front of the door, bouncing slightly on the balls of my feet, waiting.

Stephen shut off the water.

I was ready. He would be drying his hands now. For a fleeting second, I wondered if he was going to come out or getting ready to shower after his morning excursion, but then the doorknob began to turn.

I hit the door with a solid roundhouse kick, sending it crashing into his face, then followed through, pushing the door out of my way as it bounced back toward me and moving into the room.

Stephen stood at a crazy angle, wailing in pain, one hand grasping at the edge of the sink counter for balance, the other clutching his nose. Blood was streaming down his face and onto his shirt.

He looked up as I came into the room, but I didn't give him time to react. Holding the revolver with my fingers and thumbs wrapped around the grip, like a supported fist below the trigger guard, I raised the weapon and to my left, then brought it down in a hard chop to the right, smacking him across the temple with the gun's wooden butt.

He crumpled to his knees, barely missing the edge of the bathtub.

I stepped forward, grabbed him by the hair, and shoved him forward, not caring too much when the top of his head hit the wall. He was starting to flail around at that point, so I pressed the revolver up against the back of his neck.

"Make me nervous, and it will be the last thing you do," I growled.

"Who are you?" he asked, his voice coming out in ragged gasps.

"The last person you expected to find you," I said. "I have some questions for you."

"D-d-deb? H-h-how?"

Maybe I'd hit him harder than I intended, but that wasn't what I expected him to say. Then again, it made sense. Deb probably was the last person Stephen would have expected.

"Move," I said, tugging him forward. When he started to get up, I shoved down on his shoulder with the barrel of the revolver. "Stay down. Crawl."

I rarely have to interrogate people – most of my information-gathering work takes place in cyberspace, and my other targets are generally of the "kill them quickly and quietly" variety. But I wanted some answers from Stephen, and the best way I knew to put a pampered brat off his game was to start by showing him just how little I cared about his welfare.

The method wasn't without its risks – sometimes they collapsed in on themselves like a black hole when faced with the reality of their situation. But most of the time they just couldn't help but talk big about whatever it was they thought they'd gotten away with.

And up until this moment, Stephen thought he'd gotten away with murder.

He crawled down the hall, turning away from the kitchen and heading down the short portion of the hall which lead into the living room. From the décor – which I generously dubbed old nineties thrift-shop – I guessed the house was a furnished rental. A massive stone wood-burning fireplace filled most of one wall, with a flat screen television mounted above it where the mantel should go. It was flanked by a pair of bookshelves holding only a scattering of books and small figurines and other knick-knacks. The front door was on the opposite wall, about a quarter of the way from the front wall.

The front wall was dominated by a floor-to-ceiling bay window, with filtered light coming in through a series of bedsheets that had been hung in lieu of curtains. A pair of unmatched easy chairs – one in worn leather, the other a frayed floral print – sat near the window, each with a small table to one side and a pole lamp positioned just behind, presumably to provide proper illumination for reading. The light blue jacket and cap he'd been wearing earlier tossed on the flowered chair, and a stack of magazines, television remote, and empty beer can on the table near the leather chair indicated Stephen's preferences.

He was heading toward the leather chair.

"Hold up there," I said. If that was where he was heading, it was exactly where I didn't want him.

A long, low sofa, with brown tweed cushions that had seen better days, sat about four feet from the wall dividing the living room from the kitchen, effectively creating a sort of faux hallway behind it. In front of the sofa was one of those short, oval coffee tables that looked more like an oversized skateboard than a piece of furniture.

I'd hurt him, but I didn't trust him. And I had no idea what he might have had hidden in the chair cushions or in his coat.

"Here," I said. "Sit on the table."

He hesitated, then continued crawling toward the chair.

I booted him in the thigh. "Did you hear me?" I asked. "Sit on the table."

"What do you want?" he asked. He'd stopped whimpering, but his bashed-in nose gave his voice a nasal sound.

"We're going to have a little chat, you and I," I said. And then, just to keep him off-balance, I added, "Seems your wife's not very happy with you."

◆

"You should have stayed in the house, like she told you to, Stephen," I said after he'd dragged himself up onto the coffee table. The spindly legs had creaked when he said, and the thin wood bowed under his weight. To be honest, I was surprised it was strong enough to hold him.

He seemed skeptical as well, and was perched on the end of it like he was poised to jump up any second. "But no, you had to go for walks, go shopping, risk everything. For what? A cup of coffee?"

He glared up at me. "Have you looked at this place? It's a dump," he said, spitting blood as he spoke. "And the coffee she left me sucks. I deserve better."

I waggled the revolver at him, like a schoolmistress waving her finger. "Tsk, tsk. Shoulda sucked it up."

"What are you going to do?" he asked. "Spank me?" A little of the old arrogant charm crept into his voice, and he grinned, seemingly unaware of just how unappealing the blood and snot dripping from his nose made him.

"Well, I *am* here to punish you," I said. He started to rise, but I leveled the revolver at him. "No, no, no. You stay right there. I have a few questions first. Call it... professional curiosity."

He shrugged, wincing. "You could have just asked. Didn't need to beat me up."

"Just doing my job," I said. "Speaking of which, that was good work, bashing in the homeless guy's face like that. A real pro job. Who gets the credit for that one?"

"She found him. Dressed him up, bought him lunch, got him to come up to the office," he said, preening a little. "But I know what my face looks like, and his wasn't a good enough match. So I got rid of it for him."

"You're a real team, you two."

"Ha! You don't know her," he said. "I do what she says."

"You expect me to believe that?" I said, though I actually thought it likely. Malia liked things to go her way, and had little patience for anyone who opposed or questioned her. "You're the one with the money, the family connections."

"You think I'd be doing this if I had any money?" Stephen said, gesturing at the room. "Everything goes to my ex – or to a lawyer."

"Not buying the pity party," I said, shaking my head. "You've never lived within your means. You've whittled down the payments to your ex to the bare minimum. And your mother's been paying for the lawyers. So what really happened? She finally threaten to cut you off?"

"I don't need her help," he said, the nasal edge making his snarl come out more like a choke. "Once the insurance pays out..." He stopped, clamping his mouth shut, realizing he'd said too much.

"You think you're going to see any of the insurance, and you're crazier than I thought you were. Your wife doesn't need you to collect the payout." I'd relaxed my stance, but now raised my left hand, cupping the butt of the revolver. "And because you wouldn't follow the rules, you've become a liability."

"So like her," he said with a little laugh. "Fine. Get it over with."

"I just have one more question," I said. "Whose idea was it to frame Deb for your murder?"

Stephen looked back at me, the expression on his face one of such actual confusion that it took me off guard. "What?"

He recovered from the split-second of uncertainty half a breath before I did. And in that moment, he turned, reaching down to grab the lightweight table, and spun, swinging it at me.

It caught me in the ribs with an audible *thwack*, sending me flying across the room. In the chaos of the moment, my finger tightened on the trigger, and the gun went off.

The report echoed in my head – not as loud as the Glock's would have, but enough to start my ears ringing. I crashed against the flowered chair, and scrambled to my feet, clutching my side.

Stephen was at the front door, scrambling with the chain lock.

I didn't stop to think about it. I didn't run after him or try any fancy moves. I just raised my gun and fired.

Chapter 30
5 years ago

Meg and her younger brother, Thomas, stood side-by side near the small casket holding their niece, Karen. They had known this day was coming, of course, but that hadn't fully prepared them for the loss.

Hadn't prepared them for the second casket.

Gary's casket.

They had died the same day – Karen from leukemia, Gary from an overdose of sleeping pills.

Meg couldn't imagine how Thomas must be feeling, his twin's pale, waxy face a mirror of his own. Gary had always been the more jovial of the two, the one responsible for leading the pair into more than their share of misadventures.

Of all her siblings, Gary was the one who laughed the most.

Meg had no idea he'd been so devastated by his daughter's death that the only way he knew to cope with the loss was to take his own life. She'd talked to him only hours before. Held him as he sobbed in the hospital parking lot. Told him to get some sleep and sent him home with his wife.

Janine.

She stood with Meg and Thomas, but apart from them at the same time, her hand trembling as she rested it on the edge of Gary's casket.

262 • LAURYN CHRISTOPHER

"How could you do this to me?" she hissed. Her voice was little more than a whisper, barely concealing her fury.

"Janine," Thomas said gently, taking a step toward her.

"Stay away from me!" she cried out, half-stumbling as she backed away from him, one hand thrust out as if to hold him back. "I tried, you know I did. I did what I thought was right for her."

Wild-eyed, Janine looked from Thomas to Gary and back. "No… No… I can't look at you and not see him," she said, her words coming out in choked sobs.

Abruptly, she turned and fled the room, her own mother casting a scathing glance toward Meg and Thomas before following her distraught daughter.

Meg put a hand on Thomas' arm. "It's not you," she said.

Thomas nodded. "I know." He glanced back at his twin. "Yeah, I know."

Meg squeezed his arm, then stepped over to Karen's casket. They'd dressed her in a frilly pink party dress – Meg remembered the excited little girl swirling it around when she pulled it from the wrapping only a few months before, and running to her room to put it on before she would open any of her other birthday presents. It was a better way to remember her – laughing and twirling around in a swirl of cotton-candy pink – than the pasty-faced porcelain doll that lay there so still… too still.

Meg reached into her bag and pulled out a well-worn, patchwork rabbit.

"What's that?" Thomas asked, coming up to stand next to her.

"She asked to be buried with it," Meg said. "I told Janine, but she refused – said it was too old and too tattered." She reached over and removed the brand new doll from the child's arms and handed it to Thomas, then tucked the bunny into its place.

Thomas slid the doll into Meg's bag. "Don't let Janine see you with that," he whispered, indicating with a nod toward the door that Janine and her mother had come back into the viewing room.

"She carried that bunny everywhere," Janine's father said, coming up to stand next to Meg. "Gary gave it to her when she was three years old. Or maybe four. It's right that she sleep with it now." He glanced over at his wife and daughter, then leaned in close to Meg. "Give me the doll. I'll see it finds a new home."

Meg passed the doll to him, then wiped a tear from her eye as the older man tucked it under his coat, then quietly slipped out of the room.

"Come on," Thomas said, tucking Meg's arm in his. "I could use some nicotine. Do you still smoke?"

Meg almost laughed at that. "You know I don't," she said. "Never did. And you shouldn't."

"It's a hard habit to kick," he said. "But, hey, I've switched to vaping. That's supposed to be easier on the system."

They went outside, shivering a little in the cool autumn air while Thomas took a few long draws from the e-cig, holding the vapor in his lungs for several seconds each time before exhaling the sweet-smelling clouds.

"Seeing anyone?" Meg asked.

"Maybe," Thomas said, between puffs.

"What's he like?"

Thomas grinned. "He's a chef."

"I asked what he's *like*, not what he *does*," Meg said. "But I suppose being a hoity-toity chef answers both questions."

"You'd think so," Thomas agreed. "But when he's not whipping up some fancy, overpriced dish – his words, not mine, I promise – he volunteers at a local soup kitchen."

"For real? Or for show?"

"Oh, it's for real. He grew up there, says just because he got out doesn't mean he should forget his roots."

"And does your chef have a name?" Meg asked with a grin.

"Darnell Williams."

"And does he treat you right?"

"What is this?" Thomas asked. "Big sister interrogation?"

"Damn straight," Meg said. She sobered. "It's just you and me now. I want to know that you're okay."

"We're good. I'll introduce you next time you come up to Chicago. Get him to cook for you."

"Not one of the hoity-toity meals, okay?"

They both laughed.

They stood there in silence for a couple of minutes, then Thomas glanced over at the mortuary doors. "I guess we should go back in," he said, tucking his e-cig into his jacket pocket.

"Yeah," Meg agreed. "After... Will you do me a favor?"

"Sure. What?"

"Come with me over to Janine's. I'm going to take Gary's iguana. She's never liked it anyway, and I hate to see her just let it die or something."

"You want Gary's iguana? You know it's gotten huge. Where are you going to put it?"

"Yes, I know it's huge – that's why I need your help. And I've got plenty of room. The back bedroom on the second floor is nice and sunny. It shouldn't be too hard to adapt for him."

"You're putting an iguana in the guest room?"

"Don't worry, little brother," she said. "You might not visit often, but I'll keep the second guest room for you... and your chef." He was taller than she was, so instead of patting him on the head like she wanted to, Meg settled for patting him on the arm as he held the door open for her.

Then, arm in arm, they went back into the mortuary to say their final farewells to their brother and his daughter.

♦

"You'd be on the street, if it wasn't for me," Eddie said. He'd never come into her bedroom before, and Maggie curled tightly into her blankets, clutching her floppy-eared stuffed

puppy.

"Is that what you want?" he asked, untying the sash on his bathrobe as he came closer to her narrow twin bed. "To be on the street, starving? For your mother and sister to have to sell their bodies or your little brothers take to thieving, just so you could eat and stay warm? I'm sure you're not that selfish."

Maggie didn't know what some of the things he said meant, but it all sounded pretty bad. Then Eddie's robe fell open and she saw that he wasn't wearing any clothes under it, and even though she'd just turned eleven and was supposed to be a big girl now, she squealed and began to scoot away.

But Eddie was too big and too fast. He ripped off the blanket, tossing it to the floor, then grabbed her by the ankle. Maggie   pulled, but his fingers squeezed tight, and she whimpered as he dragged her back.

"Shhh," he said, pressing his hand over her mouth. "Do what I tell you, and I'll make sure your whole family always has a warm place to live and plenty of food to eat. Do you understand?"

Her eyes wide, Maggie stared up at him in the dark, and nodded her head, just a tiny bit.

"Good girl," he said, removing his hand from her mouth, and brushing his fingers through her hair.

"Do you promise?" Maggie asked. Her mother was always worried about putting food on the table, always saying how they had to be very careful about what they spent, and not be wasteful. Maggie often thought her mother worried about money more than about her children. But here Eddie was giving her a way to help. Her lip trembled. "You'll take care of us?"

A feral gleam spread across his face as he lowered it to

hers, his breath nasty from the beer he always drank. He was still holding her tightly by the ankle, but now his other hand was sliding up her leg under her frilly pink nightgown. "Oh, yes, little girl, I'll take very good care of you. But this has to be our secret – you can never tell anyone, not even your Mother. Do you understand?"

Maggie nodded, squeezing her eyes closed to keep the tears from leaking out, holding the stuffed dog tighter to her chest as Eddie began to tug at her underpants...

Meg woke, clutching her pillow, the tears streaming down her face. Someone was knocking at her door.

"Meg?" It was Thomas. "Meg, are you okay?"

"Just a minute," she said. Scrubbing at her eyes only succeeded in smearing the tears around her face rather than actually drying them. She pushed herself up, out of her bed, and grabbed a robe.

Thomas was standing outside her door when she opened it, a dark shadow silhouetted by the night light that glowed softly a few feet behind him.

"Are you okay?" he asked again, the worry evident in his voice. "I heard you call out." He reached out for her, but she shied away from him, not yet ready to be touched.

"Bad dream," she said. It was embarrassing to be caught out like this; she didn't know quite how to respond.

"Come here," Thomas said, stepping forward and enfolding her in his arms. He pulled her close, and Meg let him, the tears falling freely as she buried her face against her brother's chest. He stroked her hair, making soothing sounds Meg couldn't understand while the sobs wracked her body.

She cried harder when she understood what he was saying.

"It's okay, Maggie," Thomas said gently. "You're not the only one who has bad dreams."

♦

Meg sat at the desk in her large home office, looking at the year-end numbers for her consulting firm with more than a little satisfaction. It had been risky, going out on her own in the competitive, cutthroat world of mergers and acquisitions, and she'd been a little nervous about it, but she'd ended her first year in the black. Not bad, if she said so herself.

Then she brought up the report for her side business – the off-the-books investments, under-the-table deals, and other unmentionable work she picked up from the dark web listings. The year-end numbers there put her little consulting firm to shame. The earnings were higher, the overhead lower. In a side-by-side analysis, it just took a lot more time and effort to do things the legal way. And, six-figure salary aside, it wasn't as profitable.

She pushed back from her desk, startling the iguana who had found a patch of sun near the French doors leading out to the roof deck. Glau had only been with her for a couple of months, but Meg was beginning to enjoy his quiet company – and he seemed to like being around her, too.

"Who'd have guessed?" she said, stooping down to scratch at the back of his scaly head. Glau was cool to the touch – cooler than she thought he should be. Meg rested her hand on his shoulder, and frowned.

"Okay, I know you like this spot because it looks sunny, but it's too close to the window," she told the iguana. "You're going to make yourself sick if you lay here through the winter."

She studied the room, looking for a better place for a six-foot lizard to hang out, but short of taking out a cabinet…

Meg looked at the row of four foot tall filing cabinets standing in the corner at the opposite end of the room from the French doors, and wondered if the carpenter she'd been working with to turn the spare bedroom into a suitable iguana habitat could build a ramp and shelf so he could lounge on top of the cabinets.

"What do you think, Glau? If I trade the three tall cabinets for four shorter ones, and put in a heating lamp? Would that make an acceptable perch?"

The iguana stared at her, blinking. But it didn't say no.

"I'll add it to the list. In the meantime, if you're going to stay there, you'll need this." She tossed a small flannel blanket over him, arranging it so it provided coverage to his core body without being in the way of his legs. Glau immediately turned and began tugging at it, pulling it off his hindquarters and higher onto his shoulder before he grew tired of the game and decided to leave it.

"I'll get the hang of lizard-parenting," Meg said. "I promise."

She walked over to the filing cabinets. Yes, it was much warmer over here. This would be a good place for a perch. And reorganizing the cabinets wouldn't be any trouble.

The cabinets were filled with client records, going back to her very first merger. She could set Jessica to digitizing the oldest of them. There was no need to keep the paper accessible indefinitely, especially since she no longer worked for the firm.

Those had been good years.

And the past year, on her own, had been good, too. Meg turned back and looked at her desk. She couldn't see the numbers on the monitor from this angle, but she didn't need to. Owning and running her little consulting firm had never been about the ROI.

She enjoyed her work.

The fact that it gave her the freedom to pursue her side jobs and then the ability to invest – i.e., *launder* – some of her ill-gotten gains was just a bonus.

But the earnings from the dark web jobs was more than she could launder without raising suspicions. She was going to have to find other companies to quietly invest in – maybe even buy a small business or two under one of her assumed names. She had her eye on a few offshore opportunities, and was looking at a couple of manufacturing facilities in Central America where an infusion of cash could help solve her problem and maybe even make a difference for the community. It was something to consider.

And if she made a profit there, too? Well, as long as she was making money hand-over-fist, there was no excuse not to pay taxes, donate generously – if anonymously – and generally be a good citizen. Make a difference where she could.

She just never wanted to have to explain where the money was coming from.

Chapter 31
Present day: Monday, eleven days after the murder

I thought my 8 o'clock call with SCH went quite well. James wasn't even worried about Kyle being the principal at Herriman Industries. In fact, he seemed almost relieved to be working with the younger executive. I wasn't really surprised. Kyle was a solid businessman and the company had done very well under his leadership.

I was about to call his office to set up a status check meeting when the cheerful tones of *Here Comes the Sun* brightened my office.

I hesitated through almost half a stanza before answering, gathering my thoughts before talking to Deb. I was sure she was calling to tell me that the police had found Stephen's body. There was so much I wanted to tell her, but never could. So much I'd wanted to say to him, but none of it would have mattered.

And there was still Malia to deal with.

"Hey, how are you doing? Holding up?" I asked her.

"I am actually, that's why I was calling," she said. "I had the strangest visit from Lieutenant Thackery yesterday evening."

"Can he do that – talk to you without your lawyer?"

"I don't know. He was very polite, and said he'd wait until I called my lawyer if I wanted him to. Or that I could go down to the station and meet my lawyer there."

"Harsh. What did you tell him?"

"Oh, Meg, I didn't want to go back to the police station," she said, that tremble creeping back into her voice. "Mother told him to go ahead and ask his questions, and if I felt uncomfortable, then I'd call Mr. Paoletti."

"What did he want to know?"

"He wanted to know how I spent my day, where I'd gone."

"Aren't you still wearing the ankle bracelet?" I asked. "Can't they just check their records?"

"That's what I thought," Deb said. "But when I asked him, he said they were just routine follow-up questions, to make sure the tracker was functioning correctly."

"Did you call Mr. Paoletti?"

"No. It seemed silly to bother him for such a simple matter. I told Lieutenant Thackery we went to church in the morning, then stopped to get fried chicken, and then I did a short shift at the hospital in the afternoon. I was home by dinnertime – and that their tracking software should be able to confirm it."

"So why was he checking up on you?" I asked. "Is he sweet on you or something?"

"Don't be silly," Deb said. "I called Mr. Paoletti to see if he knew anything, but his secretary says he's in court this morning and won't be able to return my call before noon. But here's were it gets weird, Meg. I just got a call from the police station. They want me to come down so they can remove the ankle bracelet."

It was really hard to play dumb. I knew perfectly well why Thackery had been to her house and why they were removing the ankle bracelet. They already knew she hadn't killed Stephen the first time, and were making sure she'd been nowhere near him the second time he was killed. It was all just a formality – dotting the I's and crossing the T's. For obvious reasons, I try to stay as far away from the investigative process as possible, but suspected that Uncle Jim's voicemail was probably overflowing with messages.

"So that's good news, right?" I asked, trying to convey an appropriate level of confusion.

"Yeah," Deb said. "It's good news to me. Anyway, I was wondering if you could come with me..." her voice trailed off as she said, "What the hell?"

In the background I faintly heard the sound of screeching tires. Then a car door slammed

"Deb?" I asked. "What's going on?"

"I don't know... What? Why is *she* here?"

"Who's there, Deb?"

"It's Malia. Hold on, I'll get rid of her."

"Deb, wait, I said, already levering myself gingerly up out of my chair as quickly as I could, but she wasn't answering — from the sound, I thought she had set the phone down.

Then I heard Malia's voice, shrill, but slightly distant, screaming, "You killed him. You killed him. I know you killed him," over and over.

"I don't know what you're talking about. Malia," Deb said. She was using the same calming tone I'd heard her use at the gym, when talking to some of the more anxious members of the class.

It didn't work on Malia.

Any further conversation was drowned out by the sound of fighting and incoherent shouting, and then car doors slammed, tires squealed again, and everything got quiet.

◆

I headed down the stairs more slowly and painfully than I like to admit, barely pausing long enough to slide my feet into my sneakers and grab my wrist-wallet, keys, and a zippered sweatshirt before I was out the door. Just as the forecast had predicted, it was raining, and I hurriedly pulled on the sweatshirt as I crossed the small yard to my car.

The Smith & Wesson revolver was still in the locked gun

safe under the front seat – I hadn't disassembled it yet, and now I was glad. I was going to need it.

I raced through the morning traffic toward Deb's house, cursing myself for letting my injury slow me down and not having dealt with Malia the night before. But after learning that she'd been the one to mastermind the scheme in the first place, I really thought Malia would have had more sense than to have gone after Deb. If she'd just stayed calm, she would have come to the conclusion that there was a good chance she might still get away with it.

I just wished I'd known about the life insurance policy earlier, so I could have switched the beneficiary over to Deb's children. Malia's reaction to that betrayal would have been absolutely perfect.

It was beyond my skills, but I wondered if it was too late for the Researcher or one of his super-specialists to pull it off...

Here Comes the Sun blasted on the phone, startling me. I grabbed for it, punching the speaker button.

"Deb? Are you all right?" I demanded.

"It's Barbara. That woman, that vile woman, she took her," she said. She sounded like she was halfway to tears, her righteous anger the only thing keeping her even marginally coherent.

"Who took her, Barbara?"

"Malia," Mary said, practically spitting the name. "She took my Deb. I was upstairs, and saw it all from the bedroom window. By the time I got down, got to the door they were... She shoved her into the car." Barbara was barely slowing down to breathe. "Oh, Meg, I think she had a gun."

"Okay, Barbara, calm down," I said, pulling the car off to the side of the road. I had a good guess where Malia was headed, but needed to make sure. "Deb still has the ankle bracelet on, right?"

"Yes. She said she was supposed to get it off today."

"Well, it's a good thing she still has it," I said. "Call the police—"

"Yes, yes, I'll call 911—"

"No," I said, cutting her off. "Call Lieutenant Thackery. You remember him, he's the one who came t see Deb yesterday, and who has been talking to her all this time. Tell him everything you just told me. He'll know what to do."

"Yes, yes, of course," Barbara said. "Thank you. She had a gun, a big, black one. I'm sure of it. And she pushed Deb into the car."

"Just call Lieutenant Thackery," I told her, not wanting her to start into a full repetition of the story. "The sooner you call him, the faster he can help Deb."

While I was talking to Barbara, I grabbed the burner phone from the glove box and tapped into the GPS app connected to the tracker on Malia's car. As I suspected, the ten-second blips were taking a direct route north on Broad Street from Deb's house in South Philly — she wasn't far ahead of me. Unless I missed my guess, Malia was taking Deb to the scene of the crime.

To the house in Elkins Park.

I anchored the phone on the dashboard mounting bracket, then flipped a U-turn, tires sliding on the wet pavement, and headed the few blocks west to Broad Street, then north as fast as the traffic gods would allow — cursing at every stoplight.

Malia was volatile on a good day. If she was blaming Deb for actually killing Stephen and ruining her carefully constructed plan, there was no time to waste.

The tracking blips pinged through Center City, then Callowhill, approached and passed NoLibs. Malia was moving fast, and it wouldn't be long before the police would be right behind her.

I just hoped I caught up with her first.

♦

The traffic gods hate me. They really, *really* hate me.

Three times, I squealed to a stop, too far from the intersection when the light turned to take my chances at blowing through the cross-traffic in one piece. Even in my wildest dreams, I am not a stunt driver, and as I watched the tracking blips increasing their lead, the only consolation I had as I tapped my finger on the steering wheel in time to the *swish-swish* of the windshield wipers was that I was still alive to follow her when the light changed to green.

Between what I was fairly sure was a cracked rib and the accompanying bruising, I had to work to keep my breathing shallow but steady. Ian had taught me a number of calming techniques, but most of them weren't suitable for a car chase.

I settled for making a mental list of all the things I thought I was going to need to remember when I finally caught up with Malia and Deb.

Malia was armed. If it was big enough for Barbara to call it a "big, black gun," it was probably a Glock or a Sig. Fifteen to seventeen rounds, depending on the model, and plenty of stopping power. I had no idea what her skill level was, but at close range, it's pretty hard to miss.

I had a five-shot Smith & Wesson .38 Special revolver, and I knew how to use it.

But – and here I reached down to check my pocket, only then remembering that I was wearing track pants and not the jeans I'd been wearing the day before – I only had three shots. I'd fired two rounds yesterday, one when Stephen hit me, and one to kill him, and I hadn't reloaded. My extra ammo was in the coin pouch in my jeans pocket.

Okay, good to know that now, before I pulled the trigger and came up empty.

I started to take a deep breath, but my rib protested, so I settled for a few shallow ones, focusing on the *shush* of tires on wet pavement.

What else?

My lock picks were also at home. I hadn't locked the back door when I left Stephen's hideout house, but there was a good chance the police had.

There was also a chance that there would be a police presence at the house. I had no idea how long it took them to process a crime scene, or how many repeat visits they made during the course of an investigation. So that would be something to watch for. If I saw any cars other than Malia's in the drive, I would have to keep going and trust law enforcement to handle things.

I didn't like that idea very much.

Maybe it was selfish, but I wanted to take her down myself.

I turned off of Broad Street and started winding through the convoluted neighborhood roads. The tracker was still reliably pinging Malia's location ahead of me at ten-second intervals, and I blessed Charlie for giving me exactly the item I didn't know I was going to need.

According to the GPS, I was closing the gap, but I was still at least five minutes behind, maybe more.

I focused on my list. I was forgetting something.

I had no disguise. No hood or hat to cover my hair. If someone saw me, they would be able to describe me, describe my car. I could smear mud on the license plate, but that would be only a temporary delay, especially if the rain got any heavier.

I dismissed both as irrelevant distractions.

The tracking ping had stopped, which meant that Malia's car was no longer moving. Driving one-handed on wet, winding roads, I checked the last GPS location.

As I'd expected, she'd taken Deb to Stephen's hideout house. God only knew why.

Taking a deep breath – and immediately regretting it – I stomped on the gas. I had to get there. Needed to be there.

Now.

And then I came around the curve and was on the long, straight stretch of road where the house was. I couldn't see it

yet — nor did I see any other cars parked along the shoulder —
but I did see the one thing I had forgotten to add to my list.

The cream and burgundy Craftsman on the corner.

I could see it clearly, even through rain, because every
window was ablaze with light. That could only mean one thing:
Bonnie was there, showing the house to prospective buyers.

And I only had three bullets.

Chapter 32
Present day: Monday, eleven days after the murder

I forced myself to slow down as I neared Stephen's hideout house. Malia's car was in the drive, pulled up so far the bumper was almost touching the garage door. Much as I wanted to tear in there like some hero from an action movie, I knew bursting in on her would succeed only in encouraging her to empty her Glock into me and probably take Deb out in the process.

She'd brought Deb here – to the "scene of the crime" – for a reason. I figured I probably had a few minutes before whatever Malia had planned to come to a head. Time enough to sneak in the back way.

But first...

I pulled off the road about a car length before I reached the driveway, got out of the car, and ran down the gravel drive to Malia's car. The garage appeared to have been an afterthought, tacked onto the left-hand end of the rambler farthest from the corner, with a narrow gravel walk crossing in front of the house, past the living room window, to the front porch.

It was a poor design, for the residents, though I assumed there was probably a connecting door leading into the house inside the garage. But not having to go near the big bay window worked just fine for me. Being in full view of it the whole time was risky enough. I was grateful that Stephen had been paranoid about being found that he'd hung the bedsheets to block the view — and that no one had bothered to rip them down.

I ducked down near the rear fender, hoping no one decided to pass by at that moment and wonder what the crazy woman was doing out in the rain. The tracking device was exactly where I'd left it. It pulled free with little effort, and I was running back down the drive — and wishing I'd grabbed a hat, or at least a hooded sweatshirt — in a matter of seconds.

Seconds that might make a difference to Deb's survival.

Part of me felt guilty for thinking of my own self-preservation over hers, but it was only a very small part. Whatever happened inside the house, it wouldn't be long before there were police swarming all over the outside. I couldn't leave the tracker on her car.

I didn't look back at the house until I was back in my car. As far as I could tell, the sheets hadn't moved, so I doubted Malia had seen me. Now to get inside and finish this farce once and for all.

I tossed the now silent tracker and burner phone into the glove box, pulled back out onto the street, and drove past the rambler. When I passed the Craftsman, I took the corner a little faster than I should have, and scrambled as I felt the tires hydroplaning on the wet pavement, my cracked rib letting me know the whole time that this was not a proper way to convalesce. I ignored my body — as I often do — getting my car under control at about the same moment I spotted both Bonnie's car and a second vehicle in the Craftsman's drive. No surprise there.

But it was a little annoying to see a battered pickup truck in the driveway of the neighboring house — the one that mirrored Stephen's on this side of the Craftsman, with an equally poorly positioned garage. I'd planned to save a few possibly critical minutes by cutting through that yard.

Now I was going to have to take the path through the woods.

I pulled off onto the shoulder of the road, awkwardly retrieved the revolver from the locked safe under my seat, then grabbed my phone and wallet. I shoved the phone and gun into my pockets, trading for my gloves, and set off into the woods. Instead of sliding the stretchy wrist wallet onto my ankle, which was usually my preference, I just pulled it onto my wrist as I walked, yanking my jacket sleeve down over it, then tugging on my gloves.

It had been raining long enough that the underbrush was pretty well soaked, and the path was a lot harder to navigate quickly today than it had been the previous day. My track pants were soaked to mid-calf before I'd gone ten yards.

At least I wasn't worried about being quiet.

That thought set of a warning flag, though, and I pulled my phone out of my pocket and set it to silent. The last thing I needed was for someone to call me while I was trying to sneak up on a crazy woman with a handgun.

Speed and security battled it out in my head as I moved across the rambler's back yard. Security won, and I went the extra few feet follow the treeline along the far side of the yard. No sense inviting the neighbors to wonder why a soggy-haired blonde in muddy shoes was sneaking around the yard.

There's an odd sort of stillness being outside in the rain. Except for the swooshing of the occasional vehicle passing on the road, the white noise of the rain dampened the environment both figuratively as well as literally. I didn't hear the raised voices coming from the inside of the house, until I was almost at the back door.

I hesitated for only a moment, listening. While I couldn't completely understand what was being said, I was able to confirm that there were definitely *two* voices. The argument was punctuated by the thumps and thuds and crashes of objects being thrown – presumably at each other – and, from the sound of it, with vey poor aim.

I needed to get inside.

I hadn't yet determined what I was going to do about Deb. I didn't want her to see me any more than I wanted Bonnie to, but for some reason I was slightly less sanguine about shooting her. Maybe it was guilt for my role in her troubles. Maybe it was the irony of killing the person I'd raced across town to save.

I didn't have either an explanation or a plan. But I knew that the time to do whatever I ultimately decided on was running out.

The door was locked – of course – and I didn't have my lockpicks. With a growl, because this wasn't the sort of emergency I had anticipated needing it for, I pulled the emergency credit card out of my wrist wallet. I slid the hard plastic between the door and the jamb, and began working the old lock open, grateful that there wasn't a deadbolt or chain lock on this door, like the ones that had slowed Stephen down.

The momentary pity for yesterday's target faded as the lock gave way. I eased the door open, stuffing the card into my pocket and trading it for the revolver.

The kitchen was empty. From the sound of the shouting, Malia and Deb were in the living room. Malia was raging, something to the effect of "…you've ruined everything, just like you always have…" while Deb's part of the fight was mostly pleas for her to stop screaming and calm down.

Deb didn't know Malia very well. All she was accomplishing was the verbal equivalent of pouring gasoline on an open fire.

I'd done my best to get as much of the mud off my shoes as I could while walking in the grass, and wiped them on the rough rope mat on the back porch. I didn't want to be leaving any more of a record that I'd been here than necessary, though, so when I slipped into the house, quietly closing the door behind me, I grabbed the small towel on the counter by the sink and used it to dry my lower pant legs and wipe down my shoes one more time.

From the kitchen, there were two routes to the living room. To my right, the short segment of the L-shaped hallway that I'd made Stephen crawl down. Or to my left, passing through the dining room and under a wide arch. A stairway, leading to the basement, was open to the kitchen, but the far wall divided the two rooms.

As I crept to the end of the dividing wall at the top of the stairs, my revolver at the ready, I almost felt like my caution was unnecessary. Any sound I might have made was more than covered by Malia's shrill, almost incoherent screaming.

And then a gunshot exploded from the living room.

If it hadn't been accompanied by the sound of breaking glass and Deb's voice screaming, "What are you doing? Are you crazy?" I would have probably jumped out from my hiding place before the echo faded.

But Deb sounded angry, not injured.

And the presumably accidental discharge seemed to have shocked at least a touch of sense into Malia as well.

"I'm not ready to shoot you yet," she said. "That would be too quick. Too easy. I want you to suffer." Her voice turned nasty. "Maybe I'll go back and visit those sweet children of yours. They must be so broken up over losing their father—"

"You stay away from my children!" Deb shouted. There was the sound of movement, but she didn't get far before Malia stopped her.

"Ah-ah-ah," she said. "You're not going anywhere. In fact…" there was a pause, and it was all I could do not to look, "…yes. Go that way. In there."

A door closed.

Malia swore. "Why don't these things lock from the outside?" she said. Then louder, "Don't you open this door. I *will* shoot you. I promise it."

I heard Deb's voice then, muffled, saying, "Please let me out."

I took a chance and peered around the wall where I'd been hiding. I had to know what was happening.

A huge stone fireplace was at the center of the wall on the far side of the living room, with a pair of built-in bookcases on either side. I watched as Malia dragged the large floral armchair across the living room – the Glock an incongruous darkness against the brightly-colored cushions – and shoved it up against a section of wall behind the bookcase nearest the hall.

I vaguely remembered seeing a door there, visible from the kitchen, directly opposite the back door. A coat closet, perhaps? And Malia was using the chair to block Deb inside.

She would be uncomfortable, but she would be safe from Malia.

She would be safe from me.

◆

I should have just shot Malia and walked out. That would have been the smart thing to do.

But I was far too personally invested in this to do the smart thing. So as she finished positioning the chair against the closet door, I walked across the living room. And when she turned away from the chair, I back-handed her as hard as I could.

Malia spun around, careening into the end of the bookcase where it protruded from the wall. But she recovered well, because she grabbed hold of the shelf to stabilize herself, then started throwing books at me.

"What—" *throw*, "—the hell—" *throw*, "—are you—" *throw*, "—doing here?" she demanded, lobbing the hardbacks.

I didn't bother to respond.

It was easy enough to dodge the flying books. The pieces of broken coffee table from the previous day, and the assorted debris from Malia's earlier fight with Deb, though, had turned the floor into a minefield.

When I stepped on a previously-thrown magazine and skidded on the slick paper, she flew at me.

I was still wearing my gloves, and the silicon grip was probably the only reason the revolver didn't fly out of my hand when we collided, spinning like a pair of skaters.

She reached for the gun, I held it out of reach. She tugged at my hair, I stomped on her foot, unprotected in her trendy, end-of-season sandals.

She punched me in the side.

My ribs exploded. I dropped the revolver and fell to my knees, pulling Malia to the floor with me. I think the only thing that saved me in that moment was the fact that she was more intent on going after the gun. If she'd realized my weakness and taken advantage of it... But she didn't. Instead, she dove over me, scrabbling through the torn papers, trying to get to the revolver.

Tears blurring my vision, I rolled with her, my left arm pressed against my side to protect it from further injury, our legs tangled together, keeping her from going too far in her quest for the gun. With my right hand, I reached over and grabbed her hair, yanking her head back. If I'd had a third hand – and a knife – I would have slit her throat. I had neither.

Malia's hand landed on the gun. Somehow, in her flailing about, she'd managed to grab it just right – or just *wrong* – and it went off. I have no idea where the bullet went, but over the ringing in my ears, I thought I heard glass breaking and Deb – who had been quiet up to this point – begin to scream for help.

There were now only two bullets left in the revolver, and the pain in my ribs was making me nauseous. I had to end this.

Kicking out with one leg, I maneuvered around Malia, twisting our bodies until she was practically sitting sideways on my lap. She had the gun, but so did I, my hand around the snub-nose barrel while her finger was on the trigger. For several agonizing seconds, we struggled together, each trying to point the muzzle at the other.

Behind us, Deb was still shouting.

Outside, a shadow passed beyond the sheets covering the bay window, footsteps pounded up the porch steps, fists hammered on the door.

And then Malia looked up at me, her eyes wide, as I shoved the revolver up under her ribcage, muzzle pointing directly at her heart, and forced her finger to squeeze the trigger.

◆

My ribs were on fire. My hand, where I'd been holding the barrel of the revolver, was numb. My ears were ringing.

And the fists against the door had turned to loud, booming thuds, as someone tried to break through the heavy wood.

I shoved Malia's bloody corpse off me and scrambled to my knees, then stood on shaking legs.

Move!

I staggered toward the kitchen, reaching the wall dividing the living and dining room just as the front door cracked. I moved out of sight, pressing my back to the wall at the top of the stairs, trying catch my breath.

The living room door gave way under the onslaught, slamming against the wall as a man's voice boomed out. "What's going on in here? Is everything... Oh, my God!"

Footsteps crunched over the debris-filled floor.

A woman's voice, trembling, uncertain: "Is someone hurt?"

A different voice. Also a woman, but confident, assured, with a hint of Jersey in her voice. "There's a woman in the powder room – she's the one we heard shouting. She says she was kidnapped, brought here against her will. I told her to stay there until help comes."

Bonnie. Always cool in a crisis, now talking generically about Deb.

"I think this one's killed herself," the man said.

"Oh, dear," said the frightened woman.

"I'm calling 911," Bonnie said.

I had to get out of there before anyone decided to start looking around and found me, covered in Malia's blood. There was too much I couldn't even begin to explain.

While Bonnie called the police, I slipped around the end of the stairs and crossed the kitchen, heading toward the door, and hesitated. If Deb had opened the closet door, she would see me going out the back.

Then the man's voice again. "Let me get you some water, dear. You stay right here... No, better, you go out onto the porch with Bonnie. I'll be right there."

No choice for it then. If the man was coming into the kitchen, I had to leave.

I took the last two steps to the end of the counter, grabbing the dirty towel I'd used to wipe my shoes. I then slipped out the door, pulling it closed behind me. Pressing myself against the door so he wouldn't see me from the sink, I stood there, letting the rain sluice down over me.

Waiting.

Inside the kitchen, cupboard doors slammed, water ran, footsteps receded. When no one opened the door at my back, no one called out after me, I retraced my steps back along the far side of the yard, and into the woods.

Near the edge of the woods, I stopped near a large oak tree.

Methodically – because routine was all that was keeping me moving now – I emptied my jacket pockets. Cell phone, bent credit card, car keys. All went into the pockets of my track pants.

My gloves were ruined. I could have cleaned the blood with peroxide, but the heat of the revolver's barrel had damaged the silicone grip pads on one glove. I pulled the gloves off one at a time, rolled them up, and put them into my jacket pockets.

Thanks to the rain, it was hard to tell where the dark blue sweatshirt was just wet and where it was covered in blood. I unzipped it, intending to roll it up and put it in the trunk of the car, then changed my mind. The blood had soaked through the thin fabric, thoroughly staining the pale green t-shirt I was wearing underneath. I didn't want to get into my car covered in Malia's blood, but I couldn't drive around Philadelphia looking like an axe-murderer, either.

There was nothing to be done for it.

I used the cleanest portion of the dirty towel to wipe my face, and thanked my sacrificial glove for protecting my aching hand from being burned by the revolver's barrel. I needed some painkiller – a lot of painkiller – and a couple of bandages, a shower, a drink, and a very long nap.

As I eased onto the road, heading away from the chaos behind me, I heard the sirens approaching, and smiled.

Chapter 33
Present day: A few weeks later

I spent the next six weeks moving around like a porcelain doll, my left ribs reminding me every time I did anything strenuous, like tie my shoes.

Between them, Stephen and Malia had managed to crack two of my ribs. But there were no sharp fractures, and no organs had been punctured or damaged. As long as I was careful, the doctor assured me that everything should heal as good as new.

As far as my friends went, I blamed it on Glau.

"Well, I can't very well tell anyone the truth," I said, setting some of his favorite fresh fruit on his perch by way of apology. The story I'd devised involved me standing on a chair to change a lightbulb and him running under it for some inexplicable reason, knocking both the chair and me off balance, with painful results.

He stared at me balefully, giving me one slow blink.

"Come on," I pleaded. "You're the only one I can trust not to rat me out."

I took the sudden bobbing of his head as the equivalent of a deep belly laugh. Resting one hand on his warm, sturdy shoulder, I offered him a strawberry.

Glau might not have been talking, but everyone else was.

Bonnie regaled the crowd at McGillin's with her version of what had happened.

"Wouldn't you know it, but I had a showing all scheduled, and I get there and the house next door has police tape all over the front. Now how am I supposed to spin that as a feature?" She took a long pull of her beer while everyone laughed.

"But I managed to steer the prospects away from it," she continued. "Fortunately, they arrived from a different direction. Everything was going swimmingly – it's a beautiful house – but then the wife saw that the dining room opened onto the wraparound porch. She went outside, and we all heard screaming coming from the house next door."

"The one with the police tape?" asked one of the crowd of hangers-on who always seemed to gather whenever Bonnie was holding court.

"The very one," she said, raising her glass to him. "I knew the sale was blown right then. So we all go running over to help – did I mention that it was raining? And I was in suede Manolos. Well, they're ruined. Six hundred dollar shoes, and no coat, and I go running off in the rain after my clients."

I leaned over and whispered in her ear. "Don't mention Deb by name, okay?"

"Of course not," she whispered back with a quick wink.

"We get over there, and my client is pounding on the front door like he means to break it in, and his wife is fluttering around him, as useful as a soggy hummingbird. In the meantime, I hear calls for help coming from over by the garage, so I follow the path around and find a woman waving a hand towel out through the powder room windows."

"Why didn't she just crawl out?" someone asked.

"It was one of those tiny windows – you know, the kind that's just for decoration?" Bonnie explained. "She'd managed to break it, and had her arm shoved out to the shoulder, but waving the towel around like a flag and shouting for help was all that window was going to let her do."

"I was talking to her, trying to calm her down, when we heard a bang—"

"A gunshot?"

"Exactly," Bonnie said, pointing at him with her thumb and finger like she was shooting a small pistol. "I went running back to the front door – which my client managed to force open only moments after the gunshot – and we found the other woman sprawled on the living room floor, dead. We got my client's wife out of the house before she fainted, and called the police, but the whole thing was a terrible mess. Frankly, I was glad he didn't get inside any sooner – she might have shot him instead of herself."

I hid my smile behind my beer.

I was glad he hadn't gotten inside any sooner, as well, but for very different reasons.

"What about the woman in the window?"

"The police were very good about that. We all gave our statements, and since she was talking to me when the other one shot herself, the police couldn't very well charge her with murder. They did offer to give her a ride home, though, instead of making her take an Uber or anything."

There were general nods around the table about how that had been the right thing to do. What none of them knew was that Bonnie had taken Deb home herself, sparing her the embarrassment of arriving in her neighborhood in a black-and-white.

And even Bonnie didn't know that when he took Deb's statement at the scene, Lieutenant Thackery had removed Deb's ankle bracelet himself, calling in to the station while he did so Deb wouldn't get in any trouble over it. She'd blushed a little when she told me. On the list of "right things to do," I thought that was right up there at the top.

"What about your clients?" someone asked. It sounded like the same man who had asked a lot of the questions, but he wasn't being belligerent or annoying, so I didn't bother trying to figure out who it was.

"I sold them a lovely rowhouse in the city just last week," Bonnie said proudly. "Apparently the suburbs weren't as peaceful and quiet as they'd been led to believe."

◆

It was my rowhouse Bonnie sold to her clients.

I'd closed on the East Falls house just before Thanksgiving, and, following my doctor's advice – and Deb's, and Ian's, and Jessica's – spent the entire month of December sorting my belongings, in preparation for the big move.

As soon as the doctor had verified that I wasn't going to puncture a lung if I moved wrong, and prescribed me some painkillers strong enough to let me breathe normally without noticing that it hurt like hell, I packed up everything I didn't want anyone else to see. There wasn't that much really – the unlicensed Glock 17 from under Glau's perch, a few burner phones, the tracker, a laptop, and a handful of portable hard drives that could be problematic in the wrong hands.

All of it joined the collection of fake IDs, credit cards, and emergency cash in a safe deposit box in a bank in Trenton, New Jersey, about a half hour's drive from Philadelphia. I'd found the bank a few years ago, and set up an account and the box under one of my other names. I wasn't planning to do any work for at least a couple of months, until I was both healed and settled in the new house, so it just made sense to tuck everything safely away in the meantime.

There were too many people tromping in and out of the rowhouse to risk keeping anything even remotely confidential there – even under lock and key.

When I finally agreed to let my friends help with the actual move, their enthusiasm was almost overwhelming. Deb rounded up hands for packing, and Ian marshalled the gym rats for hauling boxes and furniture down the narrow rowhouse stairs. Aunts Maureen and Ruthie brought in coolers filled with beer and enormous soft pretzels to keep everyone fueled.

Even though it had been close to two months, and my ribs were only waiting a final doctor appointment to be pronounced fully healed, no one would let me lift anything heavier than a long-neck bottle. Instead, I was assigned the onerous tasks of labeling boxes and of keeping Glau out from underfoot – until Uncle Jim and Kyle arrived, loaded up the iguana, and carted him off to his new home, leaving me with only a box of press-on labels and a handful of permanent markers.

In a matter of hours, my entire life was boxed, labeled, loaded up onto trucks, and spirited away.

"It's been a good place," I told Bonnie when she joined me in the too-empty living room. It felt larger with everything gone – and smaller, somehow.

"It was the right place for you… then," Bonnie agreed. "But you've outgrown it."

"Have I?" I asked. "Really? I mean, what do I need with six bedrooms?"

"I don't know, but it will be great for parties. And—" she looked around like she was checking to see if there was anyone in the house who might overhear her "—I have it on good authority that we're missing one right now."

"At my house?" I asked, raising an eyebrow.

"Give the woman a prize," she said.

"And here I was hoping to find a box labeled 'bathroom stuff' filled with bath salts, shampoo, and fluffy towels. There's a jetted tub I'm looking forward to getting acquainted with."

"Wine and canapes first," Bonnie said, steering me toward the door.

"How about beer and pretzels? I think there were some left."

"I don't know – but I'm not doing the cooking. I'm just supposed to get you to your housewarming," she said, nudging me gently. "So scoot."

The majority of the work crew had gone by the time I arrived, but the people who were still there – Deb and her children, Ian, Bonnie and Peggy, Jessica, Aunt Ruthie, Jim and Maureen, and Kyle – were the ones I considered both friends and family.

They greeted me like a returning hero, with cheers and hugs and applause when I opened the door. Deb jumped slightly when a champagne cork exploded from the bottle, then laughed and cheered as Uncle Jim poured it out and Josh helped hand it around.

The laughter was contagious. It was odd to see my own furnishings next to those I'd gotten with the house, and most of my personal belongings were still in boxes, tucked discreetly in corners, out of the way. Nevertheless, in only a few minutes I felt less tired – and completely at home.

"Should they be doing that? Grilling in the house?" Aunt Maureen asked, a worried frown creasing her forehead as she watched Uncle Jim, Ian, and Kyle bonding over craft beers and barbecue in the large glass room. Glau watched them, providing quiet oversight from the safety of a perch on a large log I'd had installed for him.

I caught her arm and steered her out of the conservatory through the set of French doors leading to the dining room.

"I learned a long time ago not to come between Uncle Jim and a grill," I told her. "He says he's got it vented properly to the outside, so I've decided not to worry about it."

"Maureen, come give me a hand," Aunt Ruthie said, coming to the kitchen door. "Lovely house dear," she said to me, almost as an afterthought. She caught Maureen's arm and bustled her off into the kitchen. "Have you seen this pantry…?"

I left them to it, and wandered back to the living room. With the conservatory doors thrown open to the wide passageway connecting the living room, dining, and kitchen, the house conveyed a sense of both unity and intimacy.

"So, what's the story with Business and Pleasure over there?" Bonnie asked, tilting her chin in the general direction of the grill, where Kyle and Ian stood, drinking beer and talking while Uncle Jim tended the flank steaks.

"They're friends—" I began, but Bonnie and Deb both burst into laughter before I could get any further.

"Friends? Those two?" Deb said when her laughter had faded to chuckles. "Oh, come on."

"You are so clueless," Bonnie said.

"What?" I asked.

"Two gorgeous men just spent the day schlepping boxes up and down stairs—"

"Actually, that would be down and *then* up," Bonnie said.

"—down and up stairs for you, and now are at the same party," Deb said. "And you think that's because they want to be *friends?*"

"There are other women here," I said.

Bonnie shook her head, then began tilting her glass at the "women" in question.

Aunts Maureen and Ruthie, who had taken over the kitchen and were already in the process of deciding how my cupboards should be properly arranged. If I let them, they'd have me unpacked before bedtime. "Too old."

Jessica and Cassie, who were sitting together on a loveseat, passing their cell phones back and forth as they *oohed* and *ahhed* over photos or music or something. "Too young."

Herself and Peggy, who were, at that moment, standing arm in arm near the cozy fireplace. "Taken."

"That only leaves you two," she said, turning to me and Deb.

"Mmmm," Deb said. She looked over at Kyle and Ian as though considering a purchase. "Tempting... but I'm not on the market."

"And that brings us back to you having two dates for the same party."

I spluttered, almost choking on my drink. It hadn't occurred to me that either Ian or Kyle would think of this as a *date*.

Sure, Ian and I had been an item years ago, but it had been *years*... And I hadn't exactly invited Kyle – Jessica had let the moving day plans slip when he'd stopped by the office just after the final paperwork between Herriman Industries and SCH had been signed.

I looked over at Ian and Kyle again – really *looked* – and felt the color drain from my face. There was no denying that they were sizing each other up.

And then, as if on cue, they both looked over. At me. Ian's gaze was hot, intense; Kyle's smoldering, hungry.

"I need to sit down," I said, feeling my legs go weak. I didn't have room in my life for one man. What was I going to do with two?

◆

In that weird way that parties sometimes do, everyone seemed to decide it was time to leave all at once. In one moment, we were laughing, talking, and tossing beer bottles into my brand-new recycling bin, and ten minutes later people were putting on their coats and hugging me goodbye.

I watched from the window as the various cars jockeyed around for position and one by one moved down the curved drive. No sooner had I turned away and reached to switch off the nearest lamp than my phone was buzzing in my pocket.

Eye of the Tiger. Ian's ringtone.

"Hey," I said.

"Hey, you," Ian said. It had been our greeting years ago, back when we were dating. I waited for him to continue.

"I know a great seafood place, if you're up for it," he said.

"Sure."

"It's a bit of a drive, though... out to Ocean City." He sounded hopeful, and oddly, almost uncertain.

"I've never been there."

"We could make a weekend of it."

I moved to the edge of the window and pushed the drapes open, only a sliver. Just enough to see the taillights of Ian's car, idling about halfway down the drive.

"I'd like that," I said.

The exhale was so soft I almost didn't hear it – the man was something of a Zen master, after all. "Great," he said. "Get some sleep. I'll call you tomorrow."

Ian sped away, the red line of his taillights leaving a trail in the night.

I'd gotten as far as the dining room before my phone buzzed again, this time with an incoming text message.

> *Now that the SCH deal is closed, will you have dinner with me? You do need to eat, and there's no food in your house. I checked your refrigerator. -K.H.*

I sat down, laughing, at the ridiculously large dining room table. It was practically large enough to use as a guest bed – for someone who liked an extra-firm mattress, anyway.

> *You missed the pantry. The aunts left it well-stocked. So I'm not going to starve any time soon.*

So that's a no? -K.H.

> *Do you always sign your texts?*

Maybe. -K.H.

> *Let's try lunch. See if we have anything to talk about that's not business.*

I'm sure we'll think of something.

I laughed, because he actually managed to not sign the message. And then I laughed even harder when I got his next message.

-K.H.

I shot back a reply.

Washington Square Park, corner of 6th & Walnut, Tuesday, 11:30.

He answered with a smiley face.

I didn't date much – not at all, really – and I didn't know where either of the two dates I'd just agreed to were going, but as I wandered through my new house, shutting lights off, and making sure Glau was settled in his new space, I felt lighter than I had in a long time.

I wondered how much of that was the house, the friends. The idea of going out again, or that my body was healing. But deep in my heart I knew it wasn't any of those, because the lightness had been growing over the past couple of months.

When my father left and never came back, leaving our family prey to all that came after, something had broken inside me, something that would never – could never – fully heal. But I hadn't realized until after I killed Stephen just how much I'd been pouring salt on that wound. For years, I'd believed I was purging my pain by taking my anger out on Stephen, but I wasn't. I was holding onto it. Feeding it. Helping it grow.

And now Stephen was gone.

I was still angry with my father. Still woke in a cold sweat from bad dreams that will always haunt me. Still feel the itch at the back of my mind that drives me to the dark web listings and the jobs that keep my friends safe from the ugliness that oozes out from under the locked doors and hidden recesses of my mind.

But for this moment, with Deb safe, Bonnie alive, and the possibilities of God-knew-what might happen with Ian and Kyle, life was pretty good. I was already thinking about ways to make the conservatory better for Glau – and how to partition off an area where I could pay safely with some toxic plants I'd been researching.

There was a place between the library and the adjacent bedroom that would make a perfect secret room for things I didn't want visitors to find. And I was looking forward to exploring this quiet, peaceful neighborhood that was my new home.

I went upstairs, found the bath salts, and sank into blissful, bubbly oblivion. Some time later, a back-door neighbor's dog began to bark, the yips echoing in the stillness. I dragged myself out of the tub and found my way to my bed, pulling the comforter up over my ears.

Other than a little yapper-dog that occasionally barked in the middle of the night, it was a quiet, peaceful neighborhood.

Epilogue:
Twenty-five years ago

The police station smelled of sweat and fear, cigarettes and burned coffee, shoe polish and… peppermint? Maggie turned her head, and only then noticed the small, slightly crumpled white paper bag sitting on the corner of the detective's desk, the upper edge torn where it had been rolled down.

"Have one. It will make you feel better," the detective said, holding out the bag of plastic-wrapped candies. The sugary scent of mint was strong, even through the wrapping.

Maggie looked at him in surprise. She was *thirteen*, not three. Almost fourteen. Old enough to know that a piece of candy wasn't going to fix anything. But her mother had taught her that a lady was always gracious and polite, and Maggie always tried her best to behave properly and make her mother proud. She glanced at her mother, who was perched uncomfortably on the hard plastic chair next to her. Mrs. Harrison tilted her head in the slightest of nods, her grim expression never changing.

Maggie looked back at the officer. "Thank you," she said, then reached into the bag and took one of the peppermints. It was one of the hard kind, white with green swirls, and she carefully unwrapped it, and put it in her mouth. It made her eyes water. She blinked quickly, not wanting anyone to think she was crying.

"Can you tell me what happened?" the detective asked. His rolling chair squeaked when he turned to face her.

"I thought my mother already told you," Maggie said.

"I'd like to hear what you have to say," the detective said, not unkindly. "You might remember something your mother missed."

Maggie shrugged. "I heard a noise, and got out of bed to see what it was. When I came out of my room, I didn't see anything, and all of the other bedroom doors were closed. Shelia's, too – she's my big sister – even though she was sleeping over at a friend's."

When I came out of my room, Eddie was coming out of the twins' room. His bathrobe was open, and he had that creepy, full of himself smirk on his face he often had when he'd finished with me in the middle of the night.

"There were no lights on?"

"No. It was dark," Maggie said. "I turned on the bathroom light – I didn't want the hall light to bother anyone, and the bathroom is right there at the top of the stairs. I pulled the door mostly closed and slipped my hand in through the opening so I could flip the switch. That way only a little light got out. We do that at night all the time."

Eddie had that little plastic camping lantern he always carried when he came into our rooms at night. He said he liked to see.

The detective was writing down everything she was saying, so Maggie sucked on the peppermint, looking around the room while she waited for him to catch up. Another policeman – this one in a dark blue uniform – was walking quickly toward the door, his shiny leather shoes making a *click-slap* sound on the floor. At another desk, she could hear the tinny, crackling voices of the policemen checking in on their radios.

After a minute, the detective asked. "And then?"

Maggie looked back at him. "I didn't see anything at first – the light was too bright, and it took a second for my eyes to adjust, even after I'd turned away from the bathroom."

Eddie saw me and licked his lips. "You're too late, little girl," he said. "I've found sweeter meat tonight."

"I started to go downstairs, but that was when I saw that the rail was broken," she said, "just there between the bathroom and my brothers' room across the hall – you know, where you can look down to see who's at the front door? I was afraid someone had fallen down the stairs."

"You stay away from my brothers!" I shouted, not caring who I woke up. Eddie just grinned, and that made me so angry that I shoved him. Hard. He reached out to grab me as he fell backward, but I ducked. And then he crashed into the rail, and it snapped, with a loud crack, like a door slamming, but sharper. He wasn't smirking anymore, but I was.

"Had anyone fallen?"

"Yes."

The detective had been writing his notes in a little notebook, but somewhere else in the room someone was typing. Maggie couldn't tell where the *clickety-click* sound was coming from with looking around, and that would have been rude, so even though she was very curious, she didn't look.

"Who?"

Maggie looked down at her lap. "I went to the top of the stairs and looked down… there was just enough light, a bright stripe, you know… and I saw Eddie laying there on the floor." She looked up at the officer. "That was when Mama surprised me. She must have come out of her room just when I was turning from the bathroom, because I didn't see her."

Mama was screaming, "What have you done, Margaret? Oh my God, oh my God, Eddie!" I thought she was going to break her own neck, running down the stairs like that.

"And then what?

"I pointed down to Eddie, and Mama ran down the stairs to where he was. I didn't want to go down there, so I asked if I should call 911, but she was just screaming and crying and trying to wake Eddie. So I went into her bedroom and called from the phone by her bed."

"And then?"

"And then everyone else woke up and the ambulance came. My brothers and I watched from the top of the stairs."

"You didn't go downstairs?"

Maggie shook her head.

The camping light rolled away when it landed, but hadn't broken; it just lay there, casting strange shadows across the floor. I went downstairs, past Mama and Eddie, picked up the lamp, and turned it off.

I was going to put it out in the garage with the camping stuff, but it made me feel sick to my stomach just to touch it. So I took it into the kitchen and put it in the garbage and smashed it with a big can of pork and beans so no one would fish it out. Not that any of us would. We all hated that light almost as much as we hated Eddie.

The detective finished making his notes and offered Maggie another peppermint. She smiled and thanked him politely as she reached into the bag and pulled out a second green and white mint.

The detective had been right, Maggie thought. The candy had made her feel better, after all. As they left the police station, Maggie gave the second peppermint to her mother.

◆

Acknowledgments

Several years ago, a friend and I were part of a community outreach project focused on empowering single mothers. Many of these women were struggling to keep their children fed and housed while dealing with "deadbeat" former spouses. We heard story after story, ranging from the entirely absent second parent to the actively antagonistic. I drew on those stories, blending fact and fiction to create Deborah Markham. From there, it was all too easy to give her a motive for killing her deadbeat ex-husband.

About the same time I was gathering the "seeds" for this story, I took a mystery writing workshop from another good friend, award-winning writer Kristine Kathryn Rusch. During one of the exercises, when members of the class were speculating on possible topics for our mysteries, Kris encouraged us to look at the things that "don't get talked about" in polite society, and the unwritten rules that drive family dynamics. She encouraged us all – and me, particularly, in other conversations – not to shy away from those forbidden topics, but to use them both as catalysts for our fiction and as the conflicts that drive the characters. I've learned a great deal over the years from Kris and also her husband, Dean Wesley Smith, and it would be remiss of me to not acknowledge their contribution to the *Hit Lady for Hire* series.

This note would be incomplete if I did not thank my family — especially my husband, who unfailingly "looked after his writer," and saw to it that I was supplied with coffee, water, and far better food choices than I would have gotten for myself when the call of the manuscript was louder than that of the pantry. To my entire family: thank you so much for your love, support, and encouragement, without which this book probably would not have been written.

Thank you also to Mem Morman, who kept prodding me to write the next book, romantic suspense author Stanalei Fletcher, for many long conversations about story structure, and fellow writing group members Kent Chadwick and Stephen Barq, who routinely let me drop pages on them and let me know when they disagree with unworkable first drafts.

Finally, gratitude, hugs, and chocolate to my wonderful editor, Jana Brown, who burned through the chapters as quickly as I could give them to her and never stopped asking for more. Her comments and insights made this a better book.

best,

— *Lauryn*

About the Author

As a mystery reader, Lauryn Christopher likes figuring out "whodunit" as much as anyone – but as a mystery writer with a background in psychology, she's much more likely to write from the culprit's point of view, exploring the hidden secrets driving their choices. You can see this in her *Hit Lady for Hire* series, as well as in her short crime fiction and cozy capers, which have appeared in a variety of short fiction anthologies.

Read Lauryn's musings on storytelling, find links to more of her work, and sign up for her occasional newsletter at her website: www.laurynchristopher.com

If you enjoyed this book, please tell a friend or post a review!

Also by
Lauryn Christopher

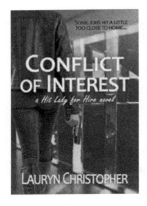

Conflict of Interest
a Hit Lady for Hire novel

**When a professional assassin has
work-related issues, someone usually
ends up dead...**

It's a bad idea to piss off a professional
assassin, and Meg Harrison – corporate
spy and sometimes assassin – is
definitely pissed off. Not only has a
new, and very irritating, client hired
her to kill her own sister, but to top it all off, Meg didn't even
know she *had* a sister.

For Meg, this is a contract that hits a little too close to home.

*"...turns the hit-man formula on its head, and in doing so
gives us a surprising and entertaining read."*
— "Big Al" (Books and Pals)

With Friends Like These
a Hit Lady for Hire short story

How well do we really know our friends? Their secret lives? Their hidden pain?

Liz, Deb, Mikki, Anna, and Meg believe they know everything about each other.

But one of them carries too many secrets — secrets that tear at her heart and eat at her friendships.

Secrets she will kill to protect.

"...a powerful piece about friendship, loss, death, and secrets."

– Kristine Kathryn Rusch

Made in the USA
Monee, IL
29 February 2024

53792579R00178